THE BOTTLE HOUSE

ENDORSEMENTS

Susan Grant takes readers on a spiritual revelation of how past regrets affect our mental health and cause individuals to lose faith. *The Bottle House* teaches us that no matter how low we feel, Jesus can forgive us, restore us, and give us comfort in every situation we go through.

—LuGina Dumas, Licensed Clinical Mental Health Counselor, Nationally Certified Counselor.

The Bottle House offers an ongoing vision of hope and comfort when we are tempted to retreat into despair and loneliness. Susan Grant understands the psychological aspects of rejection and fear and offers hope that even when carrying the heaviest burdens, we can move forward and regain a sense of purpose and direction.

—Ann W. Roach, Licensed Psychological Examiner, Certified master's level school psychologist

THE BOTTLE HOUSE

SUSAN GRANT

ELK LAKE PUBLISHING INC

PUBLISHING THE POSITIVE
Plymouth, Massachusetts

COPYRIGHT

Cover and Interior Design: Derinda Babcock
Editor(s): Sue Fairchild, Deb Haggerty

PUBLISHED BY: Elk Lake Publishing, Inc., 35 Dogwood Drive, Plymouth, MA 02360, 2021

Library Cataloging Data
Names: Grant, Susam (Susan Grant)
The Bottle House / Susan Grant
312 p. 23cm × 15cm (9in × 6 in.)
ISBN-13: 978-1-64949392-7 (paperback) | 978-1-64949-393-4 (trade hardcover) | 978-1-64949-394-1 (trade paperback) 978-1-64949-395-8 (e-book)
Key Words: Christian Fiction; Christian Mystery; Inspirational Christian Fiction; Contemporary Religious Fiction; Christian Psychological Fiction; Christian Women's Fiction; Religion and Spirituality
Library of Congress Control Number: 2021947089 Fiction

DEDICATION

For my husband, Randy, my biggest cheerleader.

ACKNOWLEDGMENTS

There are so many who have contributed to the writing of this novel, making it obvious to me that I did not write the book alone.

Thank you to Gary Magby, who made himself available to me and was the one who gently nudged me to get this novel completed.

I am grateful for the many hours of walking with Rebecca Wright as we talked through story lines and areas of the book that needed polishing.

Thank you, Sarah Grant, for sharing with me your enthusiasm for this story. Your comments as you stood by me on the playground helped to encourage me not to give up.

A special thank you to Karen Bailey, Rebecca Grant, and Erica Thompson, who are my writing cheerleaders at work.

Thank you, Johnny V. Miller, who taught me that God indeed sees our pain and longs to bring healing to the hearts of the hurting.

A thank you to both Dawn Kinzer and Jessica Snell for their hard work on the first drafts of *The Bottle House* and for the wonderful people at Elk Lake Publishing.

Thank you, Deb Haggerty and Cristel Phelps, for believing in my novel and giving it a chance and a big thank you to Sue Fairchild who has worked many hours helping *The Bottle House* be the best it can be.

CHAPTER 1

"Not guilty."

The crack of the gavel punctuated the words he'd feared most. Stefan's stomach dropped, and he quickly sat down, afraid his legs would buckle. He chanced a look at his client, Allie Barker, who sat with her hands over her face, her shoulders heaving as the waves of the verdict washed over her. Three-year-old Lauren sat in her mini wheelchair and stared at her mother, not understanding what had just happened.

Stefan looked around the courtroom, and his gaze stopped at the jury box. Two of the very people who had decided Allie's fate were now dabbing at their eyes with tissues.

Oh, Lord, how could this have happened? You know how much Allie needed a win in her personal injury case but, no! You refused to help. Now she and little Lauren will not have the funds to aid in Lauren's ongoing medical bills. I hope you're happy as you notice the suffering you could have prevented.

As the courtroom cleared, one of the jurors who had been crying walked slowly to their table, seemingly unsure she would be welcomed. Nervousness joined anger and regret in Stefan's gut. He quickly reached for his notes and folders, sure this woman would blame him for his inadequacies that ultimately lost the case for Allie. Stefan rose as she came near.

"I'm so sorry this case turned out the way it did." The juror pulled at the crumpled tissue in her hand. "Watching little Lauren, realizing she will never walk again, broke my heart." The woman's voice wavered. "I know I voted not guilty, but I want you to know I noticed the hurt, grief, and devastation Ms. Barker and Lauren have now and will continue to have to live with. In spite of how it looks, I do care."

Stefan nodded.

"It was obvious to me the recall on her car was not fixed, and there was a strong possibility the mechanic Ms. Barker spoke with acted out of spite, causing the horrible accident. I just couldn't vote guilty, because the man did not testify in court. I needed to hear from him, but I didn't." She looked down and stiffened her shoulders before turning and walking away. Her words only added to the large helping of guilt Stefan already held.

He could feel heat fill his cheeks as he sat back down and looked at his client.

Allie turned and their eyes met. Stefan's body drew back involuntarily as he saw the look of anguish on this young mother's face. Her hands, wet from tears, shook as she pulled a lock of hair out of her eyes and tucked it behind one ear.

"It's okay, Mr. Krause. You did everything you could to help me and Lauren. We'll get by. You'll see."

Allie wiped her eyes once more. Gathering her things, she rose, unlocked the brakes on Lauren's wheelchair, and slowly pushed her disabled daughter from the room.

Stefan rubbed at the stiffness in his neck. He knew he should have said something in reply or, at the very least, apologized for his failure. Instead, he began shoving papers into his briefcase, disgusted with himself.

He left the courtroom and marched to his car, pulling the knot of his tie loose as he walked. After tossing his briefcase onto the passenger seat, Stefan got in and drove down a road he traveled daily, passing the church he had attended with his late wife, Sophie. In that moment, Stefan's angered focused on God once again. He had refused to return for Sunday services since Sophie had died of colon cancer a year and a half ago. Any god who failed to extend his mercy to his beautiful wife was not a god he wanted to worship.

As his feelings of despair mounted, he stepped on the accelerator more than usual, sending his car ahead at a dangerous speed. He no longer cared. So what if he crashed the car? He'd be better off dead anyway. He no longer had his wife to live for and had heaped additional anguish on his young client. The weight of self-loathing was getting too much to carry.

Arriving at his law firm, Stefan grabbed his briefcase and walked into the building. Mrs. Warren, his secretary and paralegal, had gone home for the day, and he breathed a sigh of relief. He didn't feel like talking about the lost court case. He had other accusations to tend to.

Stefan swung his briefcase onto his desk with a bang. As he began to open the clasps, his eyes were drawn unswervingly to Sophie's picture sitting on the right corner of his desk. Stefan sat down heavily in his chair.

"What must you think of your husband today?" Stefan said, speaking to the picture. "I lost the court case. There's a part of me that's glad you aren't here to see my failure."

After a moment, his anger stirred again, and his hands curled into fists.

"How could you have continued to put your faith in a god who doesn't care about the agony of a young, single mother and her crippled daughter? One who desperately needed the financial help that a favorable ruling in her case would have provided?"

Stefan sucked in a deep breath as he realized he also felt anger for his dead wife. Repulsed at this thought, Stefan jumped up and moved away from the desk, preventing Sophie's picture from throwing accusations at him. The window in the office drew him, and Stefan took a long look out at the shade of a maple tree, gnarled with age.

As his spirit relaxed a bit, he continued his conversation with his late wife in a softer tone.

"Sophie, please tell me how you could love a god who allowed such pain to throb through your body, ultimately taking your breath permanently away."

He waited for an answer but knew none would come. After a moment, Stefan turned and walked out of the building, determined to never enter it again.

⚰✝⚰

I hope the dead cannot see all of the despair that saturate this life.

Stefan stood near his wife's headstone, his shoulders hunched.

"Oh, Sophie, I'm so ashamed. I failed you, and now I've failed Allie. When you needed encouragement and support so badly, I crumbled under my own pain. *You* were the one with colon cancer. *You* were the one who had to endure unthinkable pain, and yet, I focused on mine." Stefan's lips trembled as a tear traced the curve of his cheek. "And now I've failed Allie and Lauren too."

Stefan sat down hard under a tree and gazed at Sophie's grave. The image of little Lauren with her blonde pigtails, confined to a miniature wheelchair when she should be running and playing, filled his mind. He placed his head in his hands and cried.

How could the jury side with the car manufacturer? They knew the mechanic was vindictive and had destroyed the evidence that would have proved he had not replaced Allie's airbag.

Stefan's mind went next to Allie's face as the foreman gave the verdict. He could see the shock in her eyes and her body collapse in her chair as she covered her face with her hands. The mental picture tore at Stefan's heart, and he felt ashamed. He stood quickly and strode to his car. He drove home but, instead of going inside, marched straight to the beach.

He lifted his gaze from the ocean before him and up to the heavens. "What kind of attorney am I? I should have pursued subpoenaing the mechanic, no matter what he would testify to." He shook his head. "Now, Allie and Lauren will not have the financial protection they deserve, and it's all because of me. I've failed them."

Looking out at the water, Stefan remembered Sophie saying the waves washing in and out was the ocean's way of sweeping the clutter from the shore and making it clean once more, and what a beautiful picture of what God does for our hearts.

Stefan continued to speak to the heavens. "I don't know why my wife loved you so much, God. You've taken her away from me, broken my spirit, and now taken away my career."

He paused, lowered his eyes, and shook his head. "The Barkers would be better off without me. I did them no good. I failed Sophie when she needed me most, and you must think I'm pathetic."

His chest felt tight, as if it were suffocating him. As a wave washed over his shoes, he spoke softly, "I'm sorry, Sophie."

He staggered forward, the salty water washing over his head.

CHAPTER 2

Stacy sat next to her husband, Jack, as they waited for the sermon to begin. They'd been to this church before at the nudging of her best friend Aubree, who now sat on her other side. She scanned the order of service in the bulletin. Today's message would be grounded in John 11—the story of Jesus raising Lazarus from the dead. She enjoyed this passage and sat back in the pew, excited to see what angle Pastor Martin would take with these verses today.

As the sermon began, however, Stacy's mind wandered back to the argument she and Jack had yesterday. She'd spent the day cleaning the house. The job went slowly due to the amount clutter that had accumulated everywhere in their two-bedroom apartment. By late afternoon, she'd been exhausted. She had just sat down with a glass of iced tea when Jack came home, a golf bag hanging heavily on his shoulder.

"What's for supper?" he'd asked, throwing his bag into a corner she'd just cleared of junk.

Every muscle in her body tensed. "Is that all you can ask when you've been gone all day on the golf course while I cleaned up from your mess? What's for supper? Seriously?" Her voice rose in anger.

"Well, I see it's going to be another wonderful evening of walking on eggshells. Boy! This will be *so* much fun."

Stacy jumped up, some of her iced tea spilling over the rim of her class. "Fun? You have the nerve to say fun when my day has been anything but?"

Jack picked up his golf clubs, walked out of the room and to the closet down the hall. Stacy heard him forcefully push his bag of clubs in and then slam the door, followed by the bathroom door banging shut. The sound of flowing water in the shower announced the end to their conversation.

Stacy's attention jumped from the horrible evening to her present surroundings.

"I am the resurrection and the life. The one who believes in me will live, even though they die." Pastor Martin smiled. "Isn't it interesting Jesus spoke of 'resurrection' in the same sentence as the word 'die'? Isn't it obvious? A resurrection comes only after death. I think it's important to remember that resurrection cannot happen until someone has died."

Stacy tried to swallow but the lump in her throat made it difficult.

God, are you trying to tell me my marriage is dying, and if so, you can resurrect it?

A flutter of hope filled Stacy's stomach. *This must be a direct message from God. He will resurrect our marriage!* A smile blossomed on her face.

She hoped she hadn't missed any other important moments with her daydreaming. At the end of the service, she turned to her friend. "Hey, Aubree, I've got the dress you wanted to borrow out in the car. Why don't you stay here and keep Jack company while I go get it?"

Aubree had an interview tomorrow for a different position at Eden Behavioral Healthcare where they both worked. Aubree was hoping to move away from nursing and move to the administration department of the facility.

As Stacy returned with the garment, she could see Jack and Aubree across the room. Jack held his hand at the small of Aubree's back as her friend laughed and brushed her bangs out of her eyes. A trickle of fear washed through her stomach as she watched the exchange, but, as they saw her approach, their attention moved immediately back toward her.

Aubree accepted the dress with a hug and then turned to make her way home. Without another word, Jack strode to the car with Stacy hurrying to catch up. At home, Stacy busied herself making Sunday dinner. Jack sat on the sofa across the room from the kitchen and became engrossed with something on his phone. The feelings of yesterday returned.

Why am I always the one doing the work while he relaxes?

Glancing up from the salad she was preparing, she noticed Jack smiling at his phone. That fleeting fear she'd felt earlier returned. A panic hovered around her heart. She wondered momentarily what he was smiling about before grabbing the salad bowl and utensils and moving to the table. Perhaps his good mood would help them enjoy a conflict-free afternoon.

⚰✝⚰

Stacy looked up from the screen where she had been working on patient reports all morning. She leaned back, stretched, and glanced at the clock. Lunch hour loomed, and she smiled, thinking of her plan to get takeout from Jack's and her favorite restaurant, Gino's, and bring it home for their supper. They rarely went there because it was so expensive, but Stacy hoped this would put back some of the spark in a marriage she felt cooling. She desperately wanted to push out the fear and panic she'd been experiencing lately and, perhaps, this surprise would help. Retrieving her purse from her desk drawer, Stacy stood and headed for the office of her supervisor, Amelia Alexander.

She stuck her head in and smiled. "I'm heading out to pick up some food for our supper tonight. Would you like me to pick up something for you?" Stacy had already planned to store her takeout meal in the staff refrigerator and pop it into the oven to warm slowly as soon as she got home.

Amelia leaned back and quickly checked the clock. "I didn't realize it was lunchtime already. The morning has flown by." She removed her glasses and rubbed the bridge of her nose. "No, but thanks for the offer. I have some leftovers I plan on eating. I'll see you later."

Stacy strode out to the large parking lot of the Eden Behavioral Healthcare Facility and unlocked her car. Tossing her purse onto the passenger seat, she peered briefly into the rearview mirror. Stacy smiled, glad to see most of her hair still contained in the ponytail she often wore to work. Throwing the car into gear, she drove the short distance to Gino's.

As she entered the restaurant, Stacy breathed in the smell of garlic—her mouth began to water. She placed her order and sat down to wait, enjoying the soft sounds of Italian music playing. From her seat, she could see into the main dining room, and she looked at an area of booths beyond the lobby to her left.

She blinked in surprise. Was that Jack sitting across from Aubree?

The sick feeling of fear returned and filled her stomach as Jack caressed Aubree's hand with his. Stacy jumped from her seat and moved behind a wall in the lobby, hoping they hadn't seen her. With shaking hands and pounding heart, Stacy closed her eyes and took a deep breath. Her lower lip trembled as she remembered a time when Jack had looked at her with such tenderness.

What exactly had she seen? Surely, there was a legitimate explanation. Stacy shook her head, not convincing herself. She turned and rushed out of the restaurant, leaving her order behind. Her heart pounded as she rushed across the parking lot to her car.

I've got to get out of here before they see me!

Her hands trembled as she gripped the steering wheel, hoping the tight hold would keep her from running off the road. In minutes, she pulled back into the Eden parking lot, and the first surge of tears filled her eyes and rolled down her cheeks. She turned off her car and sat rigidly, trying to pull herself together.

Why would Aubree do this to me? What about Jack? Could they really be having an affair?

Stacy dug through her purse looking for tissues. Finding some, she dabbed at her eyes, then placed her hands back on the wheel, fighting another wave of nausea and fear.

"How could he? How could *she*?"

As her initial shock ebbed, Stacy sucked in a deep breath. She mopped her face with another wad of tissues and gazed into the rearview mirror. She frowned at the reflection of her splotchy face and red eyes, but she needed to move. Aubree would soon be returning from her lunch break, and Stacy wished to avoid her.

She slammed the door and mindlessly ran her hands down her blue scrubs. Stacy didn't know exactly what she would do, but she did know she would be proactive. "I don't care what excuse Jack gives me. I won't tolerate infidelity."

As she marched up to the main entrance, Stacy's heart filled with disgust crowding out the fear. She'd thought Aubree was her friend. They'd started going to church together!

Ugh! That's probably just so she could see Jack more.

She paused before opening the door, wiping her clammy hands on her pants again as another wave of fear washed over her anger.

What if I run into her this afternoon?

Then she remembered. Aubree was interviewing for the administration job in *her* borrowed dress. Stacy frowned but then remembered Aubree would also be conducting intake assessments on several new patients this afternoon after her interview—their paths wouldn't cross. She let out a huge breath.

Avoiding anyone's eyes, she made her way quietly to the nurses' office area. She sat down hard in her chair, stared at her computer screen, and typed in her password. In the seconds the machine took to run through its digital calisthenics, her thoughts returned to what she had seen, and the tears began again. She quickly wiped them away.

What will I do? Things hadn't been great between her and Jack, but she'd believed all married couples went through struggles from time to time.

Stacy's stomach churned. She'd chatted with Aubree often about her marriage, so she knew about their difficulties. She'd even admitted to Aubree she and Jack wanted to start a family and had been trying to get pregnant.

Her chin trembled as she worked hard not to let anyone coming in and out of the office know of her distress. *You've got to pull yourself together.*

The end of her shift finally came, and Stacy was relieved she hadn't encountered Aubree. She didn't trust herself with the anger and despair she harbored just below the layer of her professional self.

Stacy climbed into her car, pausing as a wave of dizziness flowed over her from skipping lunch. As she drove slowly home, she prayed, "God, I don't know what I'm going to do. I need your help. Please!"

She had almost an hour before Jack would come home. As she paced the living room, her mind raced over what she had seen and what she would do.

Shuddering, she remembered that day in church when she'd seen them laughing together.

"I'm so glad you could join me this morning," Aubree had said. "I hope you guys will visit my church again."

Now Stacy understood Aubree had been speaking more to Jack than her.

Clearly, Aubree's church invitations hadn't been meant to help them find one that was a better fit for them. How had she failed to put one plus one together?

"How could I have been so blind?"

⚬✝⚬

A week later, Stacy stood in her kitchen making coffee. She hadn't spoken to Jack since she'd confronted him about his affair with Aubree. He'd freely admitted they were having one and seemed relieved when Stacy asked him to pack his things and leave. Now the apartment seemed so quiet. She'd hoped the pain of her broken marriage would diminish, but so far, it hadn't.

Last week, Stacy had confessed to Amelia what had happened and asked if she knew of any openings for nursing in a different location, knowing she couldn't work in the same place as Aubree. Amelia sympathized with Stacy and promised to research other jobs for her, and, under the circumstances, encouraging Stacy to take a few days off.

With a mug of coffee in her hand, Stacy sat at the table and reached for her Bible. She turned to where she'd left off yesterday, reading from Psalm 34.

> *I sought the Lord, and he answered me; he delivered me from all my fears. Those who look to him are radiant; their faces are never covered with shame. This poor man called, and the Lord heard him; he saved him out of all his troubles. The angel of the Lord encamps around those who fear him, and he delivers them.*

Stacy had prayed through those verses every morning for the past week, desperately wanting to believe them.

She bowed her head. "I am seeking you, Lord, but I'm a poor example of a faithful follower. I just can't summon enough faith to place my situation in your hands."

The chime of the cell phone startled her, and she glanced at the caller ID.

She answered and said, "Hello, Amelia."

"Good morning, Stacy. I've missed seeing you every day. You've come to mind frequently."

"Thank you." Her heart felt soothed with the knowledge someone did care about her.

"I wanted to let you know I've been reaching out to other healthcare facilities as you've asked and have found one that has an immediate opening for a nurse. It's Bethany R&L in Klauthmos Bay, about three hours north of here."

"You found an opening for me?" At hearing the unexpected news, Stacy's voice became thick with emotion.

"Yes. On top of that, I've spoken with the nursing supervisor, Mrs. Turner, and she's very interested in interviewing you if you're willing to relocate."

"I'm willing!" Stacy said, trying to rein in her excitement.

"I told Mrs. Turner I believed you were. The job is for a full-time behavioral healthcare nurse, similar to what you do here at Eden. Another plus of this job is you could probably get by without a car. Mrs. Turner said Bethany R&L is located just off the beach, and you can walk to most places you would need, but public transportation is available too."

Stacy quickly added up how much she could bank if she sold her car. She wondered if Jack would help her sell it or how she'd accomplish the sale so far from home. In that moment, she was glad she and Jack always kept their cars in their own names.

"Mrs. Turner said to give her a call so an interview can be set up. She's also suggested you contact the chaplain of Bethany R&L, Chaplain Joseph Miller. He knows several people who would be willing to put you up for the night when you go for an interview, and he could help you find somewhere to live should the job be offered, and you accept."

Stacy jotted down Mrs. Turner's number as well as Chaplain Miller's.

She covered her mouth with her hand, containing her excitement. Just a few short minutes ago she felt so alone, and now, hope was knocking at her heart's door.

Dare she dream this might be the answer to her painful situation?

CHAPTER 3

Debbie didn't realize what she was doing then, but she began digging a hole within her heart when she was small that would get deeper in the years to come. Every time her mother said, "You're being overly dramatic" or "You idiot! You should have known better," Debbie would shovel out another piece of her heart. Before she realized, the hole had grown six feet deep. She imagined a tombstone sitting close by that held the words, *Debbie Young, Unlovable, Stupid, Flawed, and an Embarrassment.*

Tears ran down the young woman's face as she stared at her phone, her fingers cramped and still feeling the warmth from the connection to her ear after enduring another one-sided conversation with her mother.

All I wanted was to tell Mom about how our new teaching jobs were going, but as usual, the conversation changed to Mom's favorite subject—what's wrong with me.

Debbie shifted her body in discomfort from sitting so long on the steps of the house she and Josh were renting. Looking up through her tears, she quietly asked God for his deliverance from the painful idea that she was damaged goods. Yes, she was thankful he'd brought her a husband who not only loved her, but also supported her, and yet, often that didn't feel like enough. *Why can't my mother see me this way?*

The truth was, except for time she spent with Josh, Debbie often felt lonely, not only for the family she wished she had but for others as well. She wasn't good at making friends. Probably because she approached people cautiously, wondering how soon they would catch on to what a failure she was. Her judgmental voice within continued its deadly sabotage, accusing her of not living a life by faith. After all, shouldn't God's children be thankful for all blessings they received?

As she glanced around their front yard, the excitement from both Josh and her teaching jobs at Good Shepherd Christian School were fading, providing Debbie another opportunity to thrust her shovel into the dirt within her heart and pull out another mound.

When she'd told her mother about the school's requirements that she and Josh attend Good Shepherd Bible Church, her mother had said, "Still can't think for yourself, I see."

Now the idea did seem a little strict to her.

"After all," Pastor Hughes had said at their interview, "we want teachers who support the whole effort here. We also require attendance and support for all church functions."

Surely, he'd only been referring to Sunday services.

Then Josh had been informed the school also expected he take over working with the youth group at the church, requiring him to be away from home almost every night of the week. Many of the students in the youth group were Josh's regular students, and the school thought the extra activities offered the perfect opportunity for Josh to bond with them. But Debbie craved the evenings they used to have together, and she hated that Josh was now often at the church. She could also clearly see how stressed her husband had grown with the increased workload, and she resented that burden on him.

I wonder how many of the school board members would be willing to do the job they expected of Josh for no extra compensation.

Shaking her head, Debbie sighed. *I wish I didn't care so much about what Pastor Hughes, Principal Jenkins, and Mom thinks. If I could let this go, then others wouldn't be able to hurt me so much. Why couldn't Mom just say, "Oh, Debbie! Your job sounds wonderful. You are so good in the third-grade classroom, and Josh teaching high school science is perfect." Why do Principal Jenkins and Pastor Hughes have such ridiculous expectations for us?*

Debbie stood as tears pooled and her voice caught. "God, why won't you help? I hate feeling this way and I don't know what to do to lighten the load I'm carrying within my heart. Don't you care?"

Brushing the tears aside, she pulled a tissue from her pocket and blew her nose. Realizing, once again, she would hear nothing from God, she trudged into the house to start making lunch.

🍾✝🍾

Debbie paced as she waited for Josh to gather his things. She thought of their first day of school, when she'd felt a surge of hope within for a new opportunity—a clean slate. But that comfort was long gone now.

In spite of the months they had been teaching, no one at the school had befriended her or tried to be welcoming. Although she had bonded with some of her students, she still felt a nagging feeling that she'd be judged harshly by her superiors.

Debbie had hoped they could ride back and forth to work each day, but often they could not due to Josh's after school responsibilities. She longed to chat with her husband about making a difference in children's lives. But lately their conversations had mostly been vent sessions about the difficulties their schedules presented.

But today they could drive together. She smiled as Josh grabbed the keys and gave her a peck on the cheek.

When they arrived at Good Shepherd, they dropped their things off in their classrooms and then made their way to the school's chapel for a short staff meeting before the children were due.

Debbie hoped this meeting would not be long as she was eager to get back to her classroom and recheck that everything was ready for when her third graders arrived.

Principal Jered Jennings stood before the group of educators and tapped the lectern with his knuckle.

"As we are all aware, we have the privilege and responsibility of shepherding our students academically and spiritually. Remember, you are here for the students and not the other way around. Their needs are our priority." He paused a moment to let his words sink in.

After several announcements, he said, "Let us pray. God, thank you for a new day, a chance to make a difference in the students' lives here at Good Shepherd Christian School. I ask that you anoint this group of gifted educators so they will be prepared for whatever comes their way. In Jesus's name. Amen."

Debbie and Josh rose, eager to go to their classrooms. Halfway to the door, Mr. Jennings stopped Debbie. Josh hesitated, not knowing if he should stay or go.

"Go ahead, Josh," the principal stated, not asked. "We won't be but a minute."

Debbie felt her heart beat faster. Had she done something wrong? Then her eyes connected with her husband's, and a calm ran through her body. Josh squeezed her hand and smiled before walking away to begin his day.

She turned back toward Principal Jennings.

"Late yesterday afternoon, I made a tour through all the teachers' rooms, and I must say, I love the bulletin boards you have up."

"Thank you." Debbie's breathing quickened, wondering what he was going to add on that she had not gotten right.

"There is one thing, however, that concerned me. You have some beginner's chapter books. I assume you must have brought those with you. Though I think these books are appropriate for readers on the third-grade level, you should have checked with me first. Anytime you want to use supplemental materials outside of the specific curriculum that is schoolboard approved, it must be okayed with me." Mr. Jennings pushed his wire-framed glasses back up his nose.

"I'm sorry. I didn't know." Debbie moved her eyes from her boss to the door, longing to get away from the conversation.

The principal's eyes followed Debbie's to the doorway. "I can see you're anxious to get to your classroom. Have a good day, Mrs. Young."

Debbie left the chapel feeling less confident in what she had planned for her students. A frown replaced the smile she wore as she returned to her classroom.

CHAPTER 4

Stefan opened his eyes and looked at a sterile gray wall. To his right, medical instruments beeped and hissed. He looked around, confused. "Where am I? How did I get here?"

A woman in blue scrubs stepped beside him. "Hi, I'm Nurse Collins. You're in the hospital. Do you remember what happened yesterday that brought you here?"

Sophie's death, Allie's case, the verdict, and his despair came rushing back. He nodded and stared at the ceiling.

The nurse clicked the keys of her laptop recording medical information. "You just rest. Dr. Ross will be in soon to speak with you."

Stefan closed his eyes and felt a jolt of disgrace and sorrow, remembering how and why he'd tried to end his life. How he got here from that point, he didn't know. Stefan didn't have the energy to wipe away his tears, so he let them run down his face and drip onto his pillow.

In what seemed like minutes, Stefan woke to a voice he didn't recognize. "Hello, Mr. Krause, my name is Dr. Ross. How are you feeling today?"

Instead of answering the doctor's question, he asked, "How did I get here?"

The doctor gazed at his tablet and moved his attention to his patient. "A man was strolling on the beach and saw you go under. He jumped in and pulled you out. He began CPR while his wife called 911. You vomited a lot of ocean water and were breathing on your own by the time the ambulance came. He got you out just in time. He's convinced you went right in over your head on purpose. Is he right?"

Stefan nodded his head slowly, closing his eyes as another tear squeezed out.

The doctor didn't push for explanations. "The hospital chaplain will be in to see you in the morning. I'll send Nurse Collins to give you something to help you sleep."

Stefan opened his eyes as the doctor turned and quietly left the room.

His mind jumped to the night Sophie died. He had been in a room similar to this one. Grief and despair washed over him again with more force than the ocean's tides. Sobs poured from his being and echoed in the room. All he wanted to do was die.

⚰️✝️⚰️

When Stefan awoke again, his room gleamed with sunlight. He squinted and rolled his head away from the window. Remembering what had brought him here and the events leading up to it caused anguish to move through him once more.

Stefan startled when someone standing at the end of his bed spoke.

"Hello, Mr. Krause. I'm Chaplain Thomas." The older man moved closer to Stefan's bed, his brown eyes filled with concern. "I'm aware of the reason you're here, Mr. Krause, and I want to assure you I'm not here to judge."

"Thank you."

Stefan's words were barely discernible, but the chaplain nodded an acknowledgment. He brought Stefan some tissues, then poured some water into a flimsy plastic cup and handed it to him. Stefan stared at the water, realizing he had used this very thing to try and end his life. *Is water a friend or an enemy?* He raised the cup to his lips and took a sip as the chaplain sat in the chair beside the bed.

"If you want to talk, I'm here to listen. If not, that's fine too. I just want you to know I care, and so does God."

Stefan gasped as the chaplain's words sparked a bitter kindling in his soul. "Your profession stands for a god who I obviously know nothing about," he spat. "The God I know is either too weak to do anything for us here on earth or, worse than that, has the power to help and chooses not to." Stefan slammed the now empty cup back down on the side table. "All these years I've wasted, talking to a god who is indifferent to my feelings and situations."

A part of him felt ashamed for his outburst—another part felt relieved to admit it.

Chaplain Thomas sat quietly. Stefan was glad he didn't try and defend God. He didn't want to hear empty platitudes right now.

A few moments passed before the chaplain spoke again. "Mr. Krause, I'm here to help, but if my being here is causing you too much pain, I'll leave."

"No, it's fine for you to be here." Stefan wiped a hand over his face. "I'm sorry I said those things. I meant everything, but I didn't mean for my words to scorch you. My anger isn't directed toward you. I just want out of here."

"I understand, and I didn't take it personally." His eyes locked on Stefan's. "Do you think you're ready to leave here? Is home a good place for you to be right now?"

Stefan blinked, surprised at Chaplain Thomas's directness. Then he thought of his quiet, empty home.

"I want to leave, but I'm scared of facing the despair alone."

The chaplain nodded and then reached into his notebook and pulled out a brochure. "Mr. Krause, I have a suggestion for you. Here is a brochure for Bethany R&L in Klauthmos Bay, California. It's an inpatient behavioral healthcare center that offers specific treatment to people who have suffered trauma. Although I don't know your specific trauma, it's clear you're struggling. Trained counselors and medical doctors are there to help people in situations like yours. On top of that, Bethany has one of the best chaplains I've ever had the pleasure to know, Chaplain Joseph Miller. I'd like for you to consider checking yourself in there to receive some help in the healing process. You don't deserve to carry so many burdens. These people can help you put down that load."

Chaplain Thomas stood and placed the brochure on the table beside Stefan's bed. "I'll be in again to check on you. If you decide to check out the brochure and have any questions, I'll be happy to try and answer them. If I don't have the answers, I know where I can get them. I see your pain, and my prayer is you find healing. Is it okay if I pray?"

At Stefan's nod, he bowed his head. "Lord, your child is hurting. Please remind him that you love him and give him the strength to move forward. In Jesus's name, amen." The chaplain slipped quietly out of the room.

Stefan gazed up at the ceiling, overwhelmed. The idea of going to a behavioral healthcare facility made him wonder if people thought he was crazy. On the other hand, he felt nauseated at the thought of being home alone.

He picked up the brochure. As he read about Bethany, he wondered if he even wanted to get help.

A more honest question was whether he deserved help.

CHAPTER 5

Stefan was ashamed to visit Sophie, but he needed to before he drove to Klauthmos Bay. He laid a bouquet of daylilies in front of her headstone and took a seat, holding his head in his hands. He didn't remember a time when he couldn't think of what to say to his wife. Words had always come so naturally until now.

When he'd gathered his thoughts, he took a deep breath and began. "Sophie, since you left, loneliness and grief have continuously fought to rule my heart. That's why throwing myself into my work became vital. It helped me forget, but only for a time.

"Losing the Barker case makes me feel inadequate and shameful. These are heavy weights to bear on my shoulders. I should have known better, should have backtracked repeatedly just to make sure I had everything I needed to win a ruling in Allie's case. I failed her, I failed you, and I failed myself.

"If it's not bad enough telling you this, I've spoiled the Krause name by trying to end my life. In this way only, I'm glad you're not here to bear my shame."

Stefan's throat constricted, and he paused, staring at the one-word epitaph on Sophie's stone—*Beloved*. Anguish washed over him once more.

"I won't be able to visit you for a while. I hope you understand and think I'm doing the right thing by going to

Bethany R&L. I'm so tired and overwhelmed—it's the right place to be. As ever, you won't be far from my thoughts." He stood and placed his fingers lightly on her name. "Bye for now."

⚰︎✝⚰︎

Two days later, Stefan sipped some coffee as he drove down the coast. He would be in Klauthmos Bay in about twenty minutes. He'd wrestled with his feelings when he first considered going, but now felt nothing. This lack of emotion concerned him more than the lack of motivation he'd experienced these past weeks.

As he drove, he caught glimpses of the ocean from time to time. He thought of his office a block from the ocean. The lights would be off now, and Mrs. Warren's desk would be tidy—no files stacked up on one corner as they usually were. His faithful paralegal had wanted to visit her sister on the east coast, which meant closing up for a while had not been a concern for her. The doors would remain locked, and the firm's mail would be held indefinitely.

Stefan's goodbye to Mrs. Warren had been difficult for both of them. He was sure she felt as much responsibility for the loss of the Barker case as he did, even though Stefan had assured her she was not to blame.

When they closed up the office together, Mrs. Warren had stifled a sob and said, "You will be in my prayers, Mr. Krause. I hope your time away will bring you comfort." He saw her wipe her eyes as she rushed to her car.

The "Welcome to Klauthmos Bay" sign drew him back to the present. He pulled into the next gas station, checked his directions, and filled his tank. No telling when he'd need to use the car again, but it was probably wise to fill up while he was there. Stefan knew he was just dragging his feet by delaying his arrival. Regardless, he needed to get back in the car and keep going.

Stefan studied his phone and then made a couple of turns before finally pulling into the main parking lot. A large building stood in the front of the compound, and a bronze sign outside the building read "Bethany R&L."

He sat for a while and wondered again if coming here was a good idea, his stomach filling with his anxiety. *If I stay in my car, I can avoid dealing with my despair, but if I don't deal with this, it will eat me alive.* He opened the door forcefully and made his way to the trunk to retrieve his suitcase.

As he strode to the front entrance, a cool breeze brushed over him. Stefan wished it could soothe his soul. He glanced around. In the far-left corner, a small gathering of people sat in a cluster of comfortable chairs. In the opposite corner, a woman sat keying information into a computer. The nameplate on her desk read, "Elena Crockett."

He ambled over to her. "I'm Stefan Krause. I believe I'm expected today."

The woman smiled, checked her appointment log, and stood. "Nice to meet you, Mr. Krause. Welcome to Bethany R&L. I'm Mrs. Elena Crockett." She held out her hand, and Stefan shook it.

"I see all of your paperwork is complete," Mrs. Crockett said after checking his file. "Mrs. Turner will be here shortly to greet you and take you to your room. Why don't you have a seat, and I'll call you when she's ready for you."

In the split second that followed, Stefan fought the urge to run out of the building and leave. But where would he go and to what? He sat in a nearby seat. Hopefully, the wait wouldn't be long. He yearned for the privacy his own room could provide.

Stefan closed his eyes. He didn't want to think about where he was and why. Unfortunately, other thoughts crowded in—thoughts of Sophie and the suffering they both experienced jabbed a knife into his heart. The anguished face of Allie Barker pinched his chest further. Would these images haunt him the rest of his life?

"Mr. Krause? I'm Mrs. Turner. Welcome to Bethany R&L."

Stefan opened his eyes. Before him stood a woman in her thirties, dressed in a straight skirt and blouse similar to what female attorneys wore. Her brown hair was held back by two combs, one on each side of her head. She wore little jewelry, which Stefan thought practical in her position. She smiled at him, waiting for his reply.

He stood and held out his hand. "Stefan Krause." She shook his hand, never breaking eye contact.

Moving her focus to the open folder she was carrying, Mrs. Turner said, "I see we have all the information we need at this time. I'll take you to your room. This way, please."

Stefan picked up his suitcase and followed her through a set of doors.

"We're in the main building of Bethany R&L. In addition to the welcome and visitor's lounge you came into when you arrived, this building houses our cafeteria, doctors' and counselors' offices, and administration conference rooms."

They made their way out of the building and across a courtyard. Several lounge chairs were clustered in small groups surrounding a sizeable fountain spraying a cascade of water into a large circular pool. Koi swam in the clear water. Stefan wondered how many people it took to maintain a place like this. Would he ever find his way around?

Mrs. Turner paused in front of another building. "Mr. Krause, this is the Sozo building that accommodates our male guests. *Sozo* is the New Testament Greek word meaning, 'healing of the entire man.'"

He desperately wanted healing, but he didn't deserve it. The knowledge made his heart ache.

She opened the door, and they entered another lounge with several comfortable chairs, arranged, once again, in small groups. These were occupied by a few men who seemed engrossed in quiet conversation. The room's walls were painted tan, and the floor was hardwood. Several bookshelves held many volumes, and chess and checkerboard games were scattered on tables about the room.

As she made her way through another set of doors, Mrs. Turner led Stefan down a carpeted hallway, up a flight of stairs, and through a second hallway. Stefan followed until Mrs. Turner stopped at room 2023 and opened the door. She stood aside for Stefan to enter, and he stepped in, setting his suitcase down.

The walls were light brown surrounded by cream trim. One large Persian carpet covered the hardwood floor, and Stefan liked that a desk and chair sat near the large window. A simple quilt lay on the bed, and a nightstand with a lamp sat to one side. A single armoire stood against the wall opposite the bed.

"The bathroom and shower are through this door," Mrs. Turner said, pointing. "You have a couple of hours before supper is served, so why don't you unpack and get settled?"

"Thank you," Stefan said.

"You'll find a small kitchen off the lounge we saw upon entrance to this building. Juice, coffee, and tea are available there. Supper is from five thirty to six thirty in the main building. Maps of the Bethany campus are posted by the main doors of each building in case you lose your way. At this point, do you have any questions?"

Stefan shook his head. "No, thank you."

Mrs. Turner nodded and quietly shut the door behind her.

Stefan wandered over to the window and gazed out into another small courtyard. A couple of large trees grew out of a fine-trimmed carpet of grass. He opened his window and immediately smelled the salty breeze.

He closed his eyes for a moment and whispered, "I miss you so much, Sophie."

Had he done the right thing? Coming here, to this place? Would he find the help he needed to become whole again? Or would he only make a fool of himself?

Stefan sighed and wiped the moisture from his eyes.

Was it possible to find a reason to live again?

CHAPTER 6

Debbie shuffled papers around on her desk, striving to get some work done before heading home. Her class of third graders was filled with a wide spectrum of academic abilities as well as several behavioral issues, and the workload of grading papers was immense. She turned as she heard someone enter the room, thinking it was one of her students. Instead, Pastor Hughes stood just inside the door, his hands clasped in front of him.

"Debbie, I'm glad to see you today. Josh said you had quite the headache yesterday when I asked why you'd skipped services."

She felt the prickle of resentment as she stood and looked the pastor in the eye. "Though the Bible tells us in Hebrews that we should not neglect the meeting together of God's people, I don't believe this requires attendance at every service. I have been at the majority of them since Josh and I moved here."

Though Pastor Hughes said nothing more, Debbie noticed his frown as he turned and walked away.

She sat back down at her desk and heaved a sigh. She'd had confrontations with Principal Jennings many times too as they'd attempted to decide on the best course of action for teaching her students. She'd never felt so micromanaged, and they'd often had very different ideas. Tension sparked between her and the administration constantly.

Susan Grant

Each time one of these confrontations with the pastor or principal occurred, Debbie could hear her mother's voice in their words, implying she was a failure as a teacher and a Christian. The hole in her heart she was digging grew deeper with each confrontation and rejection.

Gazing out the window of her classroom, Debbie remembered the issue Mr. Jennings had brought up last week. The church was holding a Christian Growth Conference, and Debbie had done her best to attend each night, but her pile of students' work grew so large she'd skipped the second and third nights. She'd been glad for a chance to get caught up.

Mr. Jennings had come to her empty classroom the next day and told her in no uncertain terms he expected her to be in attendance for the rest of the conference.

As the months passed, Debbie felt stretched thinner and thinner. While trying to teach students with so many needs, she also had to deal with overly demanding parents who were certain they knew exactly what their child's education and class needed. Debbie found out one of her students, Larry, had been expelled from the local public school, and his parents had placed him at Good Shepherd, hoping he would be better understood.

Whenever Debbie needed to correct Larry's behavior, it was a given the child would go home and tell his version of the situation, and his parents would be right on the phone with her principal later. Also, predictably, the principal would come and question her about the latest conversation he'd had with Larry's parents. These moments always put Debbie on edge. She felt her fears of being seen as a fraud were coming to fruition. Her continual need to defend herself seeped into her conversations and reactions.

The burden of not being good enough grew as she sensed the principal losing confidence in her work. The pressure he and the pastor put on her to be at every church event also built animosity within. Just as frustrating was the fact Principal Jennings kept to his mantra of "the students' needs are the priority." Debbie agreed but began to question if the teachers' needs weren't important too. These encounters with Mr. Jennings began to happen more regularly, and Debbie often wondered how best to cope with the constant stress bombarding her every day. Although she loved teaching, she began to feel a growing lack of support from the administration.

Through winter and into spring, frustrations continued to rise from the numerous challenges, and her patience began to ebb.

Because of the frustrations Debbie felt, she often shared her aggravation with some trusted coworkers who fully understood her feelings. All were anticipating some well-deserved vacation time at the end of the school year. Her venting sessions with the other teachers had helped Debbie feel a little worthy of acceptance from her coworkers.

She turned back to her desk and began to grade papers. Just then Josh entered. She smiled. "This is a nice surprise. I didn't expect to see you—"

"Mr. Jennings asked to meet with both of us in the boardroom," he interrupted. "Willard Hughes wants to speak with us."

"Why?" She felt dread filling her body. What had she done now to garner the principal's and pastor's ire? Had another parent called to complain? Or perhaps Pastor Hughes had gone to tell on her for missing services.

Her mother's word rose to her mind. "You're always doing the wrong thing."

Josh shrugged. "I don't know. He wouldn't even give me a clue."

As Josh and Debbie made their way to the boardroom, her stomach filled with anxiety.

Mr. Jennings met them at the door. "If you both would step into the conference room, please."

Debbie paused, and Josh, perhaps sensing her emotional state, grabbed her hand and smiled.

As they stepped into the conference room, she noticed Mr. Hughes and two other board members already seated at the table. Her heart beat faster, and she had to fight the urge to turn and run from the building.

"Thank you both for coming," Mr. Hughes said as the three of them took their seats.

Debbie clenched her hands in her lap. *Did we have any choice?*

"Josh and Debbie," Mr. Hughes continued, "you know it's Good Shepherd Christian School's responsibility to make sure we're teaching the gospel of Christ, the curriculum our school has adopted, and that each staff member is living in a manner that reflects our Savior."

Mr. Hughes paused as if evaluating the comprehension of all in the room. "The biblical requirement of staying true to the cause of Christ and obeying the admonishment that we don't fail in meeting together at church is why we're having this meeting."

Mr. Hughes took a deep breath. "It concerns us, Debbie, that you are not living a life of being a servant of Christ. You have repeatedly missed services at Good Shepherd Bible Church. Several parents have called to complain. And you have been spreading animosity among our numbers by gossiping with your coworkers. Is this not true?"

Perplexed, Debbie stiffened, the feeling of doom spreading quickly through her body. "I don't understand. I have attended many services at the church. I put my students' needs first as you've asked as much as I can. But I have been vocal about the amount of work being heaped on us—not just to my coworkers but also to members of this administration."

"Yes, we are aware you are usually in attendance at church, but we expect perfect attendance. It's important to provide a united front with all our staff. Also, a few of your coworkers and Principal Jennings have let it be known on many occasions that you are often dissatisfied with decisions we have made concerning our school, and that your demeanor has been dour." Mr. Hughes looked at his notes and then at her over the tops of his spectacles.

A ringing in Debbie's ears began, and she feared she would pass out. She glanced at Josh and pleaded with her eyes. *Come on, Josh, this is your chance to speak up and tell them what our lives have been like this school year. Tell them how difficult it is to have new tasks continually dumped on you and how we've been struggling just to teach the subjects we were assigned, much less attending all church functions.*

As if reading her mind, Josh said, "Debbie has worked hard this school year and has gone out of her way to make her lessons relevant and to create an atmosphere where learning takes place. She has never missed a church service unless it was absolutely necessary."

Mr. Hughes focused on Josh. "Debbie's effectiveness in all academic areas of the third-grade curriculum is not in question here. In fact, Principal Jennings is pleased with the students' progress." Mr. Hughes turned to Debbie. "What we *are* questioning is your attitude and example among staff, church members, and toward parents, which brings me to the main reason we called this meeting. Debbie, it's obvious from your attitude and discussions with others that you have anger stored in your heart, and this is manifesting itself in your job and at church. We, the board of Good Shepherd Christian School, believe you are not following many of the precepts of God. This lack greatly affects your classroom and the children you teach. We strongly agree you need some biblical counseling for these things as well as for the obvious anger you harbor."

Debbie felt herself sway in her chair, a jolt of pain filling her. How could they decide who she was and what was within her when they hadn't taken the time to get to know her? What kind of Christians were *they*?

"The students' needs are the priority, and the obedience of the biblical standards of church attendance is vital."

Mr. Hughes's words echoed in her mind and blended with her mother's constant words of contempt. All her life, she'd never been good enough for anyone. Why had she thought being married to someone who believed she was worthy of love would change other people's opinions about her?

Debbie's face grew hot and large tears spilled out of her eyes. She stared down at the floor.

"As your spiritual leader, as your pastor, and as your employer, we think you would benefit from some concentrated counseling," Mr. Hughes said. "We've been investigating the options and believe we've found a place that would be a perfect fit for you and your needs."

What? Surely they don't think I'm unbalanced and in dire need of fixing. Debbie felt she was falling into the imaginary grave she had been digging her entire life.

He removed a pamphlet from his briefcase. "Here's a brochure for a Christian healthcare facility where we'd like to send you. Bethany R&L is in Klauthmos Bay, about two hours from here. You can get the care and counseling there we feel you need to be the Christian woman and teacher God meant for you to be." Mr. Hughes leaned forward and offered a tentative smile Debbie doubted was sincere.

"The board agrees with this plan and will pay any bills your insurance does not cover. The summer break will begin shortly, and Bethany R&L has prepared a room for you." He held out the brochure. Debbie drew back as if it were poisonous.

Josh cleared his throat and reached out with a shaky hand to take the pamphlet.

Mr. Hughes sat up straighter in his chair. "Debbie, we believe it would be in your best interest to accept this offer for counseling. So, Josh and Debbie, you'll need to make a decision. If you choose not to go this route, the board will have to reconsider both of your positions at our school."

Debbie slumped back against her seat as Josh softly stroked her hand. The room lost focus—she felt despair wash over her.

Mr. Hughes and the others stood. "We'll need your decision within the week."

🍼✝🍼

The Youngs stumbled out of the building, bewildered. Debbie couldn't comprehend the information that had just been given to her, but she knew it meant she wasn't acceptable or wanted here at Good Shepherd Christian School.

My mother was right, I am, indeed, a broken and worthless person.

Josh opened the car door, and Debbie slid in, staring straight ahead. He climbed behind the wheel but didn't start the engine. "I'm so sorry. I didn't know what those men were going to say." He turned toward her. "What's been going on? I've been so busy, I didn't realize you were struggling so much."

"I thought I'd been doing my best, but I guess it's never good enough." Debbie's voice wavered. "As to the requirement I be at every church function, you know how we both feel about this."

Josh sighed and took her hand in his. "We'll figure this out together." He turned back to the steering wheel and drove them home.

Debbie leaned back against the headrest as silent sobs shook her body.

God, do you notice my misery? Why did you let this happen? It's almost as if you agree with my mom's opinion of me. Do you see me as an utter failure? You know all that has transpired, how hard both Josh and I have worked for you and now … this? Don't you care?

The rest of the drive home, Debbie went over the meeting again in her mind. She felt hopeless. She'd never be good enough, and those men agreed. Debbie saw herself in the deep grave she had fallen into in her imagination. She looked around and saw that imperfection, inadequacy, devastation, and self-loathing were there as well. The pain for herself, and for Josh, was intense. What an embarrassment she was to Josh and everyone else. Her heart shattered into pieces as shame and grief consumed her.

When they arrived at the house, Josh steered Debbie to the kitchen without saying a word. She sat at the table and sobbed while he made tea.

A few minutes later, they sat across from each other at the table, teacups in hand.

"Do you agree with Mr. Hughes, and the others? Am I in direct disobedience to God?"

"I can tell you've been under a lot of stress, but I believe the Bible leaves it up to us to decide on how many church services we attend," Josh assured her and then paused, as if in thought. "You can't let Mr. Jennings get to you so much. He's not your mother, you know."

Josh was right. Yet his words still stung a bit, as if he too were telling her she was wrong.

"I do know Mr. Jennings has placed a lot on your plate this year and expecting you to be at every church service is ridiculous. I know you and Mr. Jennings have also butted heads several times, but I don't believe going away for several weeks is warranted. I'm guessing the stress of his expectations, added to those of your mother in the past, have stressed you out. My job hasn't been a piece of cake either. I haven't been here enough for you. And they seem to be concerned about you venting your frustrations but not enough to do anything about your concerns. I'm wondering if we should consider leaving Good Shepherd."

Debbie shook her head as fear moved into her aching heart. "What will we do for jobs if we quit?"

Josh didn't answer, and they sat silent for several minutes.

When no answers seemed to come, Josh pushed away from the table and held out his hand to her. "Why don't we sleep on this tonight and reexamine everything tomorrow?"

Debbie looked up and nodded but doubted sleep would come.

As she lay in bed that night, she prayed. *Lord, why is it I never can do the right things? You must be unhappy with me or you wouldn't have let these things happen. Forgive me, Lord, for my failures and shortcomings. I want to do what's right, but I don't seem to be able to. Will I stay in this grave I have dug permanently? Do you care about my suffering?*

CHAPTER 7

Stefan woke with a start and checked the clock on the nightstand. He'd slept for almost an hour and was glad to see he still had about that long before supper. He got up and emptied his suitcase, placing his clothes in the armoire and his toiletries in the bathroom. He took a quick shower, dressed, and headed toward the cafeteria in the main building.

When he reached the courtyard, he glanced at his watch. *Not yet time for supper.* He decided to sit near the fountain and watch the koi swim. He and Sophie had dined at a restaurant that had beautiful fish like these in a pool. Once again, the familiar ache gripped his heart.

He closed his eyes. *Will I feel this way forever?*

Fear gripped him as another thought hit him. *What if I do get over this grief and move on?* He never wanted to lose his connection with Sophie and the life and feelings they once shared. Maybe it was better to hang on to his pain.

Moving his gaze from the fountain, Stefan noticed someone unfamiliar heading his way. Perhaps the man was just passing through the courtyard. No—he was still coming toward Stefan, smiling. He held something in his hand that reflected the sun. Stefan squinted, trying to see what the man carried. The man stopped and set the object—a small bottle the color of the sky—on a nearby table.

He smiled. "Hello, I'm Chaplain Miller."

Stefan stood and shook the man's hand. "I'm Stefan Krause."

"I've been expecting you today." The chaplain motioned for Stefan to sit once more before taking another chair beside him. "Welcome. Have you settled into your room?"

"Yes." Stefan felt ashamed of his lack of conversational skills.

"I see your pain and I care, Stefan," Chaplain Miller whispered, a look of sincerity in his eyes.

Stefan's own eyes filled with tears, and he quickly lowered his gaze.

The two of them sat in silence for a few moments, and then Chaplain Miller shifted in his seat. "It's almost time for supper. Why don't I send you in the right direction, and you can find a seat for both of us while I stop by my office for a moment?"

Chaplain Miller picked up the small bottle, and they walked toward the main building. After opening the door, the chaplain pointed Stefan in the general direction of the cafeteria. "I'll meet you in a few minutes."

Stefan found the cafeteria after only making one wrong turn. About a dozen people were already eating, and about that many were waiting to go through the serving line. Stefan took his place at the end, grateful no one spoke to him.

What do you say to others in a behavioral healthcare facility? "Have you cracked up yet?" "How many personalities do you have?"

He shook his head. He shouldn't be thinking like that. He wasn't fairly evaluating the people there. What if they were thinking the same thing about him?

Stefan sighed, picked up a tray and some silverware and moved through the line. Fried chicken, slaw, and mashed potatoes had always been favorites, but would he even taste them? He couldn't remember the last time he'd enjoyed a meal. Life's pleasures seemed to have died along with Sophie.

He accepted the full plate the server offered him and put it on the tray beside a cup of coffee he'd already poured. He made his way to a table, and as he sat, he noticed Chaplain Miller in the serving line. Should Stefan go ahead and eat or wait for him? He'd wait.

"I see you found your way to the cafeteria," Chaplain Miller said, sitting down at the table. "Let's give thanks before we eat."

Stefan bowed his head.

"Lord, thank you for bringing Stefan here safely and for your love and concern for him. Bless this food and the hands that prepared it. Amen."

"How long have you been working here, Chaplain Miller?" If he began the conversation right away and focused on the chaplain, maybe Stefan wouldn't have to talk about himself.

"I've served the people of Bethany R&L for twenty years." He smiled and Stefan noticed the wrinkles beside his eyes. He wondered if they were from age or the stress of dealing with other people's heartaches.

Stefan nodded and picked up his fork.

Chaplain Miller picked up a drumstick. "Did you have a pleasant drive here today?"

"Yes, and uneventful. From the little I've seen, Klauthmos Bay is a beautiful place."

"It is. I love this area and can think of no other place I'd rather live."

Stefan wanted to keep the conversation from being about him, but if he asked too many questions, Chaplain Miller might turn them around and ask him the same things. He ate some mashed potatoes while trying to think of more conversation.

Maybe the older man sensed Stefan was uncomfortable talking about himself, because Chaplain Miller didn't press him to talk about anything personal during their meal. Stefan felt relieved and grateful. After the two men finished their meal, Chaplain Miller showed Stefan where to take his tray of dishes, and they left the cafeteria together.

"We have several evening activities that might interest you," Chaplain Miller said as they reentered the courtyard. "You'll find them listed on the bulletin board in the lounge of the Sozo building. I know you're tired, and maybe a little overwhelmed, so I'll understand if you pass up attending any of them tonight. But I want to encourage you to consider going to some of them from time to time. No one wants you to become a hermit while you're here. Being alone too much isn't healthy for any of us."

Stefan nodded, not because he agreed with Chaplain Miller's words but because he wanted to acknowledge he heard what the man had said.

"They serve breakfast between six thirty and seven thirty. Coffee and juice are also available in Sozo's lounge. Mrs. Turner will be contacting you when she's finished scheduling your appointments with Dr. Walker." Chaplain Miller stopped walking and turned toward Stefan. "Do you have any questions?"

"No, but thank you for all the information." Stefan had difficulty looking the man in the eyes and stared at the floor instead.

"That's what I'm here for. I'll see you tomorrow, and, Stefan?" He placed a hand on his shoulder. "I care."

Stefan couldn't stand the idea of being within the four small walls of his room so he ventured back to the lounge and found two men playing chess. "Excuse me. Is the ocean far from here?"

The two men paused their game. One stood, smiling, and held out his hand. "Hello. My name is Jerry Gage. This is my friend, Frank Snider."

Stefan made brief eye contact as he shook each man's hand. Jerry looked to be in his mid-forties. Frank, on the other hand, looked to be in his fifties, and the look Stefan saw in his eyes was easily identifiable—despair.

Forcing his thoughts to slow down, he said, "I'm sorry. I should have introduced myself first. I'm Stefan Krause. Nice to meet you both."

"I take it you're a new arrival here," Jerry said. "Welcome. Now, to answer your question. Yes, the ocean is just a couple of blocks over." He pointed. "If you go out that door and take a right, you'll see a trail that will T-bone Cayce Road. Turn right on Cayce, and you'll see the ocean at the end of two blocks."

"Thank you." Stefan made his way out the door. As Jerry said, he found the beach just a short hike down the road.

Stefan stopped at a bench, removed his shoes and socks and deposited them on the sand. He made his way slowly to the waterline, stopping just short of the tide.

"Will there ever be a time when my heart isn't broken?" Stefan moaned as he stared out at the water. "I can't take a breath of air without thinking of you. Wherever I am, I continually see a door open and expect to see you coming in, smiling. I faintly hear your voice, and I panic because I'm afraid of not hearing the sound ever again. I close my eyes, desperate to see your face, terrified because each day your image fades more from my mind. How can a person hold so much sadness?"

As the incoming tide crashed over his feet, so did Stefan's despair. He suddenly found breathing difficult, and he moved back to the dry sand and sat.

The smell of the sea air, the tremendous losses in his life, and this bottomless grief gave Stefan the drowning sensation he'd experienced weeks before. With knees bent, he put his head between them and wept.

When his tears had run their course, he stood. Feeling sticky from the salty air, Stefan picked up his shoes and walked back to Bethany.

The lounge was empty, so he went into the kitchen and poured some orange juice into a glass.

Although the sun was beginning to set and Stefan felt tired, it was too early to go to bed. He returned to his room, finished his juice, and took a shower to wash the salt from his skin. Stefan sighed. *If only I could take a shower on the inside.*

Now what would he do to fill his time? There was no television in his room, not that he watched TV much anyway, but he didn't want to risk going anywhere on the Bethany compound where he might encounter people. He just wanted to be alone.

Stefan climbed into bed, resolving to just get some rest. But sleep would not come easily.

CHAPTER 8

After a fitful night, Debbie was glad to see the sun coming up. With resentment in her heart, she prayed.

Lord, it's not fair! You know how hard Josh and I work, and despite that, how the school is treating us. You also know I've strived to be the best teacher to the students in my classroom. Yet they don't seem to care about those things. All they seemed concerned about is the possibility of looking bad because one of their teachers isn't at a few church functions. Knowing my heart and motives, Lord, why didn't you intervene? Why have you allowed this to happen? Do you see my wounded soul? Do you even care?

Shoving off the covers, Debbie rose and put on her robe. As the board had suggested the night before, she would stay home today and think about all that had transpired. She smelled fresh coffee brewing and heard bacon sizzling and made her way to the kitchen where she found Josh making breakfast.

Last night's meeting had been playing through her mind all night. With each remembered statement, the pain intensified, and fresh tears rolled down Debbie's cheeks.

She tried her best to sob softly, but as she hung her head, she felt solid and supportive hands on her shoulders. She turned and leaned into Josh's embrace. She wasn't sure how long they stood there, holding each other, but a rumble in Josh's stomach reminded her they hadn't eaten breakfast yet. Debbie picked up the full coffeepot and filled their mugs. They sat at the table to eat.

After a minute or two, Josh put down his fork and focused on Debbie. "I'm so sorry the school board has made an unbiblical issue of church attendance. As to your attitude concerning both of us being overworked, I completely agree with you. They're drawing conclusions without taking into consideration who you are. And I know I haven't been here enough for you, and I'm sorry. I should have spoken up and told Pastor Hughes and Mr. Jennings that running the youth group and being at all church services was asking too much of me too.

"I want you to know I don't think you're a bad person in dire need of psychological treatment, but you have carried around the heavy burden of feeling inadequate so long." Josh paused, and the couple's gazes met. "I would love for you to take the opportunity to have this weight you've carried for years lifted."

Debbie frowned. "You think I am in dire need of counseling too? Is that what you're saying? I guess my mother was right all along. I am worthless." She hung her head and wept.

Josh placed his hand on hers. "No, I don't think anything of the sort. I love you just the way you are. And you're a great teacher. But what if this might be an opportunity to be delivered from the bondage your mother placed on your heart while you were growing up? Even though the board's motives and demands aren't right, you could still benefit."

Reaching for a napkin on the table, Debbie mopped her face. Josh got up to get the coffee pot and refilled the two mugs on the table.

"Honey, I don't want you to feel you're some broken piece of pottery that's in desperate need of mending. I was just thinking of you, not what other people decided about you." Josh took a sip of coffee and stared into the cup. "I think it might be a good idea to call Pastor Bell and see what his counsel suggests. He is a wise man, and he knows us both fairly well."

Debbie nodded. Was she beginning to consider that going to Bethany wouldn't be a bad thing? "I'll give him a call."

Josh left for school, and Debbie tried to keep herself busy. As she finished each task, she'd check the clock and wonder if it was too early to put in her call. As time went by, her anxiety built. Would Pastor Bell agree with the school board? Would he believe she needed fixing? Debbie wasn't sure she could handle that right now.

As ten o'clock approached, Debbie gathered her courage. If she didn't contact their former pastor right now, she'd lose her nerve.

With shaking hands, Debbie dialed the number, and Pastor Bell's secretary put her call through.

"Good morning, Pastor Bell."

"Hello, Debbie! I hope you and Josh are well."

"Um, that's what I'm calling you about. Josh and I aren't well right now, and I'd like to speak with you about it, if this is a good time." A part of Debbie hoped Pastor Bell wouldn't be able to chat.

"I've got time. What's going on?"

Debbie described what had happened with the school board the night before. As she spoke, her throat tightened, and tears flowed once again.

Pastor Bell said nothing for a moment, and she worried she was about to hear her worsts fears confirmed—that she was in dire need of fixing.

"I'm sorry you're having to go through this, Debbie. My advice to you is to set aside all that has transpired and go to Bethany R&L, not because you're mentally or emotionally ill, but because you deserve to see yourself as God does." He sighed. "Learn all you can during your time there and accept this opportunity as a gift. What else would your employer pay for unlimited counseling *and* time at the beach in Klauthmos Bay?" He chuckled and said, "Who knows how God will use this in your future."

They continued to speak a little longer, with Debbie absorbing comfort into her troubled soul.

"Please keep in touch as you can," Pastor Bell said as they finished their conversation. "I care about you and Josh, and I want to hear what the Lord does for you in this difficult situation."

After the call, Debbie took a cup of hot tea out on the porch and sat on the step, mulling over the conversation that had just taken place. She wanted to be sure she'd remember all the details so she could pass them on to Josh when he got home. Although the school's rejection stung, what Pastor Bell said made sense and seemed to parallel Josh's thoughts. In spite of what the administration at Good Shepherd thought of her, the idea of finally dealing with her mother's rejections and criticisms gave her hope. Could it be possible she could begin crawling out of the grave she had dug? Maybe she could finally learn to love who she was, despite her mother's disapproval. Maybe God did have something more in store for her.

Taking a sip of her hot tea, she thought about being away from Josh—could she do it? But she had to try. She didn't want to live these feelings of rejection anymore.

CHAPTER 9

Stacy faced the window on the bus she had just boarded for Klauthmos Bay, hoping her seatmate would not be a talker.

Was she making the right decision? Could she make it on her own? What if she didn't like Mrs. Turner? What if her temporary landlords didn't like her? Would this pain within her ever diminish? The questions turned in Stacy's mind just like the wheels revolved beneath the bus.

The events of the last several days crashed over her spirit like hurricane waves on the shore. Once again, she couldn't stop the silent moan within her heart. She positioned her body away from the other travelers, wanting to hide her distress if she could, especially from the woman sitting next to her.

Almost hypnotized, Stacy watched as the drops of rain hit the window and ran down it, reflecting her feelings.

As they approached Stacy's destination, the older lady sitting beside her nudged Stacy gently. "Where are you headed, dear?" she whispered.

"I'm going to Klauthmos Bay to hopefully start a new job."

The woman clutched her purse on her lap and smiled. "Such a beautiful place. You'll love it there. That's where I'll change buses to head to my granddaughter's place. I can't wait to see her."

Stacy smiled and turned again toward the window. She didn't want to be rude, but she wasn't up for any conversation right then.

As the bus pulled into the terminal, Stacy looked at her watch and noticed they were ahead of schedule. Would Chaplain Miller already be there?

Stacy waited for her seatmate to gather her things. As the woman moved into the aisle, she smiled at Stacy. I hope this new job will work out for you."

Stacy thanked the woman.

I don't have it yet.

Stacy watched the woman step down from the bus and move in the direction of another one parked close by.

Stacy picked up her suitcase and scanned the area, hoping to see someone either with a sign, introducing himself, or searching for someone like her.

Seeing no one except for a man behind a counter, she dropped her heavy suitcase, not knowing what her next move should be.

Lifting her suitcase, she plodded over to the women's restroom and pushed through the door. She ran some water to rinse her face and stared into the mirror. *What do I do now? Does God care about me and my problems?* As she studied her chubby cheeks, she felt another jab of pain in her heart.

"If I were prettier and thinner, maybe Jack would still want me." She shook her head quickly, hoping to clear her thoughts. Then she put her hands under the warm water and splashed some on her face. Using a paper towel, Stacy dried her face and hands and then hefted her suitcase again and headed back into the terminal, avoiding the mirror on her way out.

The bus station was still empty except for the older gentleman behind the ticket counter.

Not knowing what else to do, she marched over to the ticket window.

She cleared her throat, hoping to get the man's attention. "I'm trying to find Chaplain Miller's house. Can you give me directions?"

The old man peered up at her through thick-lensed glasses. "Oh, you want to know how to get to the Bottle House. Interesting place ... interesting place." His eyes took on a faraway look as his thoughts seemed to drift for a second.

When he refocused, he smiled and said, "You're only about five blocks from there. Chaplain Miller lives across the street from Lakewood Park, so it'll be easy to find. You can't miss the house. The windows are filled with bottles upon bottles. I'll draw you a simple map." He tore off a piece of paper from a notepad on his desk and sketched out the map and then handed it to her.

"Did you call Chaplain Miller's home the Bottle House?"

"Yep! That's Chaplain Miller's house, all right." Seeing Stacy's confusion, he continued. "He is a puzzling man. Though he seems nice enough, no one has been able to find out why he has such a large collection of bottles in his house. If you were to stroll by, you would see each window filled with bottles peeking out from among the vines that are beginning to grow around the outside of his house."

"What are the bottles for?" she asked.

"I'm not sure, but a few people have been bold enough to creep up to his windows to get a peek at them, and *they* report that there are many sizes, shapes, and colors. Some of those same individuals claim each one is labeled, and they hold varying amounts of liquid."

"What do these bottles hold?"

The man shrugged. "No one knows for sure, but some have speculated that Chaplain Miller has a drinking problem, and those bottles provide him with a secret nip now and then. I don't know how much of that information is fact or fiction, though."

Stacy frowned.

"Others who have spent time with Chaplain Miller and have been guests in his home find it hard to believe he could be an alcoholic," the man continued quickly, "but they admit they haven't discovered what the bottles contain."

Stacy thanked the man for the map and moved toward the door. Was going to the Bottle House a good idea? She didn't trust her reasoning abilities. After all, they were a large part of what had brought her to this point.

"You're more than welcome to wait here until the drizzle clears out," the old man called.

"Thank you, but I think I'll go ahead."

Drizzle or no drizzle, Stacy wanted to get outside to toss a mental coin, enabling her to decide whether to try and find Chaplain Miller on her own, or buy a bus ticket and head back home.

Her stomach churned. Stacy didn't have a choice—she didn't have a home anymore.

Jesus wept beside Lazarus's grave. Will he weep beside the one I'm digging for myself?

Stacy sat on the stone bench across the street from Chaplain Miller's house as the gloomy day's mist surrounded her. The vacant playground reflected her empty life, and the painful image of Lazarus weeping brought to mind the sermon she heard the last time she and Jack had attended church together. Something had bothered her about how the pastor presented the story of Lazarus, and her heart struggled to understand it. Stacy brushed a fresh tear away. What she *could* understand was Mary and Martha's heartache. Heartache had been her constant companion since that horrible day.

THE BOTTLE HOUSE

Stacy's gaze moved from the playground in front of her to Chaplain Miller's home across the street. She studied the house as she clutched the piece of paper she had written his address on just a week before. Several objects could be seen in his windows and her eyes widened. Why did the chaplain collect those?

Stacy's thoughts traveled back to the events that had brought her there, and grief washed over her again.

CHAPTER 10

Stefan awoke the next morning to sunshine streaming through the large window in his room. He swung his feet to the floor and stretched. His stomach growled—hunger was a good thing. As he was making his way to the bathroom, his room phone rang.

"Yes?" Stefan said.

"Good morning, Mr. Krause. This is Mrs. Turner. I hope you've settled in and made yourself at home. I just wanted to let you know you have a therapy session with Dr. Walker this morning at nine o'clock. Directions to his office can be found on the maps posted by all the main doors."

Stefan thanked her and ended the call.

After a quick shower, he arrived at breakfast, wishing to be anywhere other than in Klauthmos Bay. He knew his stay here would be painful. His emotional and spiritual wounds were deep. Stefan scanned the room. Did most of the people present wish the same thing? He filled his tray, then found a seat at an empty table.

Jerry, the man he'd met last night, strolled over, tray in hand. "Do you mind if I join you?"

Stefan shook his head and moved his coffee mug closer to his tray.

"Did you find Klauthmos Beach yesterday?"

"Yes, it was a simple straight shot down the road, just as you said. I expected to see more people around."

"It's a public beach." Jerry paused with a spoonful of oatmeal halfway to his mouth. "But most of the locals go to the main pier a couple of miles up the shore. I love Klauthmos Beach, but if you want a change and get tired of washing salt off your skin, you can always travel the opposite way on Cayce Road, and you'll find Lakewood Park. It's right across the street from the Bottle House."

"The Bottle House?"

"It's the nickname the locals have given Chaplain Miller's home. He has hundreds of tiny bottles in his house. You can see many of them in the windows."

"Oh?" Stefan's heartbeat sped up as he remembered the sky-blue bottle he'd seen the chaplain carrying.

Jerry nodded. "Some say Chaplain Miller just collects bottles like others collect coins. I've seen them in his office too. Anyway, Lakewood Park has many beautiful flowers, shaded pathways, and benches throughout. It's a nice place to read, reflect, and soak up the sun."

Jerry slurped his last sip of coffee, wiped his mouth with a napkin, and stood. "I'm sure I'll be seeing you around."

As he watched Jerry walk away, Stefan noticed a very pregnant nurse making her way toward him, and he stood out of respect. Stefan was an old-fashioned man who always stood when a lady approached. Sophie had loved that about him.

"Hello, I'm Nurse Carson. Are you Stefan Krause?"

He nodded. "Please, have a seat."

Relief flashed across the woman's face, and she lowered herself onto the chair.

Nurse Carson consulted her clipboard. "If you haven't guessed, I'll be going on maternity leave very soon, and another nurse will be replacing me. When it's determined who will be filling in, you'll see both of us together while she learns her routine and patient load."

Stefan nodded, saying nothing.

"I see you have an appointment with Dr. Walker at nine o'clock. If you're finished eating, I'll show you where his office is located. Then you'll know exactly where to go. Oh, and Chaplain Miller asked me to give you a message. He said to tell you he has you down to meet with him at two this afternoon. If that doesn't work, you can change your time. His schedule is on his door. We'll go right by his office on the way to Dr. Walker's."

Stefan took care of his tray and followed Nurse Carson out of the cafeteria. They made their way through a simple maze of hallways until they came to a closed door with a simple cross.

"This is Chaplain Miller's office. Since his door is closed, he has someone with him. Here's his schedule." Nurse Carson pointed at the door. "Any time you need to change times or schedule future appointments, this is where you do it."

Stefan nodded. He thought he heard someone crying within the office and his heart ached, knowing intimately what suffering felt like. He felt relieved when Nurse Carson continued down the hall.

After lunch, Stefan had some time to kill before meeting with Chaplain Miller. He decided to take Jerry's advice and head to Lakewood Park.

As he made his way down Cayce Road toward the park, he thought about his initial meeting with Dr. Walker. He hadn't realized how much he'd dreaded that appointment until after it was over.

Stefan had been surprised Dr. Walker seemed to be about his own age, but his kind eyes had reflected his intelligence. Stefan liked that the man hadn't dilly-dallied with small talk too. Instead, the doctor had asked him many straightforward questions, recording Stefan's answers on his pad of paper.

When the doctor had asked Stefan if he still thought suicide was an answer to his suffering, he'd squirmed a bit in his seat. He had simply answered that he didn't know. Dr. Walker had written more—more than just "I don't know" Stefan was sure—on his pad and then scheduled Stefan's next appointment for tomorrow morning.

"If you find yourself teetering on the edge of despair, you have an emergency number on the phone in your room. Chaplain Miller's number is there as well. You can call anytime you're in need. Don't hesitate."

Stefan replayed the doctor's words in his head as he walked, and before he knew, he'd arrived at the park. Stefan looked around at the stone benches, trails—even some playground equipment—chose a bench that was well out of the way of the trail and sat down.

He stretched out his legs as he noticed a mother and child at the swings. The girl pumped her legs with every ounce of energy she could while her mother pushed. When the swing rose higher, the child squealed with delight.

As he continued to watch, he pictured Allie Barker and Lauren. He frowned as once again pain gripped his heart. Lauren would never know the joy this girl was experiencing on the swing. Stefan lowered his head in shame.

Stefan stood to make his way back to Bethany and his eyes traveled across the street. His gaze landed on a window that contained shelves holding all sorts of bottles.

Chaplain Miller's house! Stefan moved across the street to get a better view. Every window held shelves of bottles. He studied them as he traveled the width of the house. The bottles were in all shapes and colors and no bigger than his hand. Stefan forced himself away when he felt someone might think he was snooping.

As he made his way back slowly to Bethany, his curiosity over the Bottle House grew. Why did Chaplain

Miller have so many small bottles? Was he just a collector? It seemed an unusual hobby.

Stefan checked his watch and thought about his appointment this afternoon with the owner of this unique house.

CHAPTER 11

Stacy shifted on the stone bench and reached down to massage her calf muscle. It'd been a while since she'd walked any distance. She needed to muster the strength and courage to head over to Chaplain Miller's house, but she felt frightened. She'd spoken with him on the phone only a couple of times, but she'd have to trust this stranger because she needed his help. Trust was something Stacy felt a little short of, and she didn't like not having a choice under the circumstances.

Moving her gaze again to the empty playground, the words of the first two verses of Psalm 13 ran through her mind. *Oh Lord, how long will you forget me? Forever? How long will you look the other way? How long must I struggle with anguish in my soul, with sorrow in my heart every day?*

Stacy had never felt such extreme emotions—anger, hurt, embarrassment, and betrayal. She felt angry at Jack and Aubree for what they'd done. Her cheeks burned with embarrassment when she thought of what her friends and coworkers must think of her. After all, many say when someone cheats, it's because their spouse didn't measure up. But the most unsettling thing for Stacy was realizing she felt hurt and angry that God seemed so distant when she needed him so much.

Lord, all the hurt, fear, and betrayal are overwhelming, and it keeps going on and on. I don't know how much longer

I can stand it. I cry out to you, but all I receive is silence. I'm dying on the inside, Lord. You wept at Lazarus's grave. Do you even care enough to weep at mine?

She put her head in her hands as the weight of her circumstances pulled her down, and her tears returned. Her clothes and hair were damp from the mist, and though the air temperature wasn't terribly cool, she shivered.

Wiping her hair and tears out of her eyes, Stacy suddenly noticed someone standing nearby. She gasped.

"I'm sorry if I frightened you," the man said.

He was tall with gray hair and green eyes magnified through the lenses of his glasses. He wore dark-blue work pants and a checkered shirt. The stranger bent down and placed something on the ground. Then he removed his glasses and wiped the moisture off them with a handkerchief, giving Stacy a few moments to catch her breath.

"I'm Chaplain Joseph Miller," he said as he stuffed his handkerchief back in his pocket and then offered his hand.

Stacy stood and stammered. "I'm Stacy Meadows." She shook his hand.

Chaplain Miller smiled. "I'm sorry I didn't meet you at the bus station," he said softly. "I was held up because of an emergency with a patient situation at Bethany, and hurrying home, I saw you sitting here. I wondered if you might be the nurse I was waiting for."

Stacy stared at the ground and her eyes immediately found the object Chaplain Miller had set down moments before. She frowned at the small, delicate, dark-red bottle.

Chaplain Miller drew her attention back. "How about if we head over to my terrace, and I'll make us some hot tea? It won't take but a minute to brew some, and you can relax and regroup a little."

She nodded.

"May I?" Chaplain Miller asked, reaching for her suitcase.

"Thank you."

Chaplain Miller led the way over to his house with her suitcase in one hand and the bottle he'd retrieved in his other. Stacy wanted to ask him about the bottle, but she didn't want to pry into something that was none of her business.

Chaplain Miller set down her suitcase outside the terrace door and then dried off the seats and the small round table that sat nearby. "Make yourself comfortable. I'll bring out the tea as soon as it's ready." He moved quietly into his house, the small bottle still in his hand.

Stacy sat in the chair the chaplain had just dried. *Comfortable? Will I ever be comfortable again?*

She turned and studied the chaplain's house. Now she could see the bottles of all different sized, shapes, and colors—just as the ticket man had said. *What an unusual hobby.*

A few moments later, Chaplain Miller came out with a tray. Stacy turned her attention away from the windows and watched as he poured the tea and offered cream and sugar.

"Thank you." Stacy took a sip and sat back, teacup in hand, and closed her eyes for a minute, having little strength to do anything else.

They sat quietly sipping their tea for several moments. Chaplain Miller didn't appear to be ill at ease, nor did he ask prying questions. Stacy knew she needed to speak but didn't know how to begin.

"Would you like more tea?" Chaplain Miller asked.

"No, thank you. This was just what I needed." Stacy focused on the chaplain, and he returned her gaze. His green eyes were full of compassion and concern, but he still didn't push her to say anything.

"I suppose you're wondering why I didn't come directly here but chose to sit on that stone bench," Stacy said.

The chaplain smiled. "The thought occurred to me."

"The short version of the story is I needed time to think. I'm worried about my job interview and finding a place to live if the job is offered to me, because I no longer have a job or a home since my marriage fell apart."

Chaplain Miller continued to stare at her for a moment before speaking. "Those who have suffered greatly lose the ability to compare. The circumstances that brought your suffering on, at this point, are irrelevant. Suffering is suffering, Stacy." He paused. "I can see you're hurt, and I care—and so does God. He is deeply concerned about you."

She frowned as she weighed the claim God was deeply concerned about her. Was he really?

After a moment, Chaplain Miller set his cup on the table and relaxed back into his chair. "As I mentioned on the phone, I know a retired couple down the road, Charles and Ruth Lewis. They're happy to have you in their home tonight, and if you find work at Bethany, they're open to having you with them until you can figure things out. So, that's taken care of." He swatted at a fly buzzing around his head. "How long have you worked in behavioral healthcare?"

"I've been a nurse for five years." Stacy chuckled to herself when she realized the irony of being a trained nurse in mental healthcare, and now, desperately needing that very thing.

"I know Bethany R&L has an opening for a nurse with your qualifications. It's a wonderful place to work. I've been a chaplain there for more than twenty years." He sat up straight in his chair once more. "To give you a feel for the area, Bethany is only two blocks from here, near the ocean. How about I take you to the Lewis's and see that you get acquainted? Then if you'd like, I could pop over in the morning and show you the way to Bethany for your interview."

As his words sank in, Stacy blinked back the tears gathering in her eyes, grateful for somewhere to stay and possibly work. Was this a sign that God really did care about her? Stacy didn't know, but she got up and went with Chaplain Miller to the Lewises' house.

What am I doing? I'm on my way to the home of people I've never met with a man I've known less than an hour. If I were in my right mind, I'd run in the opposite direction. But where would I go, and how would I survive?

Despite these thoughts, Stacy followed Chaplain Miller. She just didn't have the energy to think beyond the immediate.

Before she knew it—or was ready—they'd arrived. They climbed up the front steps and Chaplain Miller rang the bell. An older woman with brown hair and eyes opened the door, and her face lit up in welcome.

"Hello! Come in. Come in!"

Chaplain Miller picked up Stacy's suitcase and stood aside, letting Stacy pass into the house before him.

"Welcome," the woman said warmly.

"Let me officially introduce you two," Chaplain Miller said. "Ruth, this is Stacy Meadows. Stacy—Ruth Lewis. Ruth, I know Mrs. Turner arranged with you and Charles for Stacy to stay with you."

"She did indeed, and Charles and I are thrilled to have you, Stacy. Welcome to Klauthmos Bay."

Stacy forced what she hoped was a smile. "Nice to meet you."

"Why don't we go to the patio out back so you can meet Charles and get to know us a little before settling in? It might make you feel more at ease." Ruth gestured toward the hallway. "We have a lovely guest room with its own bathroom all ready for you, and I'll take you there in a bit. Joseph, just leave Stacy's suitcase here."

Stacy blinked, her eyes filling with tears of gratitude. Ruth quietly grabbed some tissues and handed them to her, patting her hand in the exchange. The kindness of these strangers touched Stacy deeply.

They were being so kind to her, but there she was, crying again. Stacy was so tired of not being in control of her feelings. What must they think of her?

As they walked onto the patio, an older man looked up from a book and smiled. Removing his reading glasses, he stood. "Hello, Joseph!"

Chaplain Miller smiled. "I'd like you to meet Stacy Meadows. Stacy, this is Charles Lewis." Charles held out his hand, and Stacy accepted the shake.

"Hello, Stacy. It's nice to meet you."

Stacy looked at the older gentleman. He had little hair, except for small patches of gray hair on either side. "Nice to meet you and your wife."

"Have a seat, both of you," Ruth said, gesturing toward several empty chairs. "I'll get us all some hot tea. I baked some banana bread this morning that I'll bring along too."

"Thank you." Stacy wondered how she could hold more tea, but she didn't want to turn down Ruth's offer. She glanced over at Chaplain Miller to see if he was thinking the same thing, but he and Charles were already deep in conversation.

"Did you get in a round of golf yesterday, Charles?"

"Yes, I scored an eighty-two. Pretty good for an old guy."

Chaplain Miller laughed, and they carried on a little more about the game.

Ruth came to the patio shortly with a tray, and Charles rose quickly to take it from his wife. He set it on the matching rattan coffee table.

Stacy smiled and took the tea and plate Ruth offered her. "Thank you," she said softly. "I really appreciate you both for providing a place for me to stay, assuming I get the job."

Ruth's eyes lit up. "We're so glad to have you. Have you been to Klauthmos Bay before?"

Stacy felt relieved that the first question asked was not about her dire circumstances. She felt herself exhale before responding. "No, this is the first time I've been here."

"It's a beautiful town," Charles said, "and first-time visitors often say they feel at home quickly here. I hope that will be true of you."

"There are several boutiques and seafood restaurants," Ruth said, "and our sunsets here have been painted and photographed by many."

They continued to enjoy their tea, until Chaplain Miller consulted his watch. "I need to head to Bethany R&L. If you feel comfortable, Stacy, I'll leave you in the hands of these gracious people. I'll come by here at eight tomorrow morning, and I'll escort you to Bethany. Mrs. Turner is expecting you." Chaplain Miller stood.

Stacy nodded and rose, hating the fact tears were gathering once again.

Chaplain Miller picked up his plate and saucer and walked toward the kitchen.

"I can see you out," Ruth said as she followed. Within a few seconds, she'd returned to the patio.

"Stacy, I can tell you're in difficult circumstances." She clasped her hands in front of her and tilted her head. "Charles and I won't ask you about them, but we want you to know it's not because we don't care. We'll let you decide if and when you want to share some of your burdens with us." She paused a moment and then smiled. "Why don't I take you to your room, and you can freshen up and rest? We won't have supper for a couple of hours."

Stacy nodded, and Ruth turned to her husband. "Charles, could you get her suitcase from the foyer while I show Stacy her room?"

"Of course, dear."

The older woman led Stacy from the patio and down a hallway where she opened the last door on the right. Stacy gasped at the large and airy room. A four-poster bed and matching dresser, small desk, and an oval mirror, all made of polished mahogany, stood perfectly positioned in the space. The bedding had embroidered flowers on a simple white background. Rugs were scattered on the hardwood floor, and draperies surrounded two large windows that allowed elegance and light to permeate the room.

Ruth paused while Stacy looked around, and then, Ruth moved to another doorway. "Here is your own private bathroom. Everything you need is here—towels, hair dryer, shampoo, and more. If you find there's something additional that you want or need, just let me know."

Stacy stepped into the bathroom. Her eyes grew large at the sight of a full garden tub, separate shower, and fluffy white towels hanging from several rods. She could almost picture herself in the tub, soaking away some of her aches and pains.

Ruth smiled at Stacy and patted her arm. "Please, make yourself at home. I'll call you in a couple of hours when supper is ready. I'll be praying God blesses you with rest from your travels."

In a voice no more than a whisper, Stacy murmured her thanks, and Ruth shut the door behind herself.

Stacy took one more look around the two rooms, wiped away some tears, slipped off her shoes, and climbed into the soft bed. Her head sank into the pillow, and she closed her eyes, hoping she was too tired for her mind to wander.

Such a short time ago, her life had been orderly. She'd loved her job, her husband, and her life. She shook her head as she thought how quickly everything had changed. She pictured a plate of fine china smashed into hundreds of pieces, lying on the floor. That was her life now.

"Yes, I want some rest from my travels, but will I ever have rest for my soul?"

Tears flowed down the sides of her face and onto the pillow. She tried her best to keep her sobbing quiet so Charles and Ruth wouldn't hear. Finally, her weeping gave way to exhaustion, and she fell into a deep sleep.

When Stacy awoke, she didn't know where she was at first, but then the soft comforter and warm furniture reminded her. Her eyes moved to the window, and she could see twilight had fallen. The clock on the nightstand showed 7:00 p.m.

"I've been asleep for more than three hours!"

Stacy rose and went into the bathroom to freshen up. She cringed, seeing the reflection of a young woman whose eyes mirrored despair. She moved out of the bedroom and down the hall, following the sound of conversation. She found the Lewises in the family room.

"Hello, Stacy," Charles said as he looked up from the table he had been sitting at. "Were you able to get some rest?"

"Yes, but I didn't mean to sleep this long. I'm sorry."

"You have nothing to apologize for." Ruth stood from a flowered couch. "You were still asleep when supper was ready, so we went ahead and ate. I've saved a plate for you. There's roast beef, mashed potatoes, carrots, and some yeast rolls I made this afternoon."

The thought of food made Stacy feel queasy. She hadn't been able to eat properly since that horrible day when she knew her marriage was over, but she didn't want to be a bad guest. Stacy followed Ruth into the kitchen.

"Please sit there at the island." Ruth opened the oven and pulled out a plate covered in aluminum foil. "Would you like some iced tea?"

"Yes, that would be nice," Stacy said as she climbed onto the stool. She surveyed the roomy black and white kitchen and liked the decorative effect. The stainless-steel sink was empty, and all the matching appliances shone with cleanliness. She shook her head, catching her breath as she thought of her own messy kitchen, a place that was no longer hers. Ruth set down the plate of food on the placemat in front of Stacy and brought over a glass of iced tea. Ruth poured herself a glass and stood across from her.

"I'm glad you had a good nap. Amazing how much a short sleep can revitalize a person." Ruth took a sip of her tea. "I'll set up an ironing board and iron in the laundry room in case you have anything you need to press. I bet a nice hot soak in the tub would do you a world of good too. Enjoy your meal, and I'll be back in a bit." Ruth finished her tea, placed the glass in the sink, and left.

While taking small bites of food, Stacy's eyes roamed the kitchen, noticing more details. In addition to the stainless-steel appliances and sink, soffit lights above the white painted cabinets brightened the room. Small appliances were scattered on the gray marble countertops, and expensive pots and pans hung from the rack above the island.

Oh, how I wish Jack and I could have a kitchen like this one with enough room for a family to spend time together ... laughing ... creating memories ...

Stacy caught her breath, and the food in her mouth suddenly tasted bitter. She and Jack would never have anything together again.

⌂✝⌂

Stacy shut the door to the guest bedroom and leaned against it, closing her eyes. Her mind immediately went to the nightmare that was her life these last several weeks. "I would give anything to keep my mind from constantly returning to Jack and Aubree and what they did and are doing," she whispered.

Stacy quickly moved into the bathroom and turned on the hot water in the tub, hoping to distract herself from her thoughts. She poured some of the eucalyptus bath crystals into the water and climbed in when the tub was filled. Leaning back, the hot water bubbling around her, Stacy yearned for comfort as she prayed.

Lord, please help me! I feel as though the waters of my life are poised to cover my spirit and drown me. I hurt so bad. How could Jack and Aubree, the people I loved and cared about the most, betray me? I didn't have a clue what they were doing. I gave Jack my whole heart and now I feel as if he ripped it right out of me. Please help me, Lord!

She was glad the sound of the whirlpool covered the sobs pouring from her body.

In time, Stacy reached up and turned off the jets, shivering now the water had cooled. She climbed out and wrapped a fluffy white towel around herself. She padded into the bedroom and opened her suitcase. Her hands quickly found the maroon nightie Jack loved to see her wear.

I knew Jack and I had some problems to work out. Our communication needed to improve, but what married couple doesn't have problems? Other than that, I thought Jack and I had a wonderful marriage. Boy, was I wrong. Stacy bit her lip to keep it from quivering. She dropped the towel and slipped into the gown.

Stacy searched her suitcase and found a top and skirt that might be decent enough to wear to Bethany R&L tomorrow. She shook them out, hoping to avoid ironing, and laid them over the chair. After placing the suitcase on the floor, she stepped over to the desk. She fingered a few magazines, and her eyes moved to the books standing on the small shelf. Among them was a Bible. Stacy picked it up and climbed into bed.

"Please, Lord, send me some comfort and direction," she whispered.

Stacy opened to the first Scripture that came to mind—Psalm 23.

"'The Lord is my shepherd; I shall not want,'" she read aloud. "Lord, you say you are my shepherd and that my needs will be taken care of. Yes, I have a place to stay for now and a good possibility for a job. I'm grateful, but I'd trade both of those things to not feel so much pain."

She turned back to the Scripture. "'He leadeth me beside the still waters.'

"Lord, I'm thinking that sheep probably scare easily so, therefore, the shepherd leads them to a peaceful place. I'm terrified right now and in desperate need of peace, but all I feel is anguish. Where are my still waters?

"'He restoreth my soul.'"

Restore? Is that even possible?

Stacy closed the Bible and placed it on the table beside the bed. She couldn't read more right now. She reached over to turn off the lamp, slid down under the covers, and laid her head on the pillow.

As had been true of every night at bedtime over the last few weeks, she pictured that broken china plate, uttering the only words she could at this time, "Help me!"

CHAPTER 12

Debbie had not expected the amount of anxiety building within her as they made their way toward Bethany R&L. The voices in her head screamed her insecurities causing her to wonder if she could, indeed, get out of this imaginary grave she had fallen into. What if these people confirmed her mother's opinions about her? What if they agreed with the administrators? What if they confirmed what she'd heard her entire life—she wasn't good enough. She *must* be flawed. There was no hope for her. She'd never be a person anyone could be proud of—including God. Demoralization joined her in her grave.

Tears ran down her cheeks as the pressure of pain needed a release. Josh said nothing as he drove down the winding roads toward Klauthmos Bay. Maybe he didn't know what would be helpful or healing, but he laid his hand on hers which offered some comfort.

I lift up my eyes to the hills. From where does my help come? My help comes from the Lord, who made heaven and earth. The beginning of Psalm 121 spoke gently through her mind. Debbie needed help from the Lord—she just wasn't convinced that help needed to come from Klauthmos Bay.

Sooner than Debbie was ready to, they pulled into the parking lot of Bethany R&L and the ringing in her ears returned, playing a tune Debbie feared. Josh had the envelope of information they'd received and pulled out the greetings letter and the map of the facility. Though Debbie couldn't see the ocean because of the buildings, she could smell the salty sea air. From this point on, would she associate this difficult time with the smell of the ocean? She hoped not.

"It says you report to the check-in desk in the main lobby right here," Josh said, pointing to a place on the map.

They got out of the car, and Josh grabbed Debbie's hand and her suitcase.

"Can you do this?" Josh asked. When she didn't respond, Josh squeezed her hand gently. "Remember what Pastor Bell said. Think of this as a gift, not a punishment."

Debbie nodded, then bit her lip to keep it from quivering and wiped away a tear. As they entered the lobby, Debbie felt some tension give way in response to the pleasant sight of deep peach-painted walls and the creamy-white trim. She noticed the cream, plush carpet and wondered how they kept a floor like that so clean. Comfortable chairs were arranged in small groups, allowing people a place to meet for semi-private conversations.

Josh and Debbie made their way to what they assumed to be the check-in desk.

"My wife, Debbie Young, is here to check in for a while. I believe you already have her paperwork."

The woman at the desk smiled. "Hello, Mr. and Mrs. Young. My name is Elena Crockett." Debbie rocked from one foot to the other. "Yes, I have Mrs. Young's paperwork. If you'll find a seat, I'll send for Mrs. Turner. She's our inpatient coordinator and the supervisor of our nursing staff. She'll take you to your room and see that you get settled."

Josh thanked her and led Debbie to some chairs across the room. As they sat down, Debbie's hands shook.

"Debbie, it's okay." Josh pulled her closer. "I'm here for you. If you decide this is more than you can bear, let me know, and we'll go straight home. Any time of the night or day, you call me, and I promise, I'll come right away."

"Thank you." What else could she say? If she didn't stay, both she and Josh would suffer financially. Would they both be able to find teaching jobs in the area? And what if this stay really did help her with the insecurities she felt?

They sat about ten minutes before a middle-aged woman approached with a smile on her face and a file in her hand.

"Hello, Mr. and Mrs. Young. I'm Mrs. Turner."

Both Josh and Debbie stood and shook hands with her.

"I'm here to take you to your room, Mrs. Young, and to answer any questions either of you have. We'll leave this main building and make our way toward Iaomai, the building that houses our woman. *Iaomai* is Greek for 'divine healing.' Follow me, please."

Josh held Debbie's arm for emotional and physical support as they followed Mrs. Turner out of the main building and through a courtyard where a sparkling fountain flowed and many tables with chairs were scattered around.

They soon came to a building whose plaque held the word Iaomai. Debbie looked at the word on the sign and felt hope move across her heart a second before shame and inadequacy quickly rushed in and shoved it out. As they stepped through the door, Debbie saw a lounge that had several couches and shelves full of books. In a room off to the left stood a small kitchen that included a refrigerator and stove. Everything seemed so cozy and welcoming, yet Debbie couldn't feel completely at ease.

"Mrs. Young, this is the women's lounge. Many enjoy gathering here in the evenings for reading, conversation, or for snacks. I hope you'll feel welcomed here."

Would Debbie experience something different here than what she had at the school? Was it possible someone other than Josh and her students would ever be glad to see and welcome her?

Mrs. Turner motioned for them to follow her out of the lounge and down a hallway. Debbie's feet felt like they weighed a thousand pounds. At her hesitation, Josh again took her elbow for support and walked beside her. They made their way through several halls.

Good grief! Would she ever find her way around?

They soon came to room number 1135, and Mrs. Turner opened the door.

Debbie was surprised to see a cozy room with seafoam-colored walls, not anything like she would expect of a room in a mental healthcare facility. A beautiful coverlet with embroidered flowers that included yellows, whites, and the same color green as the walls covered the double bed. Sunlight poured through a large window, and Debbie was glad to see a small desk, lamp, and chair in one corner. There was also a simple chest with five drawers on the wall opposite the bed. Had local artists painted the watercolor seascapes hanging in the room? She was pleased to see she had her own bathroom, complete with a shower.

Mrs. Turner must have been explaining the meal schedule, but lost in thought, Debbie had missed some of it.

"There is always coffee, tea, and juice available in the kitchen of the woman's lounge, and supper is from five thirty to six thirty p.m. in the cafeteria located in the main building."

"Thank you," Debbie murmured.

"Dr. Benjamin Murphy will be working with you in the days ahead, and we'll set up therapy sessions with him in the morning. Nurse Carson will be assigned to you until her maternity leave. You'll also meet Chaplain Joseph Miller, either tonight or in the morning. Many here find him to be a great comfort. We're fortunate to have him on staff."

"How soon would these sessions with Dr. Murphy begin?" Josh asked.

Mrs. Turner smiled. "As soon as tomorrow."

Debbie's heart wrenched as she was reminded of why she was there. Feeling almost physically assaulted, she sat down on the edge of the bed, and Josh sat beside her, putting his arm around her.

Mrs. Turner moved her gaze to Josh. "We ask all visitors to be out of the building by nine." She smiled at them and shut the door on her way out of the room.

"I don't know if I can go through with this, Josh. I'm terrified of being left here alone."

"I know, honey. I understand."

"What are you going to say when people from school and church ask you where I am? This is so humiliating." Tears of shame ran down her face.

"Debbie ..." Josh gently turned her face so he could look her in the eye. "It's no one's business where you are and why. There is nothing to be humiliated about. All of us are imperfect. There is no person who is better than another, and that includes anyone at Good Shepherd Christian School. God loves us all."

They sat like that for a while as Debbie cried. She longed for acceptance and was surprised when she realized she also needed the same from herself.

Would she ever have peace with and confidence in herself? Was this even possible?

Debbie and Josh sat quietly in her room, his arm around her and her head nestled against his chest, when there was a soft knock on the door.

"Come in," Josh called, and a tall man with gray hair and kind green eyes entered. Debbie's focus moved from the man's face down to his hand. Her eyebrows raised as she saw he held a small light green bottle. He set it on the small desk and smiled.

"My name is Chaplain Joseph Miller. You must be Josh and Debbie Young." He held out his hand. They stood, and while Josh was shaking the chaplain's hand, Debbie wiped away her tears.

Chaplain Miller moved to her and looked her in the eyes. "I see your pain, and I care, Mrs. Young."

Debbie held his gaze for a moment and felt a brief sense of peace. Maybe this man *could* understand her anguish. She held out her hand, and Chaplain Miller took it.

"Debbie, even though I'm a chaplain here at Bethany R&L, I'm available to talk about anything, spiritual or otherwise. I have a sign-up schedule on my office door, and you can make an appointment to see me. I'm also on call after-hours. My contact information is by the phone on the desk. Don't hesitate to use it, any time of the night or day."

"Thank you," Debbie said.

Chaplain Miller returned to the desk and picked up the light green bottle. The sunlight beaming in through the window bounced off the glass and Debbie noticed the color was the exact shade of the ocean. How beautiful! Then Debbie's breath caught. Her name was written on a label affixed to the side of the bottle. What could the chaplain possibly use this bottle for?

Before she could ask, Josh had walked the chaplain to the door. "Thank you for coming in, Chaplain Miller. It's a comfort that Debbie will have spiritual support here."

Josh shut the door behind Chaplain Miller, and panic filled Debbie. The time was coming closer for Josh to leave, and her eyes filled, knowing she'd soon be left behind.

⚗✝⚗

Later that night, Debbie sat alone on her bed, her stomach full of anxiety. Josh had stayed for dinner after helping her find the cafeteria. But that was hours ago, and Josh would probably be close to home by now. Her heart ached as she contemplated sleeping without his strong arms around her.

Despite the emotional upheaval of the day, Debbie wasn't ready to get in bed for the night. She had noticed books in the woman's lounge. Maybe she could find something interesting to read.

Debbie stepped out into the hallway and made her way to the lounge with only one wrong turn. Just as she was about to enter the room, she stopped short. A young woman, around twenty years old, sobbed quietly while Chaplain Miller sat beside her, praying.

Debbie's heart raced and then empathy filled it. She understood the apparent pain the young woman had. Just when she was about to turn around and head back to her room, Debbie noticed a beautiful purple bottle on the table in front of the chaplain. Curiosity trumped any other feelings for a moment.

The bottle, though a different shape and color, was about the size of the one the chaplain had when he'd visited Debbie earlier. Did the bottles belong to the chaplain? If so, why did he have them?

She slowly made her way back to her room and readied for bed. She'd have to forgo reading tonight.

She dreaded this part of the day without Josh beside her. Every night, they would share evening prayers, say good night, and sleep would soon engulf her—content to be in the security Josh gave her. Tonight, Debbie had to pray alone, surprised that speaking with God on her own felt unfamiliar.

The words of Psalm 121 came to mind. *I lift up my eyes to the hills. From where does my help come? My help comes from the Lord, who made heaven and earth.*

"Lord, though I don't understand so much of why you do the things you do," Debbie prayed, "you do, and you even know why you allow them to happen. I confess I'm scared right now and don't understand any of the whys."

Debbie wrung her hands.

"Please send the help you promised. You know I don't handle change well, and there's been too much of it in my life recently. You say you love and accept me, but I don't feel it right now. Will I ever feel that you or anyone else will accept me for who I am? It seems like neither my mother nor the people at Good Shepherd do. Oh, Lord, it hurts so much."

Silent, hot tears of rejection ran down Debbie's cheeks and gathered on the pillow. Her mind went to the circumstances that led her there, and she burned in shame once more.

CHAPTER 13

Stacy had finished her breakfast and waited now in her room for Chaplain Miller to arrive. She picked up the Bible she'd left on the nightstand and opened it again to Psalm 23. "'Yea, though I walk through the valley of the shadow of death, I will fear no evil: for thou art with me.'"

Stacy closed the book and laid it back on the table.

Lord, I know what death feels like. I'm living it right now. I'm an emotional wreck, and I'm supposed to keep putting one foot in front of the other. How will I do this? My stomach is in knots, and I feel so alone. You are with me, Lord, I believe that, but I also feel like I'm balancing on a tightrope with no net below me. I'm ashamed to say I need to see a net right now. I want to feel you're with me, but I can't. Help me!

A light tap sounded on her door.

"Chaplain Miller is here, Stacy," Ruth said.

Stacy grabbed her purse and followed Ruth to the front door.

Chaplain Miller smiled at her from the front door. "I trust you got some rest last night, Stacy."

"I did, thank you."

Ruth put her hand on Stacy's shoulder. "Charles and I are praying for you today. We'll be waiting to hear of the Lord's provision for you."

Stacy nodded her thanks and then followed the chaplain out the door.

As they walked down the street, Stacy struggled to think of conversation topics.

Thankfully, Chaplain Miller broke the silence. "Let me tell you a little about Bethany so you'll feel more informed as you discuss the possibility of working there with Mrs. Turner."

"I'd be glad for anything you can tell me," she said.

Chaplain Miller smiled and then nodded. "Bethany R&L has been here in Klauthmos Bay for over twenty-five years. It provides both inpatient and outpatient services to those in need. The founders of Bethany had a vision that just as our bodies and minds sometimes need treatment, so do our souls.

"At Bethany, you'll find a staff that seeks to meet the emotional, mental, and physical needs of our patients, as well as their spiritual ones. As the chaplain, I work hand in hand with the doctors and nurses, providing counsel for our patients' spiritual needs."

"It sounds like a wonderful place. How many patients are there?"

"There are around forty patients in residence, with a few new people coming in this week, in addition to many outpatients who come for therapy and other such treatments. I'd guess there are over a hundred people who receive treatment at Bethany during the week. We have six therapists, three general practitioners, and around twelve mental health nurses on duty in a twenty-four-hour period."

Stacy was impressed with what she heard. It sounded like just the place she'd love to work.

But then her mind went back to her own personal trauma. How could she do her best work when she felt as if she needed counseling herself?

"You know, Stacy, one of the best ways for us to deal with our own difficulties is to help others with theirs."

She gaped at the chaplain. *How did he know what I was thinking?*

"As a mental healthcare nurse, you have the unique opportunity to do just that. I'm not implying that your present circumstances aren't difficult. I only seek to encourage you."

Stacy nodded as they took the last steps up to the front door of Bethany R&L. She prayed Chaplain Miller was right and that this would be the beginning of her healing too.

$$\text{⌂†⌂}$$

"If I were to ask Mrs. Alexander what kind of nurse you've been, what would she tell me?"

So far the interview had been standard, but thorough. Mrs. Turner had asked about her qualifications and job experience already but now seemed intent on digging deeper.

Stacy sat up straighter in her chair. "Mrs. Alexander would say I'm committed to the patients in my care. She never had to check up on the work I did during my shift because she knew I'm dependable. She'd say I'm organized, prompt, and competent in my duties."

"Good." Mrs. Turner scribbled something on her notepad. "Did you like working there? If so, why did you leave?"

Stacy knew this question was coming, and her stomach soured. She took a deep breath. "I loved my job, but I needed to leave the area for personal reasons."

After a few more questions and answers, Mrs. Turner stood. "I've already called your references, and they've confirmed what Mrs. Alexander and you have told me."

Smiling, Mrs. Turner picked up a file from her desk. "I'd like to offer you a position as a mental healthcare nurse here at Bethany R&L. Here is a contract outlining your salary and benefits. If you're ready to sign, I'll make a schedule for you to begin tomorrow morning at eight if that suits you. We provide uniforms for you to wear while working. Pick them up from the supply office near the main entrance before you leave. You must furnish your own shoes, however."

Stacy clasped the file. "That's wonderful! Thank you, Mrs. Turner. I'd love to work with you and the other staff here. And I'm fine with starting tomorrow." Stacy looked over the contract, then signed the document and handed it back.

"You'll be taking over Nurse Cindy Carson's caseload, as she'll be leaving shortly on maternity leave. Here's a list of patients and brief summations of each case you'll be responsible for. Take it with you and read it closely. It will help you tremendously."

Stacy took the list and stood. "Can you tell me where Chaplain Miller's office is located?" Stacy felt a bit unsteady at the sudden change in her life and needed a little shot of security. "I'd like to tell him that I'm going back to the Lewises' house."

Mrs. Turner nodded, opened her office door, and stepped out. Stacy followed. "Turn left here, go to the end of the hall, and make a right. His office is on the right. If his office door is closed, he's either with someone or he's gone. He always has his schedule posted on the door though. I know I need not tell you to be sensitive to our patients' privacy, so always double-check to see if he has a patient counseling appointment before knocking."

Stacy thanked Mrs. Turner and made her way to Chaplain Miller's office. She turned the corner and saw an office with an open door. Stacy drew closer to see Chaplain Miller's name and a small cross on the door. Peeking in to make sure he was there and not speaking with anyone, she felt relieved to see him alone.

Stacy knocked softly. Chaplain Miller's fingers stopped typing and he stood. "Hello, Stacy! Are you done with Mrs. Turner?"

"Yes, I am."

"Well, how about taking a seat for a minute while I finish up this message, and then I want to hear all about it."

While Chaplain Miller continued his work, Stacy studied the room filled with books, diplomas on display, and filing cabinets. A few plants and a Bible sitting on his desk made her smile. Two tall table lamps brought a comforting feel that no overhead fluorescent lights could provide.

Then, she noticed five bottles of different colors and sizes, including a dark red one beside his desk. Was this the bottle Chaplain Miller had with him when they first met in the park yesterday? When she peered closer she noticed they all had a small label displaying one word. She couldn't make out the text and moving any closer to examine them would seem rude. Each bottle held some sort of liquid, just like the man at the bus ticket counter had described.

"I trust your interview with Mrs. Turner went well." Chaplain Miller's voice jolted her from her thoughts. "Would you like some coffee while we talk? I have a fresh pot."

"Yes, I would. Thank you," Stacy said, sending a quick glance back to the bottles.

Chaplain Miller filled two cups, offered cream and sugar, and then sat back down. "How did the interview go?"

"Good. I must have represented myself well because Mrs. Turner offered me the job. I signed the contract and will start working tomorrow morning."

He let out a whoop. "Well done! You must be excited. What an answer to prayer. Charles and Ruth will be happy to hear the news."

Stacy smiled. "I'm sure they will." She felt a glimmer of hope before remembering the broken shell of her life.

She wondered when she'd ever let herself feel excited or hopeful again.

"Stacy, by the expression on your face, I see something is bothering you," Chaplain Miller said softly. "Of course, one of my jobs here at Bethany is to be a spiritual support to the patients who come for treatment. But I'm also here to support the staff in any way I can. Please know that I see your pain, and when and if you'd like to talk about it, let me know."

Stacy bit her lower lip. "Thank you, Chaplain Miller. I may take you up on that. For now, though, I'm feeling overwhelmed and tired. I think I'll go back to the Lewises' house and rejuvenate some."

"That's a good idea. Do you think you know your way back to their house? If not, I can go back with you."

"No, I'm sure I can find the way. Thank you again for all you've done for me. Your kindness touches me." Stacy stood, glancing again at the bottles as she turned to go.

Stacy made her way back to her hosts' house, thankful for the new job but sad she had no one to share her good news with. She'd always shared everything with Jack, but now, she had no one.

Oh, Lord, I am grateful for all you have done. Please help me deal with the burden of sorrow that lies on my heart. Amen.

CHAPTER 14

Stefan found Chaplain Miller's office with little difficulty. Glancing at his watch, he was glad to see he was on time. He peered in through the open door. Upon seeing him, Chaplain Miller stood from his desk and smiled.

"Stefan! Welcome. Come right in," Chaplain Miller said, holding out his hand.

Stefan shook hands with him, trying to produce at least half a smile in return.

"Sit down and make yourself comfortable. I've got a fresh pot of coffee that just finished brewing. Would you like some?"

"Yes, thank you."

Chaplain Miller made his way over to the coffee maker. He returned with two mugs and handed one to Stefan.

The mug felt warm and inviting in Stefan's hands, and he wondered if Chaplain Miller hated Styrofoam as much as he did.

"Are you finding your way around?" When Stefan nodded, Chaplain Miller continued. "Once you've been through each building a few times, you'll find it's not complicated."

Stefan placed the mug on a glass coaster on the chaplain's desk. "You're right. I've even found my way to Klauthmos Beach and Lakewood Park."

"Both good places to rest and reflect. I've always felt closer to the Lord in the great outdoors, especially at the ocean."

Chaplain Miller took a sip of his coffee and then leaned back in his chair. "I don't request any prior information about individuals I counsel here at Bethany other than what I need to know, but I've been informed the beach holds some painful memories for you. Is that correct?"

Stefan contemplated his answer and opened his mouth to speak but then shut it. Picking up his mug, he took a sip and then traced its rim with his finger while searching for words. Chaplain Miller waited quietly.

"I guess you can say the ocean was supposed to be my coffin," Stefan said quietly, "but it didn't work out the way I planned."

Chaplain Miller nodded and waited a few moments before he spoke again. "Is it correct that you're a personal injury attorney?"

"Yes." Stefan felt caught off guard by the question but was happy to change the subject.

"What is the most unusual case you've come across?"

Stefan thought for a moment and then chuckled. "In law school, a professor told us of a case where a woman sued a meteorologist because his forecast had been wrong. She claimed that the subsequent flu she caught and medication expenses should not be her responsibility but his. She testified she didn't dress properly because she had faith in his prediction, and he was wrong."

"Let me guess." Chaplain Miller held up a finger. "She won her case."

"Yep, and she was also awarded funds for ongoing psychiatric treatment for the anxiety she developed because she no longer had faith in the forecasts."

"It still amazes me what a litigious society we have," Chaplain Miller said. "I'm sure you remember, as I do, a day when you made a verbal commitment, shook hands on it, and your word was as good as gold."

"I do." Stefan stared at the wall for a moment. "On one hand, it's a sad reflection on our country. A person's word no longer holds the weight it used to. On the other hand, it's job security for me."

Chaplain Miller chuckled, stood, and moved to the coffee maker. "That it is. Would you like some more coffee?"

"No, thank you." Stefan relaxed back against the chair while the chaplain poured more coffee.

Chaplain Miller picked up his replenished mug and returned to his seat. "If we're conditioned to have no faith in mere verbal agreements in our society, we also transfer this into our personal relationships. We find it difficult, in many cases, to take another's word concerning any given thing of importance."

Stefan nodded, knowing how many people went to court for this very thing.

"There are a few exceptions, however. Is there anyone in your life, Stefan, whom you trust to keep his or her word?"

Stefan frowned as he thought about Sophie. She'd been the only person he could trust.

Pulling himself out of the past and back to the present, he cleared his throat. "Yes, there was one person I could depend on, knowing she meant what she said and said what she meant."

"You're using the past tense. Do you speak of your wife?" Chaplain Miller asked.

"Yes." Stefan's voice faltered as the image of his wife lit up his mind, producing an ache that he believed would never leave. He slumped a little in his chair, cleared his throat again and looked down, desperately seeking to hide his hurt from the chaplain and himself. "My wife, Sophie. She was the one person I could count on. She never told me just what I wanted to hear. She had a gentle way of speaking and yet at the same time, she didn't sugarcoat her words. But now ... she's gone."

"I'm sorry for your loss," Chaplain Miller said in a soothing tone. "Tell me more about her."

Stefan pressed his lips together, seeking to stop their trembling. When he'd regained some control, he sat up again, blew out a breath, and continued.

"I met Sophie when I was completing my undergraduate work. She attended the same church I did, and we were introduced to each other at a singles mixer the church sponsored. We started dating and were married the following year." Stefan paused, picturing a young Sophie and feeling the joy of their wedding day.

"That was more than forty years ago. In many ways, I consider myself lucky to have had that many years with her. Sophie was fiercely loyal to me and our sons."

Stefan clenched his hands into fists. "She never wavered in her faith in God, even when I believe she had a right to. I wonder if she would still be as dedicated to God if our roles were reversed, and she was left here alone."

Chaplain Miller didn't challenge Stefan's words. Instead, he changed the subject again. "Tell me about your sons."

"Our two boys are grown and out on their own. Robert lives in New York with his wife, Catherine, and their three children. Mark lives in Virginia and is married to Colleen—they don't have any children yet. Both sons are CPAs."

Chaplain Miller drew a notebook close and began to write notes. Stefan often did the same with his own clients to keep the facts straight.

"When was the last time you saw your sons?" Chaplain Miller asked.

Stefan paused and tried to swallow the lump that gathered in his throat. Holding back his grief drained his energy. He sat back in his chair feeling defeated.

"They were with me the two weeks prior to my wife's death and stayed through the week that followed her funeral. It was a hard thing to see them grieving so much for their mother. Then we had some disagreements, and there were words that were said in anger."

"Oh? What was the conflict about?"

"It was clear we were all raw with emotion and when Robert said we should rely on God's strength to get us through this, I lost it."

"What did losing it look like?"

"My first knee-jerk reaction was to say I didn't find a reason to rely on a God who did not help their mother in her biggest time of need. The pain was so bad at times she would pass out." Stefan shook his head and looked down. "And then Mark said perhaps God did send help by taking his mother home to heaven with him."

"Do you no longer believe in God and the afterlife with him for those who are his children?"

"That's the problem. I still believe in God and the life to come, but now, I think God is a cruel and distant God, and I said so to both of my sons. When they left at the end of the week, it was clear my relationship with each one was strained, and they have not been here for a visit since."

"Have you reached out to them? Have they called?"

"We've spoken every few weeks, and both of them have suggested several times they come out here for a visit, but I have discouraged that. It's clear there is a barrier between us."

"Are they aware of your desperate decision to end your life, and your subsequent hospitalization?"

He doesn't beat around the bush. Stefan ran his hand over his face. "No, they know nothing about it, and they also don't know I'm here."

Chaplain Miller paused in his questioning while he continued to write, giving Stefan a few seconds to gain control of his emotions.

Finally, the chaplain laid down his pen and returned his gaze to Stefan. Taking a deep breath, he said, "You know, we were talking about how it's hard to take people at their word these days."

Stefan nodded.

"When God tells us something like, *I will never leave you nor forsake you,* because we have learned from our experiences that taking someone at his word isn't prudent, it's easy to conclude we can't trust God's word either. This can make it seem like God is not good or reliable, and in reaction to this, we may be angry at God."

Chaplain Miller paused and stared at Stefan as if waiting for his full attention.

"Are you angry with God, Stefan?"

A fresh wave of grief and anger flowed over Stefan. When he answered, his tone sounded sharp. "Yes. I am."

The chaplain offered a curt nod. "Your reaction to God is normal because you have learned that people frequently break promises. What we must do as Christians is not judge God's actions or inactions based on our experiences with the human race." Chaplain Miller paused for a moment, letting his words sink in. "Here's my challenge to you." He reached for a piece of paper from a stack on his desk.

Stefan's eyes followed his movements, and suddenly, he spotted a sky-blue bottle among others on the table beside Chaplain Miller's papers. Was this the bottle he had seen earlier? Stefan looked closer and saw the bottles held varying amounts of liquid, and they all had labels. His breath quickened as he noticed the label had his name on it.

Chaplain Miller followed Stefan's eyes to the bottle as he handed him the paper. "Take this list of some of God's promises and read them as you would any other words. Then, step back a moment, and test these words. Are they true? Is the speaker trustworthy? Have you seen in your life evidence that God does keep his promises? We tend to look at God the way we've learned to look at people because experience has taught us people are flawed, but when we consider a subject who is not flawed, we need to change how we look at God's promises."

With these words, the chaplain stood. "Think over what I've said, and we'll discuss it at your next appointment. My schedule is full tomorrow and I have a funeral service the day after, but I have several slots open for the following day."

Stefan cleared his throat and stood. "Thank you for your time. I'll give careful consideration to the things you've said."

As Stefan made his way back to the door, he glanced again at the sky-blue bottle.

Why does the chaplain have that? And why is my name on it? Stefan wanted to ask about it but something inside him felt afraid.

As he walked out of the room, the chaplain called softly to him. "Remember, Stefan, God sees and cares."

CHAPTER 15

Stacy arrived back at the Lewises' home, exhausted. She briefly told Ruth how the interview had gone, that Mrs. Turner had offered her the position, and that she'd signed a contract.

"Wonderful! I'm so glad." Ruth studied Stacy's face and frowned. "You must be tired. Why don't you go back to your room and get some rest? Charles will be home from playing golf later this afternoon, and we'll want to hear about your morning."

Stacy felt relieved at the suggestion and headed down the hall and into her room.

She quickly hung up her uniforms, to keep from wrinkling them. She took off her shoes, and the thought of a bath in the garden tub tempted her. *No, I'll save that for tonight. I'll just rest for a while.*

Stacy climbed into bed and lifted the Bible from the table beside her. She turned back to Psalm 23. The fourth verse caught her eye.

"Yea, though I walk through the valley of the shadow of death, I will fear no evil."

Stacy leaned back against the headboard, and her face crumbled as pain squeezed out from her closed eyes.

Lord, I haven't thought of this before, but in a sense, I've experienced death these last several weeks. The life I knew and thought was good is dead, along with my relationship with Jack. On top of that, I've lost my best friend, Aubree. All these things, dead.

You say, "Yea, though I walk through the valley." I don't feel I can even walk through this valley. Lord, I've collapsed on the ground. I'm so wounded. Help me, Lord.

Stacy continued to cry until she fell asleep.

🍾✝🍾

Stacy awoke to a knock at the door. She rose, quickly smoothed her hair, and opened the door.

Ruth stood there smiling. "Supper is ready."

"Thank you. I'll be right there."

Stacy went back to the mirror in the bathroom and combed her hair. Though she'd rested, she could see the marks of tiredness in her face. She turned away and joined her hosts in the dining room. Even though she didn't have much of an appetite, she'd try to eat something. She needed to build up her strength again to start her new job.

"I hear that congratulations are in order," Charles said after they'd filled their plates and blessed the food. "Tell me all about it."

Stacy finished the piece of chicken she was chewing and smiled. "Well, as you know, Chaplain Miller accompanied me to Bethany, and Mrs. Turner was waiting for me."

"How did you like Mrs. Turner?" Ruth asked.

Stacy thought for a moment, searching for the words that best described her impression of her new supervisor. "Mrs. Turner is friendly, but she's definitely a no-nonsense kind of person. She reminds me of my former supervisor, Mrs. Alexander, in several ways. She helped me feel comfortable right away.

"Mrs. Turner asked many questions about my qualifications, of course, but she also wanted to know what kind of reputation, as a worker, I had at my former position at Eden."

"That's an interesting question," Charles said, slathering butter on his dinner roll. "I'm guessing she wanted to see how you viewed your own work ethic and was comparing it to what she'd already learned was your former supervisor's view of your work."

"That makes sense." Stacy reflected on his explanation for a moment. "Whatever her reason, she offered me the job, and I signed a contract."

"I made a strawberry pie to celebrate your good news," Ruth said. "So save room for it!"

"Oh, that's my favorite."

Stacy savored every bite of the delicious dessert and then laid down her fork feeling like she'd eaten more food tonight than all the last several weeks combined.

"May I help you with the dishes?"

"Thank you for your offer," Ruth said, picking up several plates from the table. "I'll take you up on it in the days to come. But tonight, you might like to get outdoors and become acquainted with the immediate area where you'll be working. If you'd like to go to the beach, take a right on Cayce Road, if you want to visit Lakewood Park, take a left."

Charles went to the patio with the evening paper, and Stacy wondered if they were following their normal routine or if this was for her benefit.

"All right," Stacy said, "I think I will. Thank you."

As soon as Stacy walked out the front door, she smelled the sea air. Wanting to see Klauthmos Beach, she set out in that direction.

As she strolled past Bethany R&L, she thought about all that had transpired there earlier in the day. Would her new job be similar to where she used to work? She'd loved working there and missed many of the people. Even Aubree. Her heart lurched at how quickly her life had turned upside down.

She observed the healthcare facility she'd soon become intimately acquainted with and was impressed with the neat and welcoming grounds. The grass was trimmed, the pathways were bordered with flowers and plants, and numerous large trees offered cool shade from the hot sun. She could see how this place would be a soothing balm for troubled souls.

Some people were sitting about, talking in hushed tones, and Stacy believed many of them also knew their way into "the valley of the shadow of death."

She forced herself not to let her thoughts head in that direction right then and focused instead on the yards and houses she passed as she continued to the beach.

It didn't take long before Stacy reached the small dunes that bordered the beach of Klauthmos Bay. She took off her sandals and walked toward the waves gently rolling toward her.

Stacy let the tide wash over her feet, the wind blowing her blonde hair back from her face. She closed her eyes and breathed in the salty air. If she didn't know better, Stacy would have thought she was at home in Monterey. Hopefully, she would not associate the painful memories there with the sights and smells of her new town.

Monterey was no longer her home. Without her permission, the memory of seeing Jack with Aubree flooded her mind again. The waves of anguish, despair, and hurt pounded against her heart. Nausea moved over her stomach, and for a moment, she thought she'd be sick. Stacy sat down on the sand and lowered her head, crying. Slowly, the queasiness passed.

Stacy's thoughts returned to Psalm 23, and she turned her eyes heavenward.

Why, Lord? Why did these horrible things happen? The psalmist said that even though he was walking through the valley of the shadow of death, he feared no evil. I'm sorry, Lord, but I fear everything.

Are you disgusted with me because I am so full of fear? Are you disappointed with me? I know I am.

On top of that, I'm not sure I have the strength to start a new job, a position where I'm supposed to help other people. I can't even seem to help myself. Will Mrs. Turner be sorry for hiring me?

I've lost so much, Lord. My husband and best friend. I'm not sure I have anything left to give. This is too much to bear, Lord. Your word tells me you miraculously healed a blind man with a little mud, how about healing me?

She listened for a response, but none came, and she wondered if God had abandoned her like Jack had. She sat for a while, watching the waves roll back and forth across the sand. When she felt another wave of tiredness wash over her, she rose and returned to the Lewises'.

She found Ruth sitting out on the patio reading.

"Hi. I just wanted to let you know I was back."

Ruth closed her book and set it in her lap. "Sit down, dear, and keep me company a bit. Charles has gone to a meeting at church, and I'd love to get to know you better. Along with the job, what brought you to our town?"

Stacy sat on a chair across from her host. "It's a little complicated." She fought to swallow the lump that had appeared in her throat.

"If you're uncomfortable sharing, you don't have to."

"I know, but I think it would be good for both of us if I tell you. It just won't be easy."

"Take your time, dear. We have the whole house to ourselves for at least another hour."

Stacy swallowed again. "I wound up coming here because my former supervisor at Eden Behavioral Healthcare Center discovered that Bethany R&L had an opening. She knew I needed to leave, and she helped me.

"You see, one day, on a whim, I went on my lunch break to get some of my husband's favorite food for our supper. I found Jack with my best friend, Aubree." Stacy's vision blurred, and she stopped for a moment to brush the moisture from her eyes.

When she looked up again at Ruth, she felt touched to see tears also forming in her eyes.

"When I confronted Jack, he admitted he was having an affair with Aubree, and he was filing for divorce. I was so hurt and humiliated. Not only did my husband betray me, so did my best friend. I worked with Aubree, so I knew it would be hard to keep working there."

Ruth reached out and patted her hand. "Stacy, I'm so sorry to hear this. I have no words I can say to make this better for you, but the Lord can make good come out of the bad of this life. I'll pray he will help you see this as your life unfolds."

Stacy hoped so too, but she couldn't see how.

⚱️✝⚱️

Later that evening, Stacy sat down at the small desk in her room and took out the list of patients Mrs. Turner had given her and read through the brief bios of each one. When she read about Debbie Young—a woman in her twenties—and a brief summary of why she was at Bethany, Stacy's heart went out to her. Here was someone who suffered from rejection too. She'd do everything she could to help Debbie feel accepted.

Putting the papers aside, Stacy couldn't believe how weary she felt. *I must be really out of sync, feeling so worn out after this relatively easy day.*

She pondered all that had transpired that day. She reflected on Bethany R&L and compared the little she had seen to Eden. She hoped working for Mrs. Turner would be at least as good as the working relationship she had with Mrs. Alexander. Then, her thoughts went to Jack and Aubree.

The pain rushed through her like a jolt of electricity. Stacy rose and looked out the window, fighting back unanswered questions.

THE BOTTLE HOUSE

Why had Jack cheated on her? Stacy had always gone out of her way to give him what he wanted. Apparently, she wasn't as good as Aubree. Stacy's body was so far from perfect, but on a scale of one to ten, Aubree's was an eleven. But didn't inner beauty count for anything? She and Jack had shared so much, and he'd thrown it all away.

She felt humiliated. Aubree got a part of Jack that was only supposed to be Stacy's. Her best friend—the very person she regularly confided in—had betrayed her, and now, Stacy had nothing.

She should have noticed Jack had stopped doing the little things that couples do for each other. How long would it have taken her to find out what was going on if she hadn't seen them together that day in the restaurant?

She lay down on the bed and pushed her sobs into her pillow.

Stacy awoke sometime later and saw the darkness through the window. The house seemed quiet as she consulted the clock. 1:20 a.m.

Wide awake now, she picked up her Bible, flipping back to the Twenty-third Psalm. She ran her eyes through the verses and stopped at verse four again.

"Yea, though I walk through the valley of the shadow of death, I will fear no evil."

Being a nurse, she'd seen death triumph over her patients. It was so final—something beyond anyone's control. Forceful. Irreversible.

Lately, Lord, I've been walking through the valley of the shadow. I'm scared this hurt I'm feeling will be as unchangeable as death. I'm afraid of everything.

You must be disappointed in me because I'm fearful of the evil that has played out in my life. I'm so hurt and angry right now. I want this to be over, but it keeps going on and on.

I don't know how much longer I can take it, but it seems as if you're saying, "Oh, yeah? You'll make it. You might almost die, but you'll make it." Don't you care? You seem so detached from me, so uninvolved. Please, Lord, I need encouragement.

I know it may not sound like it but I'm grateful for this job. Thank you for providing it, but I just wish for the comfort of having a husband around to share my life with— the good and the bad.

Stacy remembered the time Jack had gotten a long-overdue promotion. They'd cheered while twirling around in each other's arms. Then, as quick as the memory came to her mind, it disappeared in what felt like a puff of smoke. Stacy's eyes went back to the psalm.

"For thou art with me; thy rod and thy staff they comfort me."

Stacy hung her head, ashamed of her lack of faith. She didn't have the energy to dispute her thoughts with these words.

Where are you, Lord? You say you are with me, but I just can't feel it. I need your comfort. I hurt so bad. Will it always be this way?

CHAPTER 16

Debbie found her way to the cafeteria at breakfast and waited in line to get her meal. Though the food smelled good, the acid in her stomach held her appetite hostage. Ever since the meeting with the board at school, Debbie had no desire for food. She selected a few small dishes and sides she hoped would tempt her, then picked up a glass of ice water and sat down.

She didn't know what she dreaded most about mealtimes—having someone join her or having people avoid her. If someone sat with her, Debbie was afraid they'd ask why she really wasn't eating much, but if no one sat with her, she'd feel even more alone.

She bowed her head briefly in a prayer of thanks for the food, then opened her eyes and glanced around the room. A nurse smiled and walked toward Debbie's table.

"I believe you're Debbie Young?" After seeing Debbie nod, she added, "Do you mind if I join you?"

"No, please do." Debbie moved over to make room for the pregnant nurse.

"Mrs. Turner has assigned me to you. I'm Nurse Cindy Carson." Nurse Carson sat with the heaviness of her unborn baby. "Are you finding your way around here?"

Debbie smiled, realizing that asking for directions around here must be similar to asking about the weather elsewhere. "I think I am. I plan to venture out to Klauthmos Beach today. I hear it's beautiful."

"The beach is one of my favorite places here. I'm not sure I can articulate why, but there's great comfort for me while standing at the edge of the ocean."

"Me, too. I know I'll be visiting there regularly."

"I'm glad I ran into you," Nurse Carson said. "Mrs. Turner let me know they've hired a new nurse. Her name is Stacy Meadows. She'll work with me a few days and then will take over for me during my maternity leave. I'll introduce you shortly, but in the meantime, I'd like to go over your schedule with you after we finish our breakfast."

"Whatever we need to do." Debbie tried offering a genuine smile, but she couldn't help but feel some disappointment because she was immediately drawn to this young nurse.

"Are you excited about the coming baby?" Debbie asked, trying to think of something else to talk about.

"Yes, Brad and I are so excited," the nurse said, almost bubbling over with enthusiasm. "Do you and your husband have any children?"

"Not yet." Debbie took a sip of her some coffee. "We've only been married two years, and we wanted to wait a bit. Plus, I'm teaching third grade, and I'd like to get a few more years of experience in first."

The two women continued their meal, chatting about everyday things. When they finished eating, they collected their dishes and deposited them where others were stacked.

As they left the cafeteria, Nurse Carson said, "It's nice and sunny today. How about we find a place in the courtyard and go over your schedule? Once we make a plan you agree to, it will remain the same when Nurse Meadows takes over. We can also make some other decisions."

Debbie hesitated for a moment. Maybe she'd miss Josh's call—no, it was too early. He had a meeting at Good Shepherd he needed to attend concerning summer school.

She nodded.

The two women made their way to the courtyard, stopping only at the nurse's station to pick up Cindy's schedule. They found a quiet area and sat down, making themselves as comfortable as either of them could be.

"Dr. Murphy has you scheduled for eleven this morning. I'd like to finish filling out your paperwork and then, this afternoon, Nurse Meadows will join us in order to complete some assessments on you."

Debbie opened her mouth and quickly shut it, clenching her teeth.

"What's wrong?" Nurse Carson asked. "Tell me what you're thinking."

The nurse waited a moment and then leaned forward, as much as her bulk would allow, and gently said, "Something has upset you, Debbie, and I'd like to help. Don't worry, I've been in this type of job a long time. Nothing you can say will shock me. All I want from you is honesty. What's troubling you?"

Hurt spilled out of Debbie's mouth. "It's these assessments. It's just I've heard from my mother all my life that I'm not good enough, and what if these assessments show she was right?" Two tears made their way silently down Debbie's cheeks.

"I don't know you very well," Nurse Carson said softly, "but I've seen your registration papers, and I noticed you didn't come here solely by your own prompting. If this were true of me, I'd feel angry and hurt too. It's okay to feel that way. The assessments won't determine your mental state. Rather, they'll give us an idea of how you think. They'll also be used, in conjunction with the work you'll be doing with Dr. Murphy, to help you, not to put you down."

Seeing the nurse had genuine compassion and concern in her eyes, Debbie simply stated, "I understand."

Nurse Carson smiled. "I understand too."

Just then, Chaplain Miller entered the courtyard, walked toward them.

Debbie thought the man seemed to radiate dignity. His graying hair was neatly trimmed, and his kind green eyes, seen through his glasses, communicated understanding and compassion.

"Good morning, ladies."

"I think you've met Debbie Young," Cindy said. "She just arrived last night."

"Yes, I met Mrs. Young and her husband last night. Good morning," Chaplain Miller said while shaking her hand.

"Good morning." Debbie hoped that her effort to put a pleasant look on her face was successful.

"I won't take away from your time together, but I wanted to check in with you both as I tentatively made an appointment with Debbie this afternoon." Chaplain Miller raised his eyebrows.

Nurse Carson consulted her planner. "Debbie has an appointment with Dr. Murphy at eleven and some assessments at one. Aside from that, her schedule is open. So, I guess, it's really up to her."

Debbie sat for a moment, trying to get her thoughts in order. She glanced up at his face and saw genuine kindness. "Yes, that would be nice. What time would be good for me to drop by?"

"I have three written on my schedule. Does that work?" the chaplain asked.

"I'll be there if I don't get lost." Debbie worked hard to make her voice sound light.

Chaplain Miller laughed. "I'll send out the rescue dogs if you don't show up." He gave a small salute, then left.

At that moment, something inside her spirit moved. Debbie sensed this man was different than many pastors she had known.

Nurse Carson turned to Debbie. "Chaplain Miller was the first person I met when I arrived in Klauthmos Bay. He's a good, kindhearted man. We're lucky to have him here."

THE BOTTLE HOUSE

Debbie sat back and reflected on the nurse's words. Something made her want to trust this man of God.

After they had finished creating Debbie's schedule, Nurse Carson went back to work while Debbie continued to sit in the courtyard.

What should she do now? She checked her watch. She had time before her eleven o'clock appointment with Dr. Murphy, so she decided to set out for the beach.

She gathered a towel, put on a light sweater, and strolled down Cayce Road. As she made her way to the beach, she saw a two-story house with a wraparound porch. Debbie sighed. *Josh and I would love to have a place like this!* Why did she feel such yearning just from seeing a house, of all things?

After a moment, she continued to the beach. She could hear the waves and smell the salt water before she could see it.

Debbie slipped off her flip-flops and let her feet sink into the sand. She made her way closer to the ocean, put down her towel, and then dropped to the ground, shifting herself in the sand a bit to make her seating more comfortable. Taking a deep breath of the fresh, salty air, she surveyed the area.

There was no one on her right, but when she turned her head around, her heart lurched. An older man sat on the sand not ten yards from her with his head between his knees, weeping.

He didn't seem to notice the incoming tide was just beginning to wash around him.

Debbie recognized his despair. She didn't know what caused this display of raw emotion, but she knew the feeling intimately.

Debbie lifted her eyes and prayed.

Lord, it is clear I'm not the only one seeking help from the hills of Psalm 121. I know you alone bring help. This man's heart must also be full of pain. There is so much of it here on the earth. Surely you know this. How do you feel about it? Does it stir a well of tears within you?

Debbie shook her head, not knowing the answers to her questions.

A few minutes later, she made her way off the beach, hoping her presence wouldn't be noticed by the man.

This time, Debbie ached for someone else.

CHAPTER 17

Morning came all too soon for Stacy. She sat up in bed and rubbed her temples. A headache had started sometime in the middle of the night. She had just enough time for a shower before she needed to leave the house to be on time for work.

Making her way into the bathroom, she suddenly felt faint and slightly nauseous, so she sat on the edge of the tub. Even though she'd eaten fairly well at supper the night before, it probably hadn't been enough to make up for her poor eating habits the past few days. Stacy made a mental note to eat a little better than she had been in order to do the job she now had.

Fresh from the shower, she made her way toward the kitchen where the smell of homemade waffles greeted her.

"Good morning, Stacy. Have a seat right there with Charles, and I'll bring you some coffee. If you're nice to him, maybe he'll share his newspaper with you." Ruth reached for the coffeepot. "The waffles will be ready soon. Did you sleep well?"

"I did, thank you." Stacy took a sip from the mug of coffee Ruth set before her. "I didn't know people read from a physical paper much anymore."

Charles lowered his paper and smiled. "I guess I'm probably one of the few people who do. I like to feel it in my hands and then fold it up and reuse it for other things around the house."

Stacy smiled and moved her gaze back toward Ruth. "If I'm going to live here, at least for the time being, I'd like to take on some of the household responsibilities. What chores can I take over so I can help pull my own weight around here?"

The older lady smiled as she brought two plates of waffles to the table.

"That's nice you want to help out here, Stacy. Let me give it some thought, and then you and I can come up with a plan that will work for each of us."

The two women finished their breakfast with some small talk, and then Stacy took her dishes to the sink.

She quickly dressed in her nurse's uniform, grabbed her purse, and said a hasty goodbye to her hosts.

As soon as Stacy stepped out to the street, the hurt and betrayal hit her again like an arrow that found the bullseye in her heart. Her thoughts went to Jack, how they always had breakfast together and discussed what each anticipated about the day ahead. Now, she wasn't sure she even cared about the day ahead.

Jack, what you did makes me so sad. Everyone at home must be aware now of what happened. It's humiliating and embarrassing. I must not have ever really known you. Did I just think of you as the man I wanted you to be rather than who you are?

I asked so many times for notes from you, like you used to do when we first got together, but you never wrote any. I bet you write them for Aubree. The times we were intimate, were you only thinking of her?

Stacy forced her thoughts away from Jack and Aubree. She didn't want to show up at Bethany an emotional mess. Just as she had herself under control, she saw Chaplain Miller coming her way.

"Hello, Stacy. Good morning to you."

"Good morning."

"Do you mind if I keep you company the rest of the way to Bethany?"

"Not at all." Stacy was glad she had her emotions under control, at least for the time being.

"Are you ready for your first full day?"

"I think so. Mrs. Turner gave me a good idea of where I needed to be and what I'll do. She's paired me with Cindy Carson for a few days before she goes on maternity leave, so I think I'll be ready."

"You'll be ready," Chaplain Miller said with more confidence than Stacy felt.

"Mrs. Turner gave me a list and brief bios of those who will be on my caseload. I've already found one young lady who, after reading her brief story, I feel drawn to, as if God specially put her on my list."

"Though I'm not asking for a name, don't worry about confidentiality. Part of the agreement when patients come to Bethany is that their records can be shared among the staff that work with them."

"That's good to know. That's the way it worked at my last job, but I didn't think to ask if the same policy applied here. The patient I was referring to, Debbie Young, is suffering in a way I especially can relate to. She has been told most of her life that she's flawed. It's my hope that I can somehow help alleviate her pain—at least to some degree."

"There's always plenty of suffering in the world." Chaplain Miller nodded. "People need to find meaning in their suffering, and we can guide our charges to sort this out. This is a process, as you know, that works in different ways, depending on the person."

"You're right. My goal for today is to meet Debbie and the others on my list." Stacy hoped she'd have the strength to help others through their pain while she still wrestled with her own.

"You know, Stacy, suffering on this earth wasn't God's plan. He created everything for mankind and gave it all to them, with one exception. Because this exception was violated, suffering and death entered the world. God didn't create evil, yet he did provide a way to save people from it. For that, I'm truly grateful."

Chaplain Miller held the door to the main entrance open for Stacy. She smiled her thanks as they parted. She heard his last words, almost as if they were softly carried on the wind.

"God sees your pain."

CHAPTER 18

Debbie was grateful Nurse Carson had shown her where Dr. Murphy's office was earlier that morning. Arriving at the therapist's door, she felt dread wash over her.

Remembering the nurse's smile, Debbie recalled she had said, "It's okay. It won't be as bad as perhaps you're imagining. Think of it this way, the more you actively participate in your sessions here at Bethany, the quicker you can return home."

Debbie glanced at her phone and saw the time was exactly eleven o'clock. She knocked on the open door and, glancing into the office, entered as the doctor stood.

"Hello! You must be Debbie Young. I'm Dr. Murphy."

Debbie nodded and tried her best to smile.

"Nurse Carson told me to expect you this morning." The doctor gestured to an empty seat. "Please sit down, Mrs. Young." Debbie was grateful that the doctor paused, seeming to sense she needed a moment to pull herself together.

"I want to spend some time this first appointment getting background information about you." She nodded and the therapist opened his laptop.

After a series of questions about her family and education level, he turned to more personal questions.

"Have you ever had homicidal thoughts toward anyone? Have you contemplated taking your life? Do you ever hear voices when there is no one else around?"

Debbie felt a gamut of emotions, wondering if there were right and wrong answers. "No, I haven't."

The doctor typed her answer into his computer file.

"What are the circumstances that brought you here to Bethany?"

Her face flushed, and the experienced therapist gave her a moment.

"Debbie, whatever it is that led you to Bethany, you don't need to worry. I'm here to help ease the emotional weight you are clearly carrying."

Meeting his eyes, Debbie told the doctor the details of what transpired at her job.

Instead of judging or condemning her, he simply clicked in some notes on the computer and then offered her encouragement. "Debbie, here at Bethany R&L, we strive to model the acceptance and nonjudgmental attitude that we believe is biblical toward all our residents. You can feel safe here in the knowledge we are here to help you, not judge you."

As she walked back to her room later, Debbie felt relieved Dr. Murphy knew it was important to just chat and get acquainted with her—at least for today. She assumed this was to help make her feel more at ease in the coming days.

Debbie walked to the small desk in her room and picked up her Bible. She sat back against the headboard of the bed and turned to Psalm 121.

"I lift up my eyes to the mountains—where does my help come from?"

In a general sense, she believed that help did come from God. But she questioned why he didn't intervene in situations like hers. She turned back to the Bible and read the third and fourth verses.

"He will not let your foot slip—he who watches over you will not slumber; indeed, he who watches over Israel will neither slumber nor sleep."

She had written a note in the margin next to verse three. "This is not in reference to a physical fall."

If God is not promising protection from my physical foot moving—from physically falling—it must mean emotionally, mentally, or spiritually falling. I'm not sure this is true. It seems as if God knows I've "fallen" but hasn't done much about it.

Debbie's thoughts were interrupted by a knock at her door.

"Good afternoon, Debbie," Nurse Carson said, smiling. "I want to introduce you to Stacy Meadows. She'll be the nurse assigned to you from this point on."

She invited them in and held out her hand to Stacy. Their eyes met, and Debbie quickly recognized a broken heart in this nurse, who appeared to be around her own age. Debbie was comforted in the idea that she was not alone.

Cindy continued, bringing Debbie's thoughts back in focus. "There are several things we need to assess right away so we can set up a treatment schedule that's best for you."

Cindy consulted her file. "We have some time before your appointment with Chaplain Miller at three. Because we need somewhere to spread out a bit, I suggest we head to the women's lounge or the courtyard. If you'd rather be in total privacy, the conference room is also available. It's your call."

Debbie quickly weighed her options. The women's lounge was more comfortable. Although it would be nice to sit in the sunshine, the courtyard wouldn't afford the privacy she was seeking right now. Neither would the lounge. She opted for the conference room.

As they made their way there, Stacy said, "I understand you've only been at Bethany one full day. This is my first day of working here, so maybe we can help each other find our way around."

Appreciating the offer, Debbie gave her a small smile. "Thanks. I'm still getting turned around a little."

"That's understandable. I would have never found my way to your room without Cindy's help."

"Oh, yes, you would have, Stacy. Maps are posted at all the main doors," Cindy said. "It won't take either one of you long to find your way around without needing to use them. Now, I'm going to leave and let Stacy take the lead. If you have any questions, please let me know."

Nurse Carson patted Stacy on the shoulder and then walked out of the room. Debbie perched on the edge of one of the chairs with her fingers laced together on the table.

Stacy opened her laptop and clicked into what must be Debbie's file. "I see you had your psychological evaluation this morning with Dr. Murphy and have an appointment with Dr. Fletcher at three tomorrow afternoon for your physical evaluation."

"Why do I need a physical evaluation?" Debbie asked.

"That's a good question. A physical evaluation is important in many ways. For example, I see from your records that you have hypothyroidism."

Debbie nodded.

"Knowing this, Dr. Fletcher will want to do a TSH test to see what your thyroid levels are. As I'm sure you know, the thyroid is affected greatly by stress and other such factors. We need to know things like this so we can consider them alongside your psychological needs to create a program that will help you on multiple levels."

Stacy continued to ask questions and typed the young woman's responses into her laptop. When they'd finished, Debbie felt a little worn out.

"Are you holding up okay?" Stacy asked.

"I think so. I didn't realize how involved a treatment program would be here. I was hoping after seeing Dr. Murphy a half-dozen times, I'd be free to go home."

"I understand, but you don't want to rush the process. Think of this as if you're having a complete makeover—not to change you, but to help you feel better about yourself. I think all people could use a boost in this area."

Debbie liked this new nurse already and the idea of a complete makeover. She hoped it would include making her inside prettier too.

CHAPTER 19

Debbie's hand shook as she gently knocked on Chaplain Miller's open door. In light of her history, she felt very nervous to be in the presence of someone whose job must be closely related to being a pastor. She poked her head through the doorway and saw the chaplain rising from his chair with a smile.

"Welcome, Debbie. Come right in and make yourself comfortable."

Comfortable is the last thing I'm feeling right now. Two leather chairs sat in front of his desk, and she chose the one closest to the door.

"Would you like some coffee?"

She shook her head. "No, thank you."

"It's my biggest vice."

Chaplain Miller went over to the coffee maker and poured some into a mug, then sat back down at his desk and smiled. "So, you've been at Bethany R&L for one full day. Tell me about your first impressions."

"I-I ..." Her voice caught and she stopped to clear her throat.

"I know this is difficult, Debbie. Relax, take a deep breath, and continue when you're ready."

Debbie felt fear and excitement surge simultaneously through her body. Chaplain Miller's tender attitude gave her a touch of hope, but she still felt afraid, not knowing if she could trust this man of God.

"I suppose you know why I'm here at Bethany," she said quietly.

"In a general sense, yes. Because Bethany R&L is a behavioral healthcare facility, I'm aware you've experienced some kind of trauma, but that's all I know." The chaplain moved his gaze briefly from her face to the wall beyond her. Could he be thinking about some personal trauma he experienced?

"As the chaplain here at Bethany, it's my practice not to learn too many details about patients ahead of time, except what's absolutely necessary. This is because I want to understand specific situations from my patient's viewpoint." He pushed his mug aside and clasped his hands on his desk. "So tell me about your first twenty-four hours here."

"Josh helped me get registered and settled in my room." Debbie's words faltered. She missed Josh so much already—he was her rock. How would she ever get through this without him? She couldn't even get beyond two sentences without falling apart.

Debbie leaned forward and reached for a tissue from a box on the corner of Chaplain Miller's desk. As she pulled one out, she saw several small, colorful bottles on the shelf behind him. Debbie blew her nose and rose to throw the tissue in the trash which gave her a closer view of them. Holding the tissue over the container, she stopped in midstride as she saw not only her light green bottle with her name on it but also an amber one with Josh's name on it. She let go of the tissue and sat back down, not sure what to say or ask. Her eyes meet Chaplain Miller's. He glanced over his shoulder toward the bottles, then raised his eyebrows but made no comment as he waited for her to continue.

"Those bottles on the shelf are beautiful. There's the bottle you had with you yesterday, I think, that now holds my name. I also see an amber one with Josh's name. What are they for?"

The chaplain smiled. "I have collected bottles for years. They are objects I use to remind myself and others that God is vitally interested and concerned with the heartbreak that each person experiences in this life."

Debbie sat quietly for a moment, processing what the chaplain said. His words generated so many questions but she quicky decided to wait to ask them ... for now. She didn't want to hear the sometimes-trite Christian conversation about how she needed to trust God more and everything would be better.

"I believe you asked me about my first day here at Bethany. I got settled, and this morning, I had my first session with Dr. Murphy. Afterward, I went down to the beach. It's so beautiful there."

Chaplain Miller smiled. "It's one of my favorite places in all of God's creation. It's also the place where I love to talk with God. Somehow, I sense his presence, love, and compassion there in a stronger way than anywhere else."

Debbie pictured the waves washing up on the shore and nodded in agreement.

"What are your strengths, Debbie?"

The question caught her off guard and she blinked. Chaplain Miller waited patiently for her answer. She gazed around the room, thinking. Her eyes landed on a drawing of Jesus, snuggling a lamb in his arms. A nail hole was present on the visible hand.

"I'm compassionate, loyal, and hardworking," Debbie finally answered, her eyes still on the drawing of Jesus.

"Tell me ways you use your strengths in everyday life." The chaplain's question caused Debbie to refocus on the man and what he was asking.

These questions are different than what I would expect a chaplain to ask. I thought he'd want to stick solely to the spiritual side of things.

"When I'm with hurting people, I can feel their pain. I see this a lot in my third-grade classroom."

"There is healing where compassion is present. You must be a soothing presence for those fortunate students in your care," Chaplain Miller said.

If only the men I work for would think this about me.

"I'm loyal to those in my life," Debbie continued, "and will fight to the death for anyone I'm connected with. As I said, I'm also hardworking, but sometimes, those two things make me run out of energy."

Chaplain Miller nodded. "Each strength and gift we have on this earth is also an area of vulnerability. For me, I'm an organized person, and because of that, I find it very difficult to work in an atmosphere of chaos. I'm also a good listener, and perhaps I spend too much time in my private life listening and not enough on talking. That makes it hard for people to get to know me."

Debbie pondered his words, then nodded in agreement.

"Think about these strengths you've pointed out to me. How could they be areas of vulnerability?"

Debbie paused, her eyes drawn back to the picture of Jesus and the lamb. "Well, because I'm compassionate, I sometimes empathize with others too deeply. Perhaps this diminishes my ability to see some circumstances objectively." Debbie's grip on the chair arms strengthened. The school board had been anything but compassionate in her view. The tension built within her, and she didn't know if she could continue with this conversation or even stay there at Bethany. When she moved her eyes back to the chaplain's face, she saw the tenderness and care of an individual who seemed to be listening closely. She took a deep breath.

"I guess my loyalty can blind me in some situations. I can overlook a person's actions when that may not be a good idea. And because I'm a hard worker, sometimes I feel like no one notices. This can lead to resentment."

"Good insights, Debbie," Chaplain Miller said. "I believe in the core of my being Satan loves to take the gifts and abilities God has given us and twist them. He must relish it when we get out of balance and act on the vulnerable side of them."

Debbie nodded, considering his words. The chaplain picked up his mug and took another sip.

"Sometimes Satan's even able to orchestrate, through the negative circumstances our vulnerability can cause, a permanent reluctance to use the strengths God gives us. My challenge to you is to ponder these things. Make a thorough list of the strengths, gifts, and abilities God has given you, and then, take note of vulnerabilities in these areas." He leaned forward and set the mug on his desk. "If you'd like, we can meet again the day after tomorrow and discuss what you've discovered."

Debbie stood, nodded, and smiled. She was anxious to ponder the things Chaplain Miller had shared. "Thank you for your time. You've given me a lot to reflect on."

"I'm always here," Chaplain Miller said as he stood. "I'll be praying for you."

A warmth spread through her because, somehow, she knew he meant what he said. *Maybe I will stay a little bit longer.*

She made her way through the hallways and back to her room. Noticing the time, Debbie decided to give Josh a call. She grabbed her phone, went to the courtyard, and sat in the shade near the fountain and placed the call. Josh answered right away.

"Hey, honey, I'm glad you called. I was just thinking about you."

Debbie smiled. "I had a few minutes free, and I was missing you so much. I just needed to hear your voice."

"How's your first day at Bethany going?"

"Well, I woke up feeling sort of lost. When I realized where I was ..." Debbie had remembered the circumstances of why she'd been forced to this place—the pain of the rejection. A familiar lump appeared again in her throat.

"I understand," he whispered into the phone. "I shed a few tears these last twenty-four hours too. I've just been wrestling with this whole situation and trying to figure out if we both have made the right decision for you to be at Bethany."

Debbie's heart stirred, feeling thankful for the way Josh loved and cared about her and her well-being.

"I had my first appointments today. I met with Dr. Murphy this morning and Chaplain Miller this afternoon."

"How did they go?" When she hesitated, he was quick to say, "Hon, of course I'm curious, and I have questions, but please feel free to tell me you don't want to talk about them. Okay?"

"Okay."

"So ... what's your opinion of Dr. Murphy so far?"

"Well, he surprised me by taking some time with me just to get acquainted. He asked me where I was born, what I enjoyed doing in my spare time, and how you and I met. I wasn't expecting that. He also asked me several psychological questions. My appointment with Chaplain Miller surprised me, too, but not for the same reason."

"I'm intrigued."

"Chaplain Miller centered our conversation on my strengths, and I told him I'm compassionate, loyal, and hardworking."

"That's exactly what I'd say if he asked me about you."

Debbie smiled. "But then I made the comment that sometimes being hardworking was bad, kind of like a weakness too. That's when he said that all our strengths have vulnerabilities. I knew this but somehow, when he said it, it clicked. He challenged me to make a list of all the strengths I have and to see if I can spot their vulnerabilities."

"Sounds like a wonderful assignment. I'd love it if you felt you could share your list with me when you finish."

"Of course. Oh, there was something else I felt was unusual. I noticed a small, light green bottle on his desk and an amber one right beside it. My name was on the green one and yours was on the amber one. They both held some kind of liquid. I don't know what to think of that."

"Did you ask Chaplain Miller about it?"

"I did. He said they were kind of like an object lesson about God's love and concern for his children. I don't know what the exact connection is between them and us. I hope I'll learn more in the days ahead. They piqued my curiosity."

They chatted a moment or two longer, exchanged endearments, and then said goodbye.

Debbie sat, her phone in her lap, and stared at the fountain as tears filled her eyes. She missed her husband so much.

CHAPTER 20

Stefan had awoken too early for breakfast so he'd made his way to the courtyard to study the piece of paper about God's promises Chaplain Miller had given him yesterday.

He sat in a seat by a firepit that must have been used the previous night. A faint odor of smoke still remained, and a trail of smoke rose from the mound of ash. Making sure he was alone, Stefan pulled out the folded piece of paper. His eyes went to the words from Isaiah 40:29. "He gives strength to the weary and increases the power of the weak."

Stefan crumpled the paper quickly and stuffed it back in his pocket, then stared into the firepit.

I have begged you, pleaded with you to give me strength. If anyone is weary, it's me, Lord. Why are you so distant? Why do you not act on my behalf? You could have stopped all the wrong things I've experienced if you wanted to. Instead, you did not. Why, Lord? Why?

Stefan continued to focus on the dying ashes. He couldn't help but draw a parallel between them and his heart.

A dull ache developed inside his head, so Stefan massaged the area where his nose met his forehead. As he did, the words of Chaplain Miller returned to him. *"Test God's words. Are they true? Trustworthy? Is there evidence in your life that reveals God keeps his word?"*

Stefan slowly reached into his pocket and pulled the wrinkled paper back out. He flattened it on his thigh, and reread the verse he saw earlier. "He gives strength to the weary and increases the power of the weak." His eyes returned to the firepit again. At one point in his life, he'd taken God at his word, but years of being beaten down had changed his attitude.

If I could only see these words without the skepticism I now have, maybe I could take God at his word.

Stefan pictured that ugly day when he'd tried to end his life. He'd felt like such a failure then ... and now. He'd even failed at suicide.

No. I can't take God at his word. My experience indicates he is not trustworthy. I don't feel his strength. If you count just getting by as strength, then God is not who I thought he is.

Stefan folded the paper and put it back in his pocket, convinced that Chaplain Miller's words weren't applicable to him.

Stefan frowned as he thought of how his dear Sophie had believed in and relied on God. While enduring day upon day of pain, she'd said God was her strength, that God was helping her. How could she have held onto that? What did she know that Stefan didn't and why wasn't God interested in helping him? Didn't he love everyone the same? If not, Stefan didn't blame him.

I wouldn't love me as much either.

⚰✝⚰

Later that day, Stefan decided to head back to Lakewood Park and think about the things he'd discussed with Dr. Walker in the morning's session. Although he'd dreaded the appointment, Dr. Walker had brought up some good points.

On his way to the park, he took a closer look at the surrounding houses and yards. As a child, when Stefan's father drove the family anywhere at night, he'd examine the lighted rooms of the houses they passed and wonder about the lives of the people who lived there. Today, he did the same without the benefit of light.

I wonder if everyone who lives in these houses feels as hopeless as I do. Certainly not, because then, all the behavioral healthcare places would be full, and I don't think that's the case.

His mind went to the one question Dr. Walker had asked. They had been discussing what, specifically, had led to Stefan wanting to end his life. The doctor asked if Stefan thought his decision was out of selflessness or selfishness.

Unsure of the answer, Stefan had merely stared at the doctor.

Seeing the hour was just about up, Dr. Walker had suggested that Stefan give his question some thought, and they would discuss his answer tomorrow.

Now, as Stefan arrived at the park, he sat on a stone bench to think it through.

Selflessness or selfishness? He'd wanted to immediately answer it was out of selflessness. After all, everyone would be better off without him so he would be doing them a favor by exiting their world. Yes, of course he was acting out of selflessness!

Yet, there was a small, nagging part of him that wasn't so convinced.

Stefan sat there for a time, thinking about his life and the consequences his successful suicide would have brought.

The first thing that came quickly to mind were his sons and grandchildren. The breach between Mark, Robert, and himself must be as painful for them as it was to him. *Would my suicide have added significant emotional weight to each of them? What about my three grandchildren? Would they carry this grief the rest of their lives?* Stefan felt a jolt of anguish sweep through his body. He loved his boys and grandchildren. It saddened him to think of adding more pain to them. They'd already lost their mother and grandmother and his actions would have compounded their grief.

Next, Stefan thought of his law firm. His clients on retainer could find another attorney, of course. And his head had not been in the game lately anyway. But then he thought of Mrs. Warren. She'd been a committed and faithful secretary. She'd kept his firm running smoothly and had helped in multiple ways during Sophie's illness and her death. She'd been there through everything and had put up with all his mood swings, lack of focus, and grumpy attitudes. Stefan realized now just how much Mrs. Warren had supported and helped him, professionally and personally.

Stefan knew he'd need to change his initial answer to Dr. Walker's question. His action would have been based on selfishness.

After sitting a bit longer, Stefan stood and strolled along a nearby trail which took him through a wooded area.

Stefan heard the rustle of leaves as the soft breeze blew through the trees around him. He paused, closed his eyes, and enjoyed the peaceful moment for a bit—something he hadn't experienced in a long time. Was it possible for this peace to stay in his life on a more permanent basis?

Stefan continued on the trail until he came out in a spot unfamiliar to him. He looked around, trying to get his bearings. Chaplain Miller's Bottle House stood across the street, about halfway down the block.

I think I'll get closer to Chaplain Miller's house again and see if I can find any clues as to why he collects bottles.

His eyes on the Bottle House, Stefan stepped out onto the street and heard the squeal of tires. A car had just missed hitting him. His focus had been so intent on the chaplain's house, he'd forgotten to check for traffic.

The driver had pulled the car over and stopped.

Stefan rushed over to the car. "I'm so sorry," he said. "I wasn't paying attention. Are you okay?"

The woman driver placed shaking hands on her face and took a deep breath. "I thought I was going to hit you. I came so close. I appreciate your apology, but I could never forgive myself if I'd hit and killed you."

In that moment, Stefan recognized how peoples' lives were all intertwined. All his acting and reacting spilled over into others' pathways.

"I'm really sorry to have upset you. I should have looked where I was going." Stefan took a deep breath. "Are you okay to drive, or can I call someone for you?"

"No, I'll be okay. I'm not far from home, so I'll make my way slowly." She gripped the steering wheel. "I'm glad you didn't get hurt."

Stefan watched as the woman slowly pulled away—a woman who valued a stranger's life.

He returned to Bethany, realizing he'd seen an important truth.

Everything I do affects other people.

CHAPTER 21

As Stacy returned to the Lewises' house, she reflected on her first day at Bethany R&L. She was proud she had at least met everyone on her caseload. Cindy Carson had helped with finding things and filling her in on the nurses' specific duties at Bethany.

Her thoughts moved to Debbie Young. Stacy hadn't had much time to get to know her yet, but there was something in her eyes that Stacy recognized from the years she'd worked in behavioral healthcare. Suffering.

Debbie needs to know someone cares about her.

A weariness swept over Stacy as she opened the front door and swayed a little on her feet. She was glad there was no one nearby to see her. *I need to eat better. I think it's catching up with me.*

Ruth looked up from her supper preparations and smiled as Stacy entered the kitchen. "There's the working girl. Sit down while I get you a glass of iced tea. I want to hear all about your day."

Stacy gratefully slid onto a chair.

Ruth set down the tea in front of her, and concern washed over her face. "Stacy, you're whiter than a ghost. Are you okay?"

"Yes," Stacy said after taking a swallow of her drink. "I got a little too busy and didn't eat a proper lunch."

"Well, you don't need someone telling you what to do." Ruth sighed, then patted Stacy's shoulder affectionately.

"I'm glad, however, you understand that not eating isn't good for you or anyone else you're responsible for."

Stacy nodded her head in agreement.

"Now, how did your first day go?"

"At first it was a little confusing, not knowing my way around. Mrs. Turner immediately paired me up with Nurse Cindy Carson, whose place I'll be filling, at least until her maternity leave is up. She showed me the ropes, and I was also able to meet every patient on my caseload."

"Sounds like you had a busy day."

"Yes, and a good one."

Seeing Stacy's glass was now empty, Ruth picked up the pitcher, offering to pour her more tea.

"No, thank you." Stacy set her glass on the counter. "Now, what can I do to help with supper preparations?"

"I've got a chicken baking and potatoes already peeled and on the stove. I think it would be nice to have a salad made to go with the meal. That doesn't need to be prepared quite yet, so why don't you go to your room, change your clothes, and rest a bit?"

Stacy couldn't believe how much that suggestion appealed to her. In her room, she closed her door softly, slipped off her shoes, changed her clothes, and returned her uniform to the closet before padding into the bathroom to freshen up. When she finished, she took one of the white fluffy towels and dried her hands and face, catching her eyes in the mirror.

Stacy saw the ache of betrayal there. Here was a young woman whose husband didn't want her. On top of that, she saw a chubby face with a slightly crooked tooth she tried to hide and eyes that betrayed exhaustion. *Will the pain ever go away?*

Stacy left the bathroom and climbed onto the bed. *I'll just close my eyes a minute and try to recoup some energy.*

She fell fast asleep, but her dreams held rest at bay. She saw Jack and Aubree together in her old apartment.

Aubree was sitting in Stacy's place at the dinner table, laughing with her husband.

🍾✝🍾

Morning came too soon for Stacy. She glanced at the clock. She'd slept through dinner and into the morning.

There was time to linger in bed a bit longer. She tried to focus on her day ahead but thoughts of Jack and Aubree invaded.

Do they even think of me? Are they laughing and enjoying their new life? What do their families think of their choices? Stacy knew she probably wouldn't get answers to these questions.

Her thoughts returned to the Twenty-third Psalm. She picked up the Bible from the table beside her bed and flipped to the passage, focusing on the fifth verse.

"Thou preparest a table before me in the presence of mine enemies: thou anointest my head with oil; my cup runneth over."

I guess Jack and Aubree are now my enemies. Lord, does this mean that, in spite of their choices, you will bless me? I hope so, Lord. I'm going to cling to that. I can do little else.

She pulled back the covers and swung her legs over the edge. Standing, she reached for her uniform. As she did, a dizziness hit her, and she sat down hard on the bed.

I've really got to treat myself better. I need to eat better meals, get back into exercising on a regular basis, and get better sleep.

Despite missing dinner and sleeping many hours, she didn't feel hungry but still felt exhausted.

Instead of dwelling more on the things she couldn't change, she rose to take her shower and prepare for work. When she'd showered and dressed, she made her way to the kitchen where Ruth was preparing grapefruit halves.

"Good morning, Stacy. We missed you last night at supper, but I didn't wake you because I felt sleep was a priority for you."

"Good morning. Yes, it was, thank you." Stacy filled a mug with coffee.

Charles sat at the kitchen table, reading the paper as normal, and Stacy joined him. She felt bad about missing dinner, but she'd been so tired. She hoped a good breakfast would give her the strength she needed for the day's work.

As Ruth brought plates of scrambled eggs, bacon, and toast to the table, her stomach churned.

"Stacy, you don't look so good." Ruth set the plates down and gently touched Stacy's forehead. "I've been thinking about you, and after observing a few things, I've wondered ..." Ruth stepped closed and continued in a whisper. "Could you be pregnant?"

Ruth's words hit Stacy in the gut as if she had been in the ring with Muhammad Ali.

No, I couldn't be! I can't be!

CHAPTER 22

Debbie arrived at Dr. Murphy's office on time. She wiped her clammy hands across her tan slacks before knocking on his open office door. She filled with dread knowing that the easier questions he'd asked during her first session would give way to more difficult ones today.

"Come on in, Mrs. Young." Dr. Murphy stood, indicating for Debbie to sit down. He walked over, closed his door, and returned to his desk. "Tell me how you're doing as you're getting used to a new routine here at Bethany R&L?"

Looking down, Debbie noticed her right index and middle fingers beginning to twitch. "It has been all right, so far, but I miss Josh so much, it hurts." She swallowed a lump that had grown in her throat at the mention of her husband.

"I understand, and I'm sure he misses you just as much, so let's get to work so you two can be reunited soon." The doctor paused a moment. "You shared with me at our last session the circumstances that brought you here. How do you feel about these today?"

Debbie thought while staring at the bookshelf behind the doctor's desk. Hurt and betrayal surged into her body. "My supervisors at the Christian school had some ridiculous expectations, and it seemed to me that my Christian walk was often in question." The emotion in her words rose like the red liquid in a thermometer. "All they could see is what I was doing wrong in their eyes, just like my mother always does. Why couldn't they see all the good I did this year?"

"Tell me about this good you did." Dr. Murphy smiled.

Debbie spent about a quarter of an hour describing several of her accomplishments from her first year at Good Shepherd Christian School.

"These things are wonderful, Debbie. Your students are fortunate to have you."

"Why can't my supervisors see this too?"

Dr. Murphy nodded. "Besides the things you just mentioned, what else is it you specifically think these men don't see?"

Debbie looked up at the ceiling and frowned, shaking her head. "They don't seem to notice the great progress of my students. They said they do, but I doubt it. In fact, the principal spent very little time observing me with them, and the board members sure never came in. How can you make decisions about the emotional and spiritual flaws in someone when you haven't bothered to take the time to look?"

Dr. Murphy leaned forward and the look of concern Debbie saw in his eyes touched her. "I'm sorry this has happened to you."

She could tell this man clearly cared about her. Why? In spite of her doubts, Debbie could feel her body relax a little. But not for long.

"Do you think there is any truth in what your supervisors questioned?"

With her lower lip beginning to tremble, Debbie looked at the doctor. "That's the problem. I flip-flop between thinking their concerns are unreasonable and the fact that some of them are probably true."

"I'm guessing, Debbie, that both of these things can be true."

After finishing her appointment with Dr. Murphy, Debbie decided to take a walk before lunch. She set out on Cayce Road toward the beach. As she made her way down the road that ran parallel to Bethany R&L, she thought back over the words she and Dr. Murphy had exchanged this morning in his office. Was it possible she held some responsibility for all the conflict she endured this past school year?

Putting those thoughts aside, Debbie gazed around at the houses, wanting to see "her house" again.

A smile came to her lips as she saw the simple black shutters framing the windows of the two-story white home. A swing hung from one corner of the wraparound porch, the lawn and bushes were neatly trimmed, and flower beds were filled with a variety of colorful blooms.

Whoever lived there had spent a lot of time caring for the place. She'd like them. Debbie laughed. She was probably the only person who'd ever thought such a thing solely because of a home's outer appearance.

She continued down the road and soon could hear the crash of the waves as she neared Klauthmos Beach.

Debbie stepped onto the sand, then bent over and pulled off her sandals. She closed her eyes and filled her lungs with the salty air. *Josh would love it here.* A wave of loneliness passed over her. She missed him tremendously.

She heard seagulls' cries blending with the waves. Debbie opened her eyes and wished she'd brought a towel so she could sit down for a bit.

When she noticed a young couple with their little boy, her heart lurched. She couldn't wait until she and Josh became parents, even though they'd put off plans to do so for a few years. This thought made her long for Josh even more.

On her way back, her mind automatically went to the circumstances of what brought her here to Klauthmos Bay and resentment filled her. She knew she needed to give the situation to God, but she wasn't sure how to do so and even if she wanted to.

Soon, Debbie found herself standing in front of "her house" again. This time, a woman was bending over the flower bed, working the soil.

Before Debbie realized what she was doing, she moved closer. "Good morning!"

The person working on the bed sat up slowly and smiled. "Good morning to you."

The first thing she noticed about the older woman were her kind eyes. She looked to be in her seventies, though Debbie wasn't sure. Her gray hair stuck out a bit under the brimmed hat she wore, and she was dressed in cotton blouse and khaki slacks. A muslin apron was tied around her waist, with some seed packets peeking out from a pocket.

The woman must have liked what she saw, because she stood up, with some difficulty, and approached Debbie, smiling. "My name is Patricia Harmon." She pulled off a garden glove and held out a fragile hand.

"I'm Debbie Young."

"What a beautiful day God has given us," Patricia said. "Were you enjoying some beach time today?"

"Yes," Debbie said. Then she continued in a soft, unsure voice, "As much as I love the ocean, I also like seeing houses like yours. Your flowers are stunning. It must take a lot of time to maintain all of these beds."

"That it does. I've been working in the vegetable garden most of the morning, but I love my flowers."

"I can tell. These are absolutely beautiful."

The older woman planted her hands on her hips and leaned backward, stretching. "Thank you for noticing."

"Well, I don't want to interrupt your work, but I just had to stop and meet the person who created all this beauty."

"I can't take much credit for it. It's God's creation. I'm just thankful he allows me to be the caregiver."

"Nice to meet you." She turned to continue back to Bethany.

"Nice to meet you, too, Debbie. Any time you see me out, either working or relaxing on the porch, I would love to have you stop and chat."

As Debbie headed back to Bethany, she began to dream more about living in a house like Patricia's.

I'd love to have a porch with a swing like she has. And those gardens! Josh and I could sit on the swing in the evenings, overlooking the beautiful gardens, chatting. That would be heavenly.

Debbie was startled that she felt such a light spirit within—something she hadn't experienced in a long time.

Debbie decided to explore the buildings and grounds again, attempting to obtain a better feel of her temporary home's layout.

She studied the map posted next to the cafeteria's doorway. The main building housed offices and a large lounge. She was delighted to see there was also a chapel. Debbie loved to sit in an empty chapel or church, and her soul yearned for that very thing right now.

Studying the map closer, she made a mental note of the chapel's location and then headed in that direction.

It didn't take her long to locate the chapel. She came in the back entrance, then realized it was half-full of people.

She turned away, slightly disappointed, but then she heard Chaplain Miller's voice and decided to sit quietly in an empty pew in the back.

"I know when we lose someone through death, it hurts. It's easy for us to think we'll continue on in this life indefinitely without our loved ones, but if we are followers of Christ, we need to realize that God's timeline isn't ours."

Debbie frowned in concentration. *Sounds like a memorial service, but I've never heard words like this at one.* She leaned forward, hoping Chaplain Miller would clarify what he'd just said.

"The Apostle Peter reminds us in his second book, chapter three, verse eight, that 'with the Lord a day is like a thousand years, and a thousand years are like a day.' God is not time-bound. This is good news, whether we're grieving the loss of a loved one or if we're struggling with the difficulties of life. What seems like forever to us is just a blink in time compared to eternity.

"I must admit, however, that when I was a young Christian, this kind of talk was—in my mind—hurtful." Chaplain Miller paused. "It felt as if these words washed over my pain rather than acknowledged it."

Debbie nodded her head in agreement.

"If you only read this one verse in Second Peter, you'll miss a great comfort that is tied in with the other verses there." The chaplain paused and surveyed the room.

"The whole third chapter is explaining what will happen in the 'end times,' or the time when God finally says, 'Now's the time for me to right all the wrongs on this earth.' In the midst of these things, God reminds us he has a different timeline than we do, but he also tells us in verse nine he is not slow in keeping his promise. He will always keep his promises. This is something that we, in our distress, can count on."

Chaplain Miller closed his Bible. "God promises, 'I will never leave you, nor forsake you. I will strengthen you and help you. I will take away every tear from your eyes.' I could list the promises of God all afternoon. But I'll just say this today ... God loves us and because of this, he cares about what we care about. He sees our sorrows. Let us pray."

Debbie stood quietly and tiptoed out of the chapel, heading back to her room with a tiny bit of hope in her heart.

Does God, who is holding all the universe in his hands, really care about me and what happens to me? Could it be possible to let this burden of rejection go and chose to have faith in God keeping his promise of timing and faithfulness in helping me?

CHAPTER 23

Stacy had little time to consider Ruth's question from yesterday's breakfast. She'd shrugged off her host's question and gone about her day.

With Nurse Carson's help, Stacy made rounds with all her patients, which took her most of the afternoon because she didn't want to merely visit them and check off her observations, evaluations, and their medications. She wanted her patients to know she cared about them.

She had successfully, for the most part, pushed the fear of pregnancy from her mind during the workday, but now, she couldn't avoid thinking about what would be life-changing news.

With her shift finally ended, she had to deal with the possibility of her pregnancy.

Surely, I'm not pregnant! Not now ... not after all those months Jack and I prayed and tried. What will I do if ... I'd need to call Jack ...

Stacy made her way to the drugstore, her stomach in knots.

Her path to the store took her by Chaplain Miller's Bottle House. Stacy inspected each window she could see, and indeed, all of them held bottles. She paused at one window just above her eye level and counted more than twenty bottles in this window alone.

Each bottle was unique and varied in color. Some bottles were full, and others were only partially filled.

Stacy thought of the dark-red bottle she'd seen when she first met Chaplain Miller and then again later in his office.

This is such an unusual hobby. I'll have to ask Chaplain Miller about them.

She continued to the drugstore, bought the test, and headed home. When Stacy arrived back at the Lewises' house, she took her package right to her room and placed it in the bathroom.

She changed out of her uniform and gazed in the mirror over the sink, trying to summon the courage to take the test.

If she didn't take the test, she didn't have to deal with the possibly life-changing results. Leaving the box in the bag in her room, she headed to the kitchen to help Ruth with the supper preparations instead.

"Hello, Stacy. You've come home a little later today. I hope you didn't run into too many difficulties at work."

"No." Stacy grabbed the vegetables needed for a salad and began chopping. "I made a trip to the drugstore after work."

Ruth put down the knife she was using to cut up vegetables. "What did you find out?"

"Nothing yet. I'm too scared to take it," Stacy admitted.

"Waiting isn't going to change the results, one way or the other."

"I know, but I just thought it's going to be hard enough to eat a healthy meal as it is. Finding out I'm pregnant will completely take away my appetite."

"I understand. Stacy?"

She looked over at Ruth.

"Regardless of how the test turns out, you're not alone. You have the Lord to sustain you, and Chaplain Miller, Charles, and I will all be here to support you. Everything will be all right."

When supper was over and the dishes and kitchen cleaned, Stacy could no longer put off the pregnancy test.

She went to her room, closed the door, plodded to the bathroom, and removed the box from the store's bag.

Her hands shook while she opened the box and removed one of the two tests. After reading the simple instructions, she followed each step and then left the test on the edge of the sink. The enclosed pamphlet said it would only take a minute, so Stacy watched, holding her breath, and hoping for only one red line to show up instead of two.

Before long, two lines appeared. Stacy's felt as if her stomach dropped, and she sat down on the toilet seat. She placed her head in her hands and began to sob.

Oh, no! What am I going to do? I can't be pregnant. This isn't what was supposed to happen.

Stacy left the test on the sink and began to pace the bedroom, crying.

What am I going to do? What am I going to do? What am I going to do?

In the midst of her tears, she heard a knock at her door. When she called, "Come in," Ruth stepped into her room. When she saw Stacy's tears, she guided her out of the bathroom and had her sit down on the bed. Ruth put her arm around her, saying nothing. The older woman sat with Stacy, and they cried together.

The two women held on to each other until Stacy had shed all the tears she could at the moment. Ruth went into the bathroom and returned shortly with a damp cloth in hand.

"Here, take this cool washcloth and clean off your face at bit."

Stacy did as she was told and then grabbed a fistful of tissues and blew her nose. She turned to Ruth. "What am I going to do? I can't have a baby with a soon-to-be ex-husband and no place of my own!"

Ruth put her arm around Stacy's shoulders again. "First, you need to make an appointment with a doctor to confirm this test and your due date. After that, you can make some decisions."

Stacy began to cry softly again.

"I have a wonderful ob-gyn you can see." Ruth traced small circles on Stacy's back. "Her name is Dr. Melanie Davis. You can contact her tomorrow morning and make an appointment."

Stacy nodded. Ruth stood and moved to the door.

"Stacy, I know this is going to be difficult for you, but you can trust God that he can take a difficult situation and make it good." Ruth gave Stacy a reassuring smile. "Try to get some sleep."

What about this news is good?

In spite of this, Stacy knew deep within that a baby, after all these years of yearning, could be a good thing. *God, you'll have to work on this with me.*

Stacy climbed onto her bed but was doubtful she would get rest anytime soon.

She spent the next hour thinking and crying. How ironic was it that she and Jack had tried for so many months for a baby and it never happened, and now, when she didn't want a baby, she was going to have one?

Stacy stood and walked over to the small desk. She sat down and looked at her reflection in the oval mirror. The woman she saw seemed so fragile and small. When had she lost that fire and spunk she'd once had? How in the world would she navigate through her life she felt had turned upside down?

Stacy's eyes met those in the reflection. "I'm scared."

Just as soon as she said those words, a quiet voice from within said, "But you aren't alone. I am with you."

A wave of peace passed through her. She rose and changed into her nightgown. Returning to the bed she reached for her Bible. She opened again to the Twenty-third Psalm.

"'Surely goodness and mercy shall follow me all the

days of my life.'"

Stacy looked up from the page. *Thank you for the blessing of peace, Lord. I know that this will ebb and flow in the months ahead but I appreciate it now.*

Sitting back against the headboard and pillows, several concerns went through her mind. This time she brought them to God as a request for help and not in accusations.

I am pregnant without a husband, and I don't know what the next step should be beyond telling Jack the news.

Stacy's stomach felt like she was on the world's tallest roller coaster and in the midst of the first drop. Telling Jack was not going to be easy, and Stacy realized she would now have to be in regular contact with both her ex-husband and Aubree. *What a mess, Lord.*

Tears came again, and she continued to raise her inner voice to God.

You say here in verse six that goodness is going to follow me. I don't know why you chose this point in my life to give me a baby. All I can think of are the scary and difficult things that will come along with having it. I'm not even sure, Lord, that I can do this. I know you promise to be with me. Help me to trust this is indeed true.

Stacy closed her Bible, turned off the light, and scooted under the covers, wondering how she'd ever sleep.

CHAPTER 24

Stefan gripped his tray and looked around at the sea of people in the cafeteria. He longed to just be alone, but he recognized he needed to make better choices. Instead of sulking alone in his despair, he needed to interact with others.

Then he noticed Jerry and Frank sitting at a table nearby.

"Mind if I join you?" Stefan asked, secretly hoping they were having a private conversation.

"Of course you can." Jerry, who seemed to be the more talkative of the two, pushed out a chair for Stefan to sit. "Now that you've been here a few days, are you falling into a routine that works for you?"

Stefan chuckled. You couldn't just sit down in a behavioral healthcare center and ask someone how he was doing. It somehow didn't seem right.

"I think so," Stefan said, unfolding his napkin. "Because I have appointments to occupy my time, I'm waking up earlier than I did at home. I certainly like that someone else is doing the cooking. I'm not much of a cook."

The two men laughed.

"I'm a chef at a large restaurant in San Francisco," Frank said. "It's odd for me to have other people do the cooking." Frank passed the basket that held rolls to Jerry. "What do you do for a living, Stefan?"

"I'm a personal injury attorney."

"I'm a retired CPA," Jerry piped in. "My wife and I love to go camping with the grandchildren now. I don't miss tax time, that's for sure."

Stefan nodded. "My two sons, who are also CPAs, are often overwhelmed that time of the year."

"Then you have a good idea of what I'm talking about."

The men continued to eat and make small talk. Before long, Stefan looked at the clock and realized the time had flown by. Maybe being with other people wasn't that bad after all. But if he wanted to freshen up a bit before he met with Chaplain Miller, he'd better go. He bid the men goodbye, took care of his dishes, and went to his room.

Stefan took off his shirt that bore the odor of sweat from his stroll earlier and took a fresh one off a hanger. He glanced at his reflection in the bathroom mirror while dressing and realized he was wearing a shirt Sophie had given him one Father's Day. His heart ached at the memory.

After combing his hair, he grabbed a somewhat crumpled list of God's promises that Chaplain Miller had given him and set out for his office.

A few minutes later, Stefan knocked lightly on the chaplain's open door.

Chaplain Miller rose, smiling. "Welcome, Stefan. It's good to see you. Coffee?"

"No, thanks. I'm pretty full from lunch." Stefan scanned the office, and his eyes stopped on the sky-blue bottle sitting among others on the far end of Chaplain Miller's desk. His eyes moved from the object back to the chaplain's.

"I see you have the same sky-blue bottle with my name on it I saw the other day. What's it for?"

Chaplain Miller sat for a moment and then smiled. "This bottle and the others I have collected through the years are symbols of hope for those who are hurting."

Stefan couldn't figure how little bottles could be a symbol for such a big promise.

"How are you, Stefan?" the chaplain said, changing the subject. "Do you feel a little more comfortable here at Bethany than you did when you first arrived?"

Stefan drew his eyes away from the bottle and focused on Chaplain Miller, opening his mouth to respond with a quick answer. No, better not say what first came to mind.

"Go ahead, tell me what you think." Chaplain Miller leaned forward across his desk and grinned. "Honesty is a very important part of healing."

"I was going to say I haven't felt comfortable in my skin anywhere in a long while." Stefan sighed.

"What do you think is the reason for this discomfort?"

Stefan stared down at the floor. "I guess it's because I'm such a failure, and that follows me like a shadow everywhere I go."

"That's a difficult way to live, my friend."

Stefan nodded in agreement.

"It's interesting you speak of a shadow following you. We know, of course, that shadows are made by light." Chaplain Miller stood up and moved over to one of his desk lamps. He removed the shade, then picked up the lamp by its base and moved around his desk to stand by Stefan.

"If I held this lamp above you with a big and powerful light pointing down, where would your shadow fall?"

"It would be below me," Stefan answered.

"That's right. If I moved the light to this side of you, your shadow would appear where?"

"On the other side of me."

Chaplain Miller righted the lamp, placed it on his desk, and returned the lampshade.

"God is the filler of the dark shadows you are referring to. He shines his light of love on you, and his light isn't just from one direction. Psalm 33:22 says, 'May your unfailing love be with us, Lord, even as we put our hope in you.' God's light leaves no shadows."

Stefan surveyed the lamp again.

"Have you considered the list of promises of God I gave you?" Chaplain Miller asked.

"I did a little." Stefan squirmed, worried the chaplain would think poorly of him.

"What are your thoughts, so far?"

Stefan took out the crumpled note and flattened it out on his leg. If Chaplain Miller noticed the paper's condition, he didn't say anything about it. "The Bible verse is Isaiah 40:29. It says, 'He gives strength to the weary and increases the power of the weak.'"

"What are your thoughts on this promise?"

"You want honesty, so I'm going to give it to you." Stefan tried to sound firm, confident. "What God truly gives me is just barely enough to get by. If I were to do things in a 'just getting by' manner in my practice, I wouldn't have many clients."

Chaplain Miller took a sip of his coffee and then nodded. "Do you want to tell me what specific experiences you've had that make you feel this way?"

Stefan didn't hesitate. "I had to sit by and watch the kindest and most loving person on this earth, my dear wife, Sophie, die of cancer." Stefan swallowed as tears gathered in his eyes.

"There were days during her illness and after her death that I could barely put one foot in front of the other. Some strength God gave! On top of that, Sophie always took her troubles to the Lord, while I watched her suffer and die. What kind of strength did God give her?"

"Strength comes in different forms, Stefan," Chaplain Miller said gently. "As you know, there is physical strength. Having the power to put one foot in front of the other sometimes requires more strength than a football player needs on the field." Chaplain Miller paused a moment to let his words sink in before he continued.

"There is mental strength. This is having the ability to think and reason within difficult situations. There is emotional strength. This is needed to keep someone balanced in his feelings, so they don't destroy the person or someone else. There is also spiritual strength. I call this faith. Faith that you can take God at his word. It sounds to me that God gave all of these to your dear Sophie."

Stefan nodded. "Okay, even if that's true, he certainly didn't give *me* mental, emotional, and spiritual strength. I was so weak, emotionally, I tried to take my own life, and I just don't think I have faith anymore."

"Oh, but, Stefan, God has given you emotional and spiritual strength. He saved you from the ocean waters and placed you here at Bethany so you can experience some healing. He *has* seen your pain."

Stefan frowned. Was being here at Bethany a part of God's provision of the strength he so desperately needed?

CHAPTER 25

Dr. Murphy met Debbie at the door to his office. "Good morning. Come on in and sit down."

Debbie's gaze dropped to the floor as she sat, her stomach churning. "Good morning."

Dr. Murphy sat back in his chair, his voice calm and soothing. "Tell me how you're doing right now." The doctor picked up a pen as if to make some notes.

"I'm okay." Debbie frowned.

"Just okay?"

"That's about the size of it." She felt immediately sorry to be so flippant.

"Would you like to tell me why you're agitated right now?"

Giving in to the rising turmoil, Debbie crossed her arms. "I vacillate between being very angry and feeling like I'm going to cry."

Instead of responding directly to her statement, Dr. Murphy's face softened. "What could comfort you right now?"

"All I want right now is for my husband, Josh, to take me in his arms and let me cry." Debbie brushed at the tears that had already escaped from her eyes.

"What do you think you're so angry about?"

Debbie suddenly gripped the arms on the chair and glared at the doctor. "I am so angry because all my life,

I've never been good enough. My mother never thought so and neither does my employer. He certainly didn't handle the situation at school using God's word." She could almost feel her words burning her lips on the way out.

"Which Scriptures are you referring to?"

Debbie was ready for this one. She had already spent a lot of time thinking about what the Bible had to say about a situation like this.

"Jesus said in Matthew 18, I believe, that if you have a problem with another believer, you should go to him or her first and see if that rights the situation. No one did this with me." Debbie's voice choked on her tears.

"Do you feel that their actions solidified what you already knew—that you're not a good person?"

Nodding, Debbie covered her face with her hands and cried. Dr. Murphy leaned across his desk and pushed the box of tissues closer to her. In a minute or so, Debbie looked up and reached her trembling hand for one. She dabbed at her eyes as silence engulfed the room for what seemed a long time.

After blowing her nose, Debbie looked at her therapist. "My husband, Josh, has been the only one who gets me. He is my best friend and biggest encourager. When the school board decided for me that I desperately needed help, Josh suggested we both leave there and find teaching positions elsewhere. If it hadn't been for his support, I think I would have fallen completely apart."

"If this falling apart happens, what do you envision will be the result?"

Debbie cleared her throat and whispered, "I'm afraid I will fall down alone in a black hole as permanent as a grave, my anguish engulfing me, smothering the very life out of me."

Dr. Murphy put down his pen and looked her in the eye. "Debbie, you are not alone."

She listened more to Dr. Murphy then, and her tears began to subside. She felt the people here at Bethany cared.

The nursing staff, doctors, and Chaplain Miller regularly checked in with her, making her life and pain a priority. They certainly didn't think she was worthless. Then a thought occurred to her. Debbie saw other patients here at Bethany in her mind and realized her focus was beginning to expand, allowing her to notice that others here at Bethany were suffering too. Could it be she wasn't alone?

Exiting Dr. Murphy's office and the building, Debbie looked at the calendar on her phone. There was a reminder her meeting with Chaplain Miller had been switched to tomorrow, so she had time to ponder his challenge to list her strengths and their corresponding vulnerabilities.

She loved the ocean, and the best place for her to think was the beach. She stopped in her room to get a towel, hat, and a pad of paper. She tossed everything into her tote bag and headed out.

Taking her time strolling down Cayce Road, Debbie could smell the salt in the air. She took a deep breath, closing her eyes for a moment, her spirit calming.

"Hello, there!"

She turned toward the voice and smiled when she saw Patricia Harmon waving.

"On your way to the beach? It seems like you're prepared for a pleasant visit."

Debbie smiled. "Yes. The last time I went down, I forgot to bring a towel to sit on. I remembered this time."

"I hope you have a pleasant morning. If you have time on your way back, stop by, and we'll have some lemonade."

"Thank you. I might take you up on that."

As she continued on her way, Debbie thought about Patricia. What sort of woman was she? She had such a beautiful place and disposition. Debbie wished her own personality was more like Patricia's. She didn't seem to be so controlled by what others thought of her.

Once on the beach, Debbie slipped off her sandals and put on her hat. Then she spread her towel out on the sand, sat, and stretched her legs.

She spent a few minutes staring out at the ocean and breathing in the salty air. *I want to enjoy being here, experiencing a view I wouldn't have had otherwise.*

Then she remembered how Willard Hughes had once told her she'd been living a selfish life. Was it selfish to take time for yourself? Was it selfish to need rest?

Debbie needed to redirect her thoughts to the assignment Chaplain Miller had given her.

At the top of the pad, she wrote, *My Strengths.*

Listing her weaknesses would be so much easier. *Willard Hughes and the school board would probably help with that list.*

For her strengths, she wrote down the ones she'd managed to come up with during her session with Chaplain Miller.

Compassionate, hardworking, and loyal.

She gazed at the ocean, trying to think of others.

Teaching and organizing.

Two more added to the list.

After another moment, she tossed the pad aside and sighed. What was wrong with her? Could she only come up with five strengths?

To complete the assignment, she still had to write down the potential vulnerabilities of those five.

She spent the next half hour searching for ideas. She wanted to learn from this experience and although the work was hard, she felt it necessary for her growth.

Debbie looked at her watch, thinking she'd been in the sun long enough. She didn't want to be burnt to a crisp. She gathered her things and hiked back to the road.

As she approached Patricia's house, she smiled. The older woman was waving to her from the porch swing, and Debbie made her way up the path, feeling the soft petals of a Douglas iris brushing against her leg. The colors bursting forth from the variety of flowers made her feel as if she walked through paradise.

"Place your things on that chair, dear. Help yourself to the lemonade and have a seat," Patricia said.

Debbie did as she was told and drank deeply from the offered glass. *This is so good!*

"Feel free to fill your glass again when you finish. I've got plenty."

After Debbie had refilled her glass, she sat back and relaxed. "When I met you yesterday, I mentioned how lovely your flowers were, but I've been kicking myself that I didn't tell you how much I love your home too. It's so nice, nestled among the trees and gardens, with the sound of the ocean in the distance. You must love living here."

"Oh, I do, dear. My husband, Henry, and I had this home built after we'd been married a few years. When we were first wed, we rented a small home that had no main rooms bigger than ten by ten. It was tiny! I promised myself that when we had a chance to own a home, there would be no rooms smaller than that, and this is what we built. We had a son named Wesley a few years later."

"How long have you lived here?"

"Hmm ... let me think," Patricia said. "We'd lived here eight years when Wesley was born. He's thirty now, so it's been thirty-eight years."

"What does your husband do?"

"Did. My husband died of a heart attack five years ago. Before that, ironically, he was a heart surgeon. One of the best in his field."

"Oh, I'm sorry for your loss."

She sipped on her lemonade and felt an ache for this woman she barely knew. *I'm not the only one on this earth who has suffered. I need to remember that.*

Patricia took a generous gulp of her drink. "Enough about me, tell me about yourself."

Debbie felt the stab of pain that had become so familiar to her. She dreaded telling Patricia, or anyone else, the reason she was in Klauthmos Bay. What would the older woman's reaction be? Debbie took a deep breath, seeking the right words.

"Tell me as little or as much as you want. No pressure," Patricia said softly.

The tenderness she heard in Patricia's voice touched Debbie. "I'm a third-grade teacher, and I'm married to a man named Josh, who is also a teacher at the same Christian school."

"Wonderful!" Patricia said. "How long have you been married?"

"Just over two years."

"Oh, newlyweds! I loved those first months Henry and I had together, and yet, I wouldn't want to relive the struggles of a new marriage everyone faces. Except it would mean I'd have him back with me."

"What kind of struggles?" Debbie asked.

"Oh, I was so insecure, and his parents never liked me. I often thought I was an emotional burden to Henry."

"Why didn't they like you?" How could anyone not love this friendly, kind woman?

"They felt Henry was marrying beneath himself because I was an orderly at the hospital where Henry was an intern. But we met and fell in love quickly. I'll never forget the first time he took me home to meet his parents." Patricia absentmindedly twirled the wedding band she still wore. "I was trying to be helpful, so when I offered, his mother asked me to set the table. She came in when I'd finished, observed what I'd done, and said, while moving utensils, 'I would think any mother would teach her daughter how to set a table properly. You've got the spoons on the wrong side of the plates.'" Patricia laughed.

Debbie's mouth fell open and she placed her hand on her heart. "I think I would have crawled under the rug and died. How did you ever feel good in her presence again?"

Patricia shrugged. "That is one of the main reasons why I wouldn't want to relive those years. If I'd known then what I know now about human nature, I would have handled that situation and many to come in a different manner."

"What do you mean?" Debbie asked.

"I now know that much of what people say and do to us is more a reflection of how they feel about themselves rather than a reflection of flaws within us."

Studying her glass, Debbie felt more tears gathering in her eyes. *Can this be true?*

After a moment of quiet reflection by both the ladies, Debbie rose. "Thank you for the lemonade and for a lovely time of chatting."

"Wait a moment!" Patricia ran into the house and came out with her pruning shears. "I want to give you some of my flowers."

Debbie watched as the older woman gathered a bouquet of beautiful blooms.

Handing them to Debbie, she said, "Please feel free to stop by any time. I'd love to have you."

Making her way back to the road, Patricia's words floated through the air. "God sees your pain and he cares."

CHAPTER 26

"Good morning, dear. Were you able to get any rest?" Ruth asked Stacy as she sat down at the breakfast table.

"A little," Stacy said as she placed some pancakes on her plate. "I'm still feeling dizzy off and on."

"Well, that's probably normal."

Stacy looked at Charles. Did he know about the baby? She didn't want to discuss it right now. She looked at Ruth who gave her a slight shake of her head and then smiled.

Charles folded the paper he'd been reading and turned to her. "Have you heard from your family since you've been here in Klauthmos Bay, Stacy?"

"No, my parents live in their own world of work and friends. I don't hear from them very often."

Ruth poured a cup of coffee for Stacy and handed it to her, then refilled her own cup. "Do they know you're here?"

"No, they still think I'm living in my apartment with Jack, working at Eden. I guess I should call them and let them know I've moved and why." Stacy pushed the food around on her plate, the aroma making her feel queasy.

"Are you feeling okay?" Charles asked, his voice expressing concern.

Ruth patted Stacy's hand and picked up her plate. "Now, Charles, she has a lot on her mind. Don't worry about the dishes, Stacy. You probably need to get to work."

Stacy thanked her and went back to her room to brush her teeth and grab her purse. Fifteen minutes later, as she made her way to the front door, Ruth met her in the foyer and handed her a small piece of paper.

"I haven't said anything to Charles about your news. Here is Dr. Davis's phone number in case you want to make an appointment. My thoughts and prayers are with you."

Stacy was grateful for the woman's discretion. She didn't want too many people to know just yet.

When she arrived at work, she made an appointment with Dr. Davis for late that afternoon. Stacy's hands shook as she looked at the paper Ruth had given her where she'd written her appointment time. She knew that with this confirmation, her whole life would change.

The morning flew by, and trying to make up some of the hours she'd miss that afternoon, Stacy grabbed a sandwich and some juice for a quick lunch in the courtyard.

She tried not to think about the baby and what she would do. She needed to keep her mind on her work. Even so, her eyes filled with anxious tears. She brushed them away as she saw Chaplain Miller approaching her.

He sat on the chair next to Stacy's and smiled at her. "Hello, Stacy! It's good to see you. We haven't had much contact since you officially started working here."

Although this was a chance meeting, Stacy felt as if he knew her heart. "I know. I've been staying busy. I like it here and living with the Lewises has been a blessing."

"I'm glad to hear it. You have an important role to play with the people who are in treatment here. You nurses interact with the patients more than the doctors or I do. There is one drawback, though."

"Oh?"

"Yes, it comes down to *who ministers to the ministers*? You're expected to work diligently, often, and without thanks. The job can deplete your supply of compassion and energy, so you need to be sure to refuel regularly."

"I never thought about that," Stacy said, reflecting briefly on his words.

Chaplain Miller stood. "Any time you need some refueling, I'm here to help. Just so you know, I conduct a Sunday morning service in the chapel at nine. You're more than welcome to come."

As he walked away, he turned back over his shoulder and said, "I care and so does God."

About an hour before her doctor appointment, Stacy had seen most of the patients on her caseload, but she still needed to touch base with Debbie Young. She decided to head to Debbie's room and see if she was there.

Stacy went to the Iaomai building and knocked on Debbie's door.

Debbie opened it and smiled. "Come in, Nurse Meadows. I'm just trying to relax a little."

"Please call me Stacy." She walked over to the small desk, wanting to take a whiff of the beautiful flowers there. "Where did you get these? They are stunning!"

"I was visiting a new friend on Cayce Road, and she gave these to me. I hope it's okay I borrowed a vase from the kitchen. I love flowers!" Debbie sat on the bed, and Stacy sat at the desk gazing at the flowers.

"I do, too! And yes, I'm sure it's fine." Stacy turned again and breathed in deeply the smell of the colorful blooms. "Heavenly!"

She turned her attention back to her patient. "How are you doing, Debbie?"

"My anxiety level is very high right now, so I'm trying to work on the breathing exercises Dr. Murphy taught me this morning."

"That will be very helpful." Stacy made a mental note to utilize her own when in need. "Did you discover anything about yourself during your session?"

Debbie nodded. "I guess I never realized I was so angry."

"Anger can feel like a firecracker going off, but it also creeps in gradually. I hope you'll continue to analyze this in your mind so when you meet with him again tomorrow morning, you can pick up where you left off."

Stacy consulted her tablet. "I see in today's appointment log that you're meeting with Chaplain Miller in ..." Stacy checked the time. "Another hour and a half?"

"Yes, I am."

"How do you like him?" If Stacy were honest, she'd admit she wasn't just asking this question for professional reasons. She wanted to know for herself.

Debbie rubbed her hands on her thighs for a moment, giving the appearance that she was mulling over Stacy's question. "I think there is something very different about Chaplain Miller—in a good way, not a bad one. He seems to have a discernment I think is missing in many people doing God's work."

Stacy nodded, thinking Debbie's observation accurate. "Discernment is a good thing. Someone with that gift offers good insight to a situation without passing judgment."

Yes, I think that describes Chaplain Miller well, though I wonder what insight he would offer me.

CHAPTER 27

Stefan sat with Jerry and Frank for supper and went through the motions of eating and conversation but didn't really feel hungry. Afterward, he decided to head to the beach.

As Stefan ambled in that direction, he thought about his meeting with Chaplain Miller. Stefan liked the man, and yet, he wished he didn't. His heart reminded him that if he couldn't trust God with his life, then he shouldn't trust someone working for God either.

Once he reached the sand, he removed his shoes and hiked down to the waterline. He missed sitting in his house, in his comfortable chair, watching the ocean. Memories of doing that very thing with Sophie brought heartache. They'd spent many evenings after supper enjoying their own waterfront.

He kicked at the wet sand with his foot and watched as the small hole he made quickly filled in with the surrounding wet sand. Stefan thought of how quickly any marks he made in life seemed to just fill in, not making any difference.

Stefan turned and sat on the dry sand just above the tide line. He pulled out the crumpled paper and scanned the promises of God that Chaplain Miller had given him. His eyes landed on Isaiah 43:2. "When you pass through the waters, I will be with you; and when you pass through the rivers, they will not sweep over you. When you walk through the fire, you will not be burned; the flames will not set you ablaze."

Stefan stared out at the ocean, stunned. In that moment, he felt like God had written that verse just for him. He read the words again. God didn't say he would rescue someone in those waters and that fire. Instead, God said he would be *with* that person and not allow them to be swept away or burned. He didn't say he would stop those things.

This felt like too much for Stefan to process on his own and he wished Sophie was sitting there next to him. She'd tell him what she thought of these verses. She'd give her usual brilliant insight.

If God was all powerful, why didn't he stop horrible things from happening?

Stefan lifted his eyes to the heavens. "Are these promises just your cruel way of manipulating people into following you? You're saying you'll do this or not allow that, but what's the price? There's always a price, God—a catch. What is it?"

In spite of his angry accusations, Stefan continued to hear, "I will be with you."

After returning from the beach, Stefan did not feel like going to bed yet, so he made his way to the men's lounge to maybe find a book.

He found Frank sitting at a card table in the lounge. "Hey, Frank. What are you up to?"

Frank glanced up. "I'm just having some juice and working on this puzzle. You want to join me?"

"Sure." Stefan hadn't done a puzzle in years, but maybe it'd take his mind off deeper matters. He went into the kitchen, poured some juice into a glass, and brought a folding chair over to the table where Frank was working.

"What kind of picture are we putting together?" Stefan asked, looking over the pieces.

"Here, check it out." Frank passed him the lid to the puzzle box.

Stefan studied the picture and smiled at the mountain scenery. "I guess when you don't live near the beach, your puzzles have beach scenes, and when you do, you want to see the mountains."

Frank smiled. "Never thought about it that way." He picked up the last piece he needed to complete the straight edges of the picture. "I just started it tonight. It's fifteen hundred pieces. I'm going to regret this because once I begin a puzzle, I have to finish it, no matter how many days or weeks it takes. I'm glad I can just leave it out here in the lounge."

Stefan took a piece of the sky and fit it in place.

"There's another good thing about leaving it here," Frank said as searched through unused pieces. "Other people coming by throughout the day stop and add a piece or two. It kind of becomes a group project."

Stefan continued to sort the sky-blue pieces. "I saw there was a schedule on the refrigerator for a checkers tournament. When is that?"

"There will be one tomorrow night here in the lounge. Do you play checkers?"

"My sons and I used to play the game regularly when they were growing up."

"You should sign up then."

"I might just do that." Stefan wondered if the memory of a happier time would not hurt so much.

The two men worked on the puzzle in silence for a bit, and then Frank surprised Stefan when he said, "After my daughter Linda was murdered, I tried to keep my sanity by doing puzzles. Sometimes I'd stay up all night fitting pieces together. I guess it was my way of coping with a situation that didn't fit together in my mind."

Stefan cleared his throat to clear the lump that had just filled it. "I'm sorry about your daughter."

"Thank you. I am too." Frank's voice wavered with emotion. He frowned at the puzzle, then continued working on the sky. "I just couldn't fit together in my mind how a mother could murder her own daughter," Frank said in a strained tone. "I just can't."

Stefan sagged in his chair, dropping the puzzle piece he was holding and feeling like the wind had been knocked out of him.

My God! How is Frank dealing with this? If God meant it when he said he would be with his children through the waters, rivers, and fire, this man surely needs this kind of help right now!

Shaking off the thought, he set the piece down and said, "I think I'm too tired to keep going. I'll see you tomorrow."

Frank nodded without looking up and Stefan returned to his room. Still shaken by his new friend's revelation, he sat down hard on the bed and stared at the seascape picture on the wall, trying to wrap his mind around such horror.

How in the world did Frank survive such a devastating thing? Sophie and I didn't have daughters, but if my wife murdered her own child, especially a little girl whom I would protect to the ends of the earth, I don't know how I could bear it.

After sitting for a few minutes, Stefan's mind returned to the Bible verse he'd read at the beach.

Frank sure had to pass through waters churned by hurricane-strength winds and rivers swollen with sudden rainfall. He had to have been scorched by fire. It's no surprise he came to Bethany R&L. I wonder what he thought of God's choice not to intervene and save his daughter from his wife.

For the first time while at Bethany, Stefan wept for someone else.

CHAPTER 28

The next morning, Debbie sat down at the desk and started flipping through the pages of the book she'd picked up in the lounge the night before. She skimmed sections, trying to determine if she really was interested in reading it.

Deciding she couldn't focus on words right now, she closed the book and lay down on the bed. Her thoughts went immediately to her visit with Patricia.

Debbie closed her eyes and pictured sitting on Patricia's porch. In her mind, she could see the flowerbeds in the front of the house. Debbie smiled as she realized she had not felt awkward while visiting with Patricia. She was a woman who did not judge her, nor found her flawed.

It felt good to think about something positive and fun instead of missing Josh or dwelling on the circumstances that had brought her here.

Wanting to share her feelings, Debbie picked up her cell phone and called Josh.

He picked up right away. "Hey, babe, it's good to hear from you."

"Hey, honey. I just wanted to hear your voice. I miss you so much."

"I miss you too. How are things going?"

"Well, I've had another session with Dr. Murphy. During the hour, he helped me see a part of me that I haven't seen throughout this whole situation."

"Oh?"

"He asked me about the painful circumstances that brought me here and evidently I've been harboring a lot of anger because it barged its way into my answer."

"I certainly understand why you would be angry, not only because of events in your childhood but also over that meeting at our school. I'm fighting the same demon in these circumstances."

"What do you mean?"

"When I wake up each morning and you're not there, something inside my heart hardens."

They both were silent for a moment.

"Even though it's understandable that I'm angry, I realize that it's not doing me any good letting it remain in my heart."

"You are right, Debbie, for both of us." Another silence ensued until Josh finally asked, "Has anything else of interest happened?"

"You know how I've told you the last few times we've talked that I stroll down to the beach? Remember the beautiful house I described?"

"The one with the wraparound porch?"

"Yes, that's the one. Well, I met the woman who lives there. Her name is Patricia Harmon, and I had a nice long chat with her this morning."

"That's great, babe. I know you've been lonely, so I'm glad to hear this."

They chatted for a while longer, and after the call ended, Debbie felt the usual mix of emotions—joy in connecting with Josh and hearing his voice and yearning to be home with him again.

Debbie picked up her "homework assignment" the chaplain had given her the last time they met and headed to his office.

Just outside Chaplain Miller's office door, Debbie took a deep breath. She liked the chaplain, but because of her negative interactions in her immediate past with people that represented religious authority, she felt nervous.

Debbie shyly poked her head into the office and said, "Hello."

Chaplain Miller stood from behind his desk. "Good afternoon, Debbie. It's nice to see you. Have a seat and make yourself comfortable."

"Thank you." Debbie sat in the same chair in front of Chaplain Miller's desk that she had last time she was here. He closed the folder in front of him, signaling that he was giving her his full attention.

"I assume you've been in touch with Josh. How's he doing?"

Debbie grinned. "Yes, I just spoke with him before I came over here. He's doing well. He's busy getting ready to teach Vacation Bible School at our church next week."

"Do you normally help with VBS?"

"Yes, I do. VBS was something I looked forward to every summer while I was growing up and almost as much as an adult. I'm going to miss helping this year."

"I bet, being an elementary teacher, you contribute in a vital way to the program. You definitely will be missed."

Feeling uncomfortable with the compliment, Debbie changed the subject. "Oh, I met someone in the neighborhood on my way to the beach the other day. Her name is Patricia Harmon. She's very nice."

Chaplain Miller smiled. "Patricia is a friend of mine. She's a gracious and gifted lady. I'm glad you two became acquainted." He opened a small notebook and picked up a pen. "Speaking of gifted, did you get a chance to make your list of strengths and their corresponding vulnerabilities?"

Debbie reached in her pocket and pulled out her assignment. "Yes."

"Let's hear your list of strengths."

"Well, I only came up with five," she said softly.

"That's fine."

"I have the three I told you about the first time we met. I think I'm compassionate, hardworking, and loyal." Debbie watched as Chaplain Miller wrote those down.

"And the other two?" Chaplain Miller paused, his pen ready to record her answer.

Glancing at the list in her hand, she took a deep breath. "I also have down that I'm a gifted teacher and organizer."

Chaplain Miller wrote those traits down, then laid his pen on the desk and smiled.

"These are wonderful strengths, Debbie. I can see how many of them would help you tremendously in the classroom. Now, let's discuss the potential vulnerabilities of these five things. Let's start today with compassion. Describe to me how you think being compassionate is a strength."

Debbie thought for a moment. "If I'm compassionate, it means I'm concerned about the difficulties another person is experiencing."

"Good. Compassion is a first cousin of empathy. Now tell me how being concerned with another's difficulties is a strength."

"It means I'm not talking down to them but sitting beside them in their difficulties, so to speak. I'm also not comparing their situations with mine and determining the extent of their struggles."

"Excellent thinking. You know, it's interesting that compassion comes from the Latin word, *compati*, which means, 'to suffer with.' Now, how can being compassionate be a vulnerability?"

Debbie didn't need to consult her list because she'd thought through this one completely. "If someone knows I'm compassionate, they may try and manipulate me by using a hard-luck story."

"Yes, that can happen. There have been many well-meaning pastors and churches that have someone show up on their doorsteps, claiming they need help.

Unfortunately, a lot of times, that person just wants an easy handout rather than help finding a job or something of that nature." The chaplain nodded as he continued his thought. "It's sometimes difficult to determine if this is the case with a stranger. How about the vulnerabilities you have *because* you have compassion?"

Debbie moved some hair out of her eyes. "If I'm compassionate, I may wind up taking on too much of the emotional weight the other person carries. Doing that may weigh *me* down emotionally."

"What do you mean by that?"

"I may not be able to carry all the unhappiness I sense others have. It could also be very depressing."

Chaplain Miller clapped his hands. "You got it. When a person is compassionate, he or she can give a valuable gift to those who are suffering." He paused and clicked his pen a few times. "It can feel comforting knowing that someone else cares about what they do. The problem is, compassionate people sometimes allow too much of other people's difficulties and suffering into their heart, and it becomes a heavy burden, just like you said. When I was just starting out in my chaplain ministry, I made this mistake."

"What happened?"

"In my inexperienced Christian heart and mind, I desired to help others, so I took on all the hurts and difficulties of the people I was sent to serve. This plan of action worked at first, but in time, I found that I'd filled my heart so much with these things I didn't have room to serve them. The emotional burden I'd taken on weighed me down."

"Isn't giving of ourselves and being a servant to others what God wants us to do?" Debbie asked.

Chaplain Miller narrowed his eyes in concentration. "Yes, there are dozens of verses in the Bible about being a servant to others. We are, indeed, called to be servants of Christ, and that means, in part, that we minister to others. But when we take on so much we can't function, we're hindered from being fully used by Christ, and our compassion becomes a vulnerability.

"It's ironic," he continued. "Satan can use the strength God has given you in this manner, and in doing so, take away the blessing you get from giving to other people."

"I never thought of it that way." Debbie tilted her head, thinking.

Chaplain Miller took a moment to write some things in his notebook, so Debbie let her gaze flit around the office. Several small bottles sat on the table beside Chaplain Miller's desk. The light green bottle did, indeed, have her name on it.

"I'd like you to take the other four things mentioned on your list and continue exploring each one's strength and vulnerabilities," Chaplain Miller said, drawing Debbie's attention back to him. "We'll discuss another one next time we meet."

Debbie smiled and stood. "Thank you for giving me your time. You're making me think in a way I never have before."

"You're welcome."

Debbie made for the door but turned. "Chaplain Miller, you told me that you collect bottles as a symbol that God is interested in all our lives. Why bottles?"

The chaplain smiled while standing. "Well, bottles are the object God came up with and they are also handy when you want to collect something. By the way, we have a service tomorrow in the chapel at nine."

"I'll be there."

CHAPTER 29

Stacy opened her eyes and contemplated the sun shining through her window. Too bad it wasn't cloudy. The sky would have matched how she felt.

She hadn't slept well. Who would after having your pregnancy confirmed when you're in the process of getting divorced from your baby's father? Stacy had been so heartbroken and distracted with moving and readjusting to this new norm she hadn't realized she'd missed her last two periods. She'd also thought her queasiness had been due to all the emotional trauma she'd been through.

Stacy's mind went back to last night. She'd entered the Lewises' house, dry-eyed. When she appeared in the dining room, she must have looked horrible. Charles and Ruth both jumped up quickly to help Stacy to her seat. Ruth had brought her a glass of ice water, and they sat down, one on each side of her.

"It's confirmed. I'm ten weeks pregnant." Stacy had revealed the news unemotionally.

After a few minutes of silence, Ruth stood. "What you need right now is to get some nourishment. Charles, if you can help me with the food, I'll put supper on the table, and then the three of us will put our heads together and figure out a plan."

Stacy rolled onto her side in bed and drew her knees up to her chest as she used to when things bothered her as a child. She was grateful for the Lewises' understanding as they'd patiently listened to her irrational stream of emotions.

Stacy remembered the fear in her words. "I can't have a baby now. What am I going to do? Where will I live, and how can I do this on my own?"

Then, her apprehension had morphed into anger. "Why now? After all the months Jack and I tried for a baby, and now this happens? I didn't ever want to be in contact with Jack or Aubree again, and now I get this news. Maybe he doesn't even have a right to know."

She'd fought back the lump in her throat then. "If only Jack had still loved me, we would be together right now, so happy about this news." Stacy had dissolved into tears as the Lewises tried to comfort her.

Stacy stared now at the bedroom ceiling while silent tears fell down the sides of her head and dripped into her ears. She just wanted to stay in bed—never getting up—but that wouldn't make her troubles disappear.

Wait. She hadn't considered a possible outcome from this mess.

Maybe when Jack finds out about the baby, he'll realize he should have stayed with me. He'll break it off with Aubree. I'll move back home, and everything will turn out right.

Stacy closed her eyes and pictured the scene for several minutes. Then she came to her senses. A baby wouldn't fix her broken marriage. Instead, a child brought additional complications into the mix.

Stacy remembered her breathing exercises and began them. It wasn't long before her heartrate had slowed and her mind stilled.

Lord, I need your peace again. I may not know what is the best thing to do but you have promised that goodness and mercy will follow me. Help me to focus on this and not at my own flaws.

Stacy rose, padded into the bathroom, washed her face, dressed, and then made her way to the dining room. She found Charles and Ruth at the table, drinking coffee and deep in thought. An empty cup and saucer had been placed where Stacy had sat during their previous meals together.

"Good morning, dear," Ruth said softly. "Were you able to get any sleep?"

"Not a lot," Stacy admitted. "My heart and mind were spinning continually all night. I didn't think the hurt could get any worse. Now I know otherwise, and yet, I remembered several of God's promises, including the fact that he will make everything good in his time."

"This is a hard lesson to learn when it comes to these tough things in life. Maybe you would feel some comfort in attending church with us tomorrow morning," Ruth said, buttering a biscuit.

Charles nodded as he moved the strawberry jam closer to Stacy. "Yes, we'd be happy to have you with us."

Stacy placed a biscuit on her plate and reached for some jam, hoping to trigger some kind of appetite. Reaching for the coffee carafe, Stacy immediately hesitated, knowing that caffeine would not be good for the baby.

"It's decaf, so feel free to fill your cup."

Stacy poured a cup full, smiling. "I really appreciate your offer, and I'm sure your church is a wonderful place, but I've been told about the chapel services Chaplain Miller holds on Sundays at nine. I think I'd like to attend there."

CHAPTER 30

Stefan took a deep breath of the pleasant summer evening air. Lakewood Park was fast becoming his favorite new spot to reflect on life. To his right, some children played on the swings while two women, probably the children's mothers, chatted together at a picnic table nearby. He closed his eyes and listened to the squeaks and squeals each swing's chains made as the children pumped their legs.

The sounds took Stefan back to a time when he sat in the park back home with Sophie, laughing and talking, while their two boys competed with each other to see who could swing higher.

Now Stefan listened, absorbing the comfort the sounds created in his heart. He swiped away the two tears making their way down his face. *What a mess my life is in right now.*

Stefan eventually opened his eyes and noticed Chaplain Miller sitting on a nearby bench. He wondered how long the chaplain had been waiting to speak with him. Although Stefan was angry with God about so many things, he didn't mind talking with Chaplain Miller. Could this man help him?

He wiped his face with a handkerchief and called out, "Hello, Chaplain Miller."

The chaplain stood, then came over. "Hello, Stefan. You've sure picked a nice evening to sit in the park. Do you mind if I join you, or would you rather be alone?"

"I don't mind, though I don't know what kind of company I'll be."

"I'll take my chances." Chaplain Miller chuckled as he sat down beside Stefan. "When I made my way over here from my house across the street, I saw you sitting here with your eyes closed. You must have been a million miles away."

"More like many years away. I was listening to the children." He nodded toward the swings. "The squeaking of the chains is the exact sound I remember from when my boys played in the park."

"It's kind of comforting, isn't it?" Chaplain Miller said. "The familiar, in many ways, is comfortable because it's predictable."

"Yes. Whenever Sophie and I took the boys to the park, we knew they'd immediately run to the swings and compete over who could swing the highest. Every time."

The two men smiled as they sat quietly in thought.

After a bit, Chaplain Miller shifted on the bench. "There is comfort in the predictable, but life has a way of interjecting some very unpredictable events."

Stefan nodded, saying nothing.

"When the unpredictable happens, we can feel completely out of control. That's a horrible feeling." The chaplain looked up as the two women called to the children on the swings, telling them it was time to leave. "But there is something else that can happen when the predictable is turned upside down. Just as a person can feel out of control, he can also think God has lost control of the circumstance. For some, they begin to imagine God as a weakling." Again, Chaplain Miller paused while Stefan stared off in the distance, thinking.

"What's even more scary is when the unpredictable happens and a person concludes that God *does* have control and chooses not to act. Depending on your view of the unpredictable things of life, that can be a very difficult thing for people to deal with."

Stefan cleared his throat which was tightening from the tension and anger building in his body. "I knew he could have healed my Sophie, but he didn't." The severity of the accusation surprised Stefan, yet Chaplain Miller nodded his head in understanding.

"What you've just said ultimately leads to a very important question. If God is all-powerful, why do bad things happen to his children? Some understandably conclude he must not be good. Others believe there are no answers, and they develop into bitter people.

"Here's my challenge to you, Stefan. Think of this friction within your spirit as a good thing. It is telling you, 'Examine me. Find out why I am making your heart feel so conflicted.'"

The chaplain stood. "God understands unpredictability. He didn't create it, but he allows it. This is a hard thing to understand and accept."

Taking a few steps away, Chaplain Miller called over his shoulder. "We have a service tomorrow morning in Bethany's chapel at nine. You are more than welcome."

Stefan sat for a few minutes more, looking at the now empty swing set, contemplating the chaplain's words. *I don't know if I'll ever understand how a God who is all-powerful chooses to contain that power and not intervene and help his children when they cry out to him. Is this because he is cruel or could it be he has something else in mind?*

The events of last night rushed in and filled his mind. He clearly remembered the sound of the anguish in Frank's voice when he told Stefan that his wife had murdered their daughter. He wondered what Frank thought about a God who could intervene in this life but chose not to.

How in the world does someone get over that? Stefan could not imagine ever being able to survive what happened to Frank. Did he wonder where God was when his daughter needed protection? Stefan hung his head as his thoughts weighed him down.

Stefan rose and began the trek back to Bethany. When he reached the Sozo building, he saw several men—including Frank—hanging out in the lounge. Some were working with Frank on his puzzle, and others were playing games or carrying on light conversations. He grabbed a bottle of water and joined them.

Not really knowing any of the other men, Stefan gravitated toward Jerry's table.

The older man greeted him with a nod and gestured toward the checkerboard in front of him. "Do you want to play the winner? Doug here is putting up a good fight, but I'm not so sure he can pull ahead."

"Pretty confident, aren't you, Jerry?" Doug chuckled.

Stefan pulled up a chair to watch the rest of the game.

"Jerry gets overconfident sometimes, and that's when I go in for the kill." Doug jumped two of Jerry's men, leaving him with only one red checker on the board.

"Ah, you got me. I concede." Jerry started putting his pieces back on the board. "Stefan, you play Doug, and I'll make some popcorn. I'll bring the bowl over when it's ready."

Stefan settled into the game but kept his eye protectively on Frank. What was his new friend thinking tonight?

The first game was a back and forth battle until Stefan finally pulled ahead for good. Several men had gathered to watch the intense game.

After the win, Doug stood and shook his hand. Jerry soon filled the vacated seat. "You know, Stefan, you should sign up for the checkers tournament next week. But for now, you'll have to beat me."

The two men played a fierce game, but this time, Jerry came out the victor. Doug replaced Stefan as everyone gathered to watch the final, cutthroat rematch between Jerry and Doug. With a lot of laughing and cheering, Doug came out the winner again.

THE BOTTLE HOUSE

The two men stood and shook hands, grinning at each other. They'd played in the spirit of good fun and it showed. No poor sportsmanship, no hurt feelings.

Was that because everyone here had experienced suffering and didn't seek to add to it?

Looking around the lounge and straightening his back, stiff from bending of the checkboard, Stefan realized that sometime in the final game, Frank had left the room.

CHAPTER 31

Stefan arrived at breakfast Sunday morning as most people were finishing up. He'd slept later than usual, so he was a little behind his new schedule. As he turned from the serving line with his plate of pancakes, Stefan caught Frank motioning for him to join him at his table.

"Good morning, Frank," Stefan said, setting down his tray.

"Good morning. You guys had quite the cutthroat game of checkers going last night. You gave Doug a run for his money. Not many can do that."

Stefan chuckled. "He's good at it, that's for sure. You play checkers?"

"Sometimes. But last night, I wanted to work on the jigsaw puzzle."

Stefan nodded, remembering their conversation a few evenings ago.

"I'm going to Chaplain Miller's service at nine in the chapel. You want to come?"

"I don't know. I don't have church clothes with me. I'd feel out of place." Stefan poked at a pancake with his fork and hoped Frank would buy the lame excuse.

"Oh, the chapel services are informal. Chaplain Miller has said on more than one occasion that he'd rather people come dressed comfortably than dressed up because the Lord is more interested in what someone looks like on the inside."

Stefan nodded and reached for his coffee. After taking a drink, he set the cup down and gazed at Frank. "You know, I have to be honest with you. I'm not sure God's all that interested in spending time with me. I'm not very happy with him right now. I'd feel like a hypocrite attending a service while feeling this way."

"I understand exactly what you're saying, Stefan, but I want to tell you I've discovered God wants to spend time with us in our joys, sorrows, doubts, and anger. He can take it, and he accepts us just as we are."

Stefan speared a wedge of his pancake. "Maybe I'll come. We'll see."

Sunday mornings used to be special for Stefan and Sophie. They slept an hour later than during the week and started the day off with a relaxed feeling that they carried with them to church a few hours later.

Stefan often brewed the coffee while Sophie made Belgian waffles from scratch. As he remembered their tradition, Stefan could almost smell the waffles cooking and immediately, felt a pang of resentment in his heart. Why had God allowed Sophie to die and left Stefan with the ability to frequently remember her and their life together? He shook his head. These memories were painful, and when they crowded in his heart, he sought to get busy so his mind would be occupied with something else.

Perhaps it would be a good idea to attend Chaplain Miller's service. It could be a distraction, if only for an hour.

⚰✝⚰

An hour later, Stefan entered the chapel by the back door and was surprised by the amount of people who had gathered. He quickly spotted Frank and Jerry sitting together toward the front. Stefan chose a seat in the back so he could leave quickly and unobserved by most should he choose not to stay.

The last notes from the piano faded. Chaplain Miller stood in front of the group. "This is the day that the Lord has made."

"Let us rejoice and be glad in it," the people replied.

The group stood and sang a few worship songs, and as they did, Stefan felt like a knife was jabbing him in the heart. He had sung many of the tunes with Sophie at their church but now struggled to believe the words and would not force himself to sing. After the last song ended, the congregation settled in their seats.

The chaplain stood quietly for a moment and surveyed the room before speaking. "Today, we're going to discuss a topic that many in the church think true Christians should never struggle with, and that is, what do you do when you feel like giving up on God and your Christian faith?"

Stefan frowned. *Has Chaplain Miller planned a sermon based on our earlier conversations?* He fidgeted, trying to decide if he would stay or not. The question of a possible betrayal of their conversations and a curiosity of what the chaplain would say fought within him. *Curiosity wins, for now.*

Chaplain Miller smiled. "It's interesting one of the greatest men of God felt exactly that way. His name was Elijah."

Stefan thought about the story of the prophet but couldn't remember anything about the man feeling the same desperation he did.

"Elijah was a man of tremendous faith in God," Chaplain Miller continued. "He boldly stood up to Ahab, the king of Israel, and his wicked wife, Jezebel, who both wished him dead. Elijah knew the risk he was taking in speaking against this dangerous king and his wife, but that didn't stop him.

"Sounds like Elijah was a man of God whom many of us find difficult to relate to. If you've ever been afraid—if you've ever doubted God's words—if you've ever felt all alone, Elijah may not be your choice of companions."

It's no wonder these men of the Bible boldly did God's work—they'd been given the advantage of seeing miracles first-hand. Stefan crossed his arms. *I asked God continually for a miracle, just one thing, and he wouldn't do it.*

"Elijah boldly confronted Ahab. He had a successful showdown with the prophets of Baal. What faith this man of God had!"

Forming fists, Stefan's anger grew. *Sophie had faith. Look what it did for her.*

"Sometimes readers of the Bible think this victory is the end of the story, but it's not," Chaplain Miller said. "Instead, 1 Kings 19:3 tells us Elijah ran for his life because Jezebel was determined to kill him. In fact, verse four tells us this mighty man of God sat under a tree and prayed that God would take his life. He just wanted to give up. That's shocking!"

I don't remember that happening. Stefan's heart beat faster, and he pressed his lips together in a firm line. He combed through his knowledge of biblical events, but he couldn't remember this detail about Elijah. Certainly, he would remember Elijah's desperate prayer to God.

"What had happened to the man who was so bold in his faith in God? Where are the words of courage that he often used in God's ministry? This man of God was in a short period of time falling apart, wanting to give up, and I have to ask myself, why?"

The chaplain's word surged through Stefan. *It sounds like this man of God had a crisis of faith. Certainly not! Aren't committed Christians the ones who never doubt or wander off the path of the righteous? Has my assumption about faith been wrong?*

Chaplain Miller's voice, thick with emotion, lowered to almost a whisper. "It's because Elijah felt all alone. He even tells this to God in verse fourteen when he says, 'I am the only one left and now, they are trying to kill me too.'"

Nodding, Stefan understood Elijah's feeling. It was clear the prophet, too, was questioning God. But had the prophet been as angry with God as Stefan was now? Lost in his thoughts, Stefan almost missed Chaplain Miller's next words.

"When a person has been badly hurt, one of the scariest things of all can happen, and that is feeling all alone. It doesn't matter if you've caused the pain or if someone else has, feeling isolated is terrible."

Stefan's throat tightened. He pictured the evenings he and his wife spent together in their deck chairs, watching the waves roll over the sandy beach. Living in their home alone was almost unbearable now. And he'd made it even lonelier by blocking his sons from his life. Maybe he could relate to Elijah after all.

"What complicates this loneliness is when you feel God has brought on this helpless and often heart-wrenching feeling, either by his actions or his inactions. This is how Elijah felt. And God understood Elijah's feelings. He didn't judge or punish him for them. Instead, he arranged help for Elijah and reminded him he wasn't alone."

Was it possible that God didn't judge him for his feelings and weaknesses? Was it possible that God was offering some help by sending him here to Bethany? A part of Stefan clung to these words of hope.

"This morning, I know many of you have felt like giving up, and you feel alone. Adding to that burden, some of you feel like God has deserted you."

Stefan felt ashamed because the chaplain's words were true—he did feel like God had deserted him. In the years prior to Sophie's death, a big part of his life had been spent in God's word, reading it, teaching it to his boys, and making sure his family was committed to the principles found within its pages. Since her death, though, Stefan had rarely opened his Bible.

"The good news is, God didn't abandon Elijah, and he won't abandon you. Hebrews 13:5 says that God will never leave you nor forsake you. You can count on God keeping his promises. Hope and comfort are available to all."

Could Stefan be wrong about God and his so-called reluctance to help his children when they were in need? Wouldn't he drop everything to go to either of his sons should they call for help? Even if their relationship isn't what it should be? Of course he would still go and help!

Chaplain Miller closed his Bible, bowed his head, and prayed. "The Lord bless you and keep you. The Lord make his face shine on you and be gracious to you. The Lord turn his face toward you and give you peace. Amen."

As people stood, Stefan quietly made for the door. As he left the chapel, he heard a small voice within say, "I see your heartache, and I care."

CHAPTER 32

After the Sunday service in the chapel, Stacy walked with Debbie out to the hall. "I'm glad you came, Debbie. Thanks for sitting with me and keeping me company."

"I'm glad too," Debbie said.

"I have to check my schedule for next week, so I'll see you soon, okay?" Stacy smiled at Debbie and then made her way to the nurses' station.

While consulting the calendar for the week, she felt a wave of nausea wash over her. A reminder of the little life that was growing within her.

Why couldn't this baby come along earlier in our marriage? Would it have prevented Jack and Aubree from getting together?

She wanted a few minutes of silence to calm her nerves so she made her way back to the chapel, assuming it would be deserted by now.

She slipped into a seat in the back of the now empty chapel, placed her head in her hands, and cried.

What am I going to do? What am I going to do? Stacy repeated in a silent prayer.

After sitting for a while, Stacy took some tissues from her pocket and blew her nose. As she wiped away her tears, she was startled to see Chaplain Miller sitting in a chair on the end of a row toward the front of the chapel. He turned in her direction, and their eyes met.

"Do you wish to be alone, Stacy?" he asked. "I'll leave if you do."

"No, I honestly hate being by myself."

The chaplain reached down and picked up the dark-red bottle with what Stacy assumed held her name. He stood then and moved back to where she was sitting and set the bottle on the floor.

"Why do you hate being alone so much?"

Stacy's eyes followed the chaplain's movements and then slowly moved to his face. The compassion reflected there touched her deeply, and her tears suddenly poured out. She felt ashamed for breaking down like this again in front of a man she had learned to respect, but he only wore an expression of concern.

"I miss having a husband to come home to and share things with. I also long for a best friend. I lost both at the same time."

Chaplain Miller straightened the worship song book that was on the back of the chair in front of him. "Is it that you yearn for your husband and best friend? Or is it, perhaps, that you want the kind of husband and best friend you wish you had?"

Confused, Stacy frowned.

"I'll try to explain. Sometimes we don't miss a relationship as it is, we want our idea of what it could have or should have been." Chaplain Miller raised an eyebrow and tilted his head to the right just a little bit.

Stacy nodded, agreeing with him. "I never thought of that." She gazed at the front of the chapel. "Unfortunately, I recently found out something that complicates my difficulties." Stacy began to cry again. "I'm pregnant."

Chaplain Miller lowered his head, seeming to grieve this added stress and anxiety along with Stacy.

"How in the world am I going to have a baby with no husband and no place of my own? I'll never be totally free of Jack or Aubree with a baby in the picture." Stacy's words were surrounded by pain.

"On top of that, God must be so disappointed with me because my faith wavers so much. One moment, I can trust him with this, and then, just a few moments later, I lose it and buckle under the weight of fear."

"I'm sorry to hear of your pain and difficulties," he said. "I could sit here and quote you the platitudes that we Christians know in our heads, but when it comes to the specific, difficult circumstances of life, that often doesn't bring immediate comfort. I will say, though, God understands we, as imperfect beings, will have a faith that is shaky at times."

Stacy nodded, feeling a little encouraged. She took a deep breath. "If only Jack still loved me, then I would get to rejoice in this blessing of a baby both of us had been praying more than two years for. To find out I'm pregnant now is the worst timing."

She gripped the sides of her chair. "How is it possible in God's love and care for me, he would allow me to conceive on this timetable and not all the years prior to this when Jack and I tried to start a family? Maybe if he had, Jack and I would still be together." Stacy stared at Chaplain Miller, hoping he could answer this difficult question.

"Stacy, there's never a time that God is not watching over you and acting for your good. That's not the difficult part of our faith. It's easier to trust God for a miracle in our lives, but it's much more difficult to trust when that miracle does not arrive. That is the difficulty of faith.

"God is who he is." Chaplain Miller's tone only held kindness, not judgment. "He is a God who loves us so completely that his actions or non-actions are always for our good. He loves you enough to die for you. As your baby grows and moves from your womb to your arms, you'll understand the complete love of a parent for her child. You'll also be willing to do anything for your child, even if it calls for your death. That is love."

Stacy wept quietly as she considered his words.

"Stacy, have you considered that if you and Jack had conceived earlier, your baby would be raised in a home where there is conflict raging within? I'm not saying there won't still be conflict but, perhaps, God is sparing your child from this daily environment."

Chaplain Miller bent down to pick up the dark-red bottle, then stood. "God sees your sorrow. Trust in the one who sees all and still loves us unconditionally."

As he turned to leave the chapel, Stacy asked, "Why do you have that red bottle with my name on it? What's it for?"

Chaplain Miller smiled. He glanced at the bottle, then held her gaze. "Sometimes it's hard to have faith that the God of all the universe would care about the lives of his children. When I have paused to consider this, it is an amazing thing that I, one middle-aged man, whose life is but a blip in history, matter to God. Part of the reason I have these bottles is to help us to remember that God notices his children and cares. Try to get some rest. I'll see you tomorrow."

CHAPTER 33

When Debbie left the chapel that morning, she didn't know what to feel. On the one hand, the hurt that had rooted in her heart was something she realized she was clinging to. *I should never have been treated the way I was at Good Shepherd.* On the other hand, the thought that God noticed her feelings of inadequacy and loneliness was a concept she hadn't considered. She thought of the chaplain's words again. *You are not alone.* So why did she feel so alone now? She shook her head, desperately trying to clear the fog of conflict from her mind.

Processing what Chaplain Miller had said, Debbie made her way down Cayce Road clutching her beach towel. She wanted some solitude and hoped the beach would be less crowded on a Sunday.

She felt a little disappointed when she passed by Patricia's house but didn't see her. The chords of loneliness played within her, and Debbie had hoped for the companionship and even comfort that chatting with a friend could provide.

As she approached the ocean, she immediately felt her spirit churn within as the waves moved in and out in a nautical dance.

Standing in the sand, Debbie slipped off her sandals.

What's wrong with me? Why did I have to come to Bethany when it's clear I'm not the only one with problems?

Even the members of Good Shepherd Christian School have problems and doubts. Debbie dug her toes into the sand.

I miss Josh so much. Debbie's index finger began to twitch, illustrating her anxiety within.

Just as quickly as her mind embraced her pain, it ebbed over to the words Chaplain Miller had spoken that morning. *When a person has been badly hurt, one of the scariest things of all can happen, and that is feeling all alone.*

As she stared at the water, Debbie's tears gathered once again. She did feel so abandoned. Unloved and unlovable. Clearly, the men at Good Shepherd agreed with this thought.

God, I do feel alone. Chaplain Miller told us, and deep down inside I know he's right, that I'm not. The struggle for me is that you seem unaware of my hurts. You've allowed this crisis in my life, and I don't know why.

Debbie continued to watch the waves through the convex lens of tears.

All my life I have been made to feel worthless, God. There was little I could do right in the eyes of my mother. Marrying Josh has truly been a gift from you, Lord, because he is the first person I have known that thinks I am worth something ... until we started teaching at the Christian school.

Debbie's stomach felt heavy as her throat tightened. *Mr. Jennings and Pastor Hughes made judgments about me without even asking me about the situation. I wasn't even worth the benefit of the doubt in their eyes. Maybe, instead of Josh fully accepting me, my husband is wrong in his evaluation of me too.* These thoughts caused Debbie's legs to grow weak and she sat down hard into the sand.

Her eyebrows furrowed. *This whole situation not only made things painful for me, it's brought many of these feelings Josh's way. I was surprised when he told me we should turn in our resignations and get teaching jobs somewhere else. I know he feels resentment toward those men now.*

Your spoken words to Elijah were powerful, but why can't I hear with my own ears that you care about me just as much? Do you really care about me, someone who is not a great person of faith? How do you feel, seeing your children crying out in pain?

She lowered her head, allowing her tears of confusion to continue.

Debbie sat on the beach for a long time, thinking, praying, and crying. Feeling weary and hungry, she decided to make her way slowly back to Bethany.

As she passed the home of her dreams, Patricia called out to her. "Hello, Debbie!"

She tried her best to smile and made her way over to Patricia's house. "Hello."

"I was just getting lunch together and was wondering if you'd care to join me."

"I'd love to." Debbie joined Patricia on her porch, hoping her eyes weren't too red from crying. "Can I help with anything?"

"Yes, here are some paper towels and cleaner. If you'll wipe off the little table over there, we'll sit out here and eat."

Debbie took the supplies from Patricia and cleaned the table, pulling it away from the porch railing. She maneuvered two chairs she assumed were there for this purpose and placed them around the small, glass-topped table.

Holding two plates with sandwiches and chips, Patricia asked, "Could you grab the pitcher of iced tea on the kitchen counter? Just go in through the door, and you'll see the kitchen straight ahead."

"Sure." As she made her way to the kitchen, she briefly scanned the large living room. Though it was obvious that the furniture was not new, the room looked comfy and neat. Debbie also noticed a large, framed mirror hung over the fireplace, and what appeared to be a family portrait was displayed in a stand on the mantel. In Patricia's kitchen, she noticed everything was homey and welcoming.

Picking up the pitcher, Debbie sighed. *I wish Josh and I had a place like this.*

Returning to the porch and the small table, Debbie sat beside Patricia as she bowed her head. Debbie joined her.

"Thank you, Lord, for providing this food for us this day. Thank you, also, for the things you have provided that we aren't even aware of. May we use this food and gifts you have provided in your service. Amen."

"Amen," Debbie echoed.

"We had such a wonderful service at my church this morning," Patricia said between bites of sandwich. "It was about making sure, as Christians, that we put on the full armor of God. I believe it was in the sixth chapter of Ephesians."

Debbie nodded. "I'm familiar with those verses."

"It was a good reminder to me that we need to be prepared for battle any time of the day or night." Patricia paused and took a sip of her iced tea.

Reflecting on those words, Debbie munched a potato chip.

"I was reminded the war between God and Satan continues until God ends it. In the meantime, we must be on the lookout for the enemy. Fortunately, God has provided us with the means to protect ourselves and fight." Patricia smiled.

The idea of fighting Satan gave Debbie courage. "Patricia, I haven't told you this." She looked down at her plate. "I'm a patient at Bethany R&L." Her hands shook as she raised her glass to her mouth.

Patricia's gaze showed neither shock nor pity. "It's not unusual for me to see new people ambling up and down my road on the way to the beach. Most of the locals go to another one up the road a bit, so it wasn't hard for me to put two and two together."

Debbie frowned as she listened.

"Are you worried that I might think less of you, now that you've told me?"

"I'm not sure," Debbie admitted softly.

"All of us, at one time or another, need help. There's nothing shameful about that. It may surprise you, also, that in a way, I'm jealous. You have the opportunity to interact with Chaplain Miller on a regular basis. I only get to visit with him from time to time. He's a wise man of God."

Debbie nodded. "Yes, I think he is too." She took another sip of tea. "I guess what Chaplain Miller said in his service can go hand-in-hand with what you heard today at your church."

"What was his sermon about?" Patricia asked.

"He spoke about Elijah being a powerful man, and yet, on one occasion, he just wanted to give up and die." Debbie's voice grew softer as her thoughts deepened.

"Tell me more."

"Chaplain Miller read us the verse that tells us Elijah wanted his life to end because he felt so alone."

Patricia nodded. "You know, when it comes to our thoughts, it's vital to wear the belt of truth that Paul mentions in Ephesians."

Debbie appreciated how the woman's voice rang with confidence.

"So much of our thinking is rooted in incorrect or distorted information. Truth is a vital defense against Satan's attempt to discourage us and keep us from moving forward."

Debbie leaned forward. "God told Elijah he wasn't alone, and the truth of the matter was there were seven thousand people who Elijah didn't even know were also following God. God was pointing out Elijah's false thinking."

"Yes, Debbie, that's exactly what God did."

The two women continued to eat, lost in their own thoughts. When they finished, they left the dishes on the table, picked up their tea, and moved to the swing.

"You know, Patricia, I've never felt so alone as I have this last week. It's not that no one has expressed their care and concern about me. You and Chaplain Miller have been nothing but accepting and caring."

"What's the problem then?"

"It's the reason I'm at Bethany. My husband, Josh, and I both teach at a Christian school, and there were several instances when I disagreed with the administrators' decisions. I'd watch them treat the staff, especially Josh, with such disrespect and disregard. On top of that, they required we attend every church function as if they believe it is a biblical mandate. Anger and frustration built up within me, and I exploded, protesting many things that I saw as injustices." Debbie let out her remaining breath and sat back in the swing.

"I can see how you'd feel that way."

"I only saw my venting to coworkers as a way to blow off steam, but they saw it as an indication of my weak faith. The principal and the pastor of the church affiliated with the school thought my frustration was a lack of respect toward them, but it wasn't. I was just upset at their legalistic attitudes. I thought maybe they were right about needing to be closer to God, but it still hurt. They didn't even try to get to know me or meet with me to draw up a plan to make things better. They said if I didn't come here for treatment, there was a good possibility Josh and I would both lose our jobs. I feel so betrayed and alone." Tears escaped and slid down Debbie's face.

"I'm so sorry that happened to you. If it makes you feel any better, I'd feel the same way." Using her foot to keep the swing going, Patricia leaned over and gave Debbie's hand a quick squeeze. "If you take what you heard this morning and add it to what I heard, it's clear we must get into the habit of examining our thoughts in the light of truth. The circumstances that brought you here are true, but I'd like to challenge you to examine your thoughts and see if what you're telling yourself is true."

Debbie pulled a tissue out of her pocket and blew her nose. It seemed to her that she'd cried more in this last month then she probably had in all her infancy.

"I wonder," Patricia continued, "if you could look through the lens of truth, how would you see the circumstances of what brought you here? How would your view of yourself change? Something to think about."

The two women rocked slowly in the swing as Debbie stared at the row of flowers in the front yard. Eventually, Debbie reluctantly stood. "I suppose I'll head back to Bethany and maybe read until Josh calls at two. Thank you for lunch and your good company, Patricia."

"You're welcome here any time. I'm glad you came." Patricia gave a small smile. "You know, there are times when I feel alone in the world too."

Debbie offered a small smile and then made her way back down the road. As she walked, Patricia's admission that she, too, felt alone at times echoed in her mind.

I need to remember I am not the center of the universe. Other people have hurts and difficulties and similar situations too.

CHAPTER 34

Stefan walked to the cafeteria with Jerry and Frank, dreading the afternoon. He had been told Sunday afternoons at Bethany were fairly quiet with no scheduled therapy sessions. He thought about what he could do to fill the time.

As the men ate their meal, they spoke about the Oakland A's and their chances for the World Series. They all agreed their time for getting into the playoffs and winning the series was long overdue.

They'd just finished lunch when Chaplain Miller entered the cafeteria and headed right for their table.

"Hey, fellas! I'm glad to catch you three. I need a favor. My sister visited this week, and she left a large homemade chocolate cheesecake at my house. I don't know why she makes them so big, but I could use some help eating it."

Jerry smiled. "I don't know about these other two, but I never turn down cheesecake."

"Frank? Stefan? You two interested?" Chaplain Miller asked.

"Sure, I'm game," Frank said, and Stefan nodded.

"Great! You guys come down to my house about two o'clock. Your lunch should be settled by then. You all know where it is?"

"Right across from Lakewood Park, right?" Frank asked.

"That's it. See you all at two." Chaplain Miller turned to head back out the door.

Stefan sat quietly, thinking about the invitation.

Jerry gulped down the last of his water. "Have either of you been inside Chaplain Miller's Bottle House before?"

"No," said Frank.

"Me neither," Stefan said. "I've walked by it. The windows are filled with bottles."

"I've seen them too." Jerry stood and grabbed his tray. "It'll be interesting to see the inside of his house. I want to get a closer look at those bottles he collects."

Stefan returned to his room about an hour before he was to meet back up with Jerry and Frank. He felt a little run down, so he kicked off his shoes, climbed onto the bed, and rested his head on the soft pillow.

His mind went immediately to the message Chaplain Miller had given in the chapel that morning. He did feel all alone, and it dawned on him, there was someone else he hadn't considered that he was sure felt alone as well. Allie Barker. He thought of her in the courtroom that day, her face full of pain when the not guilty verdict was given. Stefan felt contempt for himself because he knew her pain was because of him.

I just don't understand you, God. You say you will always be with us and yet you can often seem indifferent to the suffering of your people. If you do care about these things, why is it that I cannot sense that you are at work, helping me behind the scenes? Even in the story of the Prodigal Son, you give us the idea you rush right to him and throw your arms around him. Could you please show me evidence you are actively working to help me in this difficult time?

Stefan rolled over and glanced at the clock. Somehow, fifty minutes had passed, and he had only ten minutes to meet the others. He quickly ran a comb through his hair, slipped his feet into his shoes, and then rushed to meet his friends.

"Sorry if I'm late," Stefan said, hoping the men had not been waiting too long.

"No, I just arrived too." Frank put his glasses in his shirt pocket. "I was in the courtyard reading and time got away from me."

"Let's go," Jerry said.

The three men set out for the Bottle House and arrived in a matter of minutes. Stefan eyed the park across the street from the chaplain's house and smiled when he saw some kids swinging. Again, the creaking sounds from the swings immediately made him think of his own sons and his smile faded. *Would they want to see me if I called and invited them here? What would they think of me if they learn where I am and why?*

Turning his attention toward the house, he gazed at all the bottles in the window near the front door. Stefan was startled when Chaplain Miller opened the door, as if expecting them at that precise moment. He beckoned them inside.

The wallpaper in the foyer reminded Stefan of his grandmother's house. *It must be as old as this house.*

"Welcome to my home. I hope you've had enough time to digest your lunch and have plenty of room for cheesecake."

Jerry smiled. "I'll always have room for dessert." The others laughed.

"The coffee is still brewing, so if you men would like to head through this doorway, I'll bring everything in as soon as it's ready. Please make yourselves comfortable."

The three friends followed Chaplain Miller's direction, but all stopped within a few feet of the door. Stefan was not prepared for what he saw. Before them stood shelves upon shelves holding hundreds of bottles. Each bottle was no bigger than Stefan's hand and were made from various colors of glass.

He knew there were bottles in this house—he could see them in the windows—but he never would have guessed there were this many. And this was only one room. How many bottles were there in the home?

Chaplain Miller arrived with a coffee carafe, cups, saucers, and plates on a tray, interrupting Stefan's thoughts.

"Have a seat," Chaplain Miller said as he set down the tray. "I'll be right back with the cheesecake."

While their host was gone, the men sat down and again eyed all the bottles displayed.

"Now I can really see why the locals call this the Bottle House," Jerry said.

Chaplain Miller came in with the cheesecake, and Stefan couldn't believe the size of the dessert. "You were certainly right about it being a big cake."

"My sister shows her love through her baking. I must admit that I enjoy receiving it." The chaplain cut pieces of cheesecake and filled their cups with strong coffee.

Stefan took a bite of the dessert. *Delicious! Chaplain Miller's sister was, indeed, a good baker.* "I haven't had cheesecake like this in many years. When we were first married and I was still in law school, Sophie and I didn't have much money. So, when we could save up enough, we'd go to the local bakery and buy one piece of cheesecake. We'd eat the shared piece as slowly as we could, trying to make it last."

"I remember days of the extra-tight budget myself," Jerry said.

Chaplain Miller poured another round of coffee. "Help yourself if you'd like more, and I'll send a piece with each of you to enjoy later."

The four men talked about unimportant things, and Stefan felt glad to not be spending the afternoon alone in his room.

After a while, Jerry stood. "Chaplain Miller, it was kind of you to ask me to share your wonderful dessert. Thank you. But I'm going to head back to Bethany, because I've got a phone call or two I need to make."

Frank and Stefan stood as well, preparing to help Chaplain Miller take all the dishes they'd used back to the kitchen.

The chaplain shook his head. "Don't worry about these things. I'll get them in a bit. Let me take this cake back into the kitchen and cut and wrap each of you a piece to take back to your room. I'll only be a few minutes if you can wait."

Jerry laughed. "I'm pretty full already, but I won't turn down a piece to go."

"Wonderful," Chaplain Miller said, picking up the dessert and taking it into the kitchen.

As they stood there waiting, Stefan gravitated to some of the bottles on display, wanting a closer look. "Each of these bottles have labels with names on them, just like the ones in his office."

Jerry stepped closer to the window. "There are so many shapes and colors."

A gasp came from Frank's direction and Stefan turned to his friend.

Frank's face was as pale as a white sheet, and his eyes were wide and filled with grief. Stefan watched as he quietly slipped out of the room and through the front door.

The two remaining men rushed to where Frank had stood, but only saw bottles similar to the others. Stefan frowned, not understanding what had upset Frank.

"Oh, look," Jerry said quietly, pointing at three bottles. "Here's one with Frank's name on it, and this other one is labeled Linda, his daughter's name."

"What about the third bottle?" Stefan asked. "Who's Melissa?"

Jerry cleared his throat. "Melissa was Frank's wife," he said softly. "The one who murdered his daughter."

CHAPTER 35

Stacy gathered her things and set out for the Lewises' house. They were probably wondering if chapel had run long or what was keeping her.

Arriving, she popped into her room and left there the Bible she'd taken to the chapel that morning, and then headed toward the sounds of Charles' and Ruth's voices.

"Stacy, I'm glad you're here. I dislike putting salads together, and now I can leave this one in your capable hands." Charles gestured to the vegetables laid out on the counter and then headed outside to the patio.

Stacy moved to the sink and washed her hands.

Ruth chuckled. "Don't let him fool you. He doesn't mind helping at all. I think he just wanted to give us time for girl talk."

What would my life be like now if Jack had been the considerate man Charles is?

"How was church today?" Stacy asked, choosing a knife from the collection.

"It was really good. Pastor Stevenson had a wonderful sermon on the fruit of the Spirit. How was the service with Chaplain Miller?"

"It was good, and it gave me a lot to think about." Stacy reflected on the message for a moment as she worked on cutting up some carrots to add to the salad. "I need to call Jack and tell him about the baby."

Ruth kept dicing tomatoes and Stacy wondered if she'd heard the practically whispered omission.

"I know." Ruth looked up. "Have you thought about how you're going to break the news?"

"No, I haven't. How do you tell a soon-to-be ex-husband that he's going to be a father when he doesn't want a relationship with the mother-to-be?" Stacy sighed. "I'll try to call him this afternoon. He does have a right to know."

"Charles and I will be praying the Lord will give you the right words."

⚰✝⚰

Stacy sat on her bed, knowing she should go ahead and call Jack and get it over with. She took her cell phone and placed the call, her hands shaking.

The phone rang one time.

"Stacy, why are you calling? Neither Jack nor I want to hear from you."

She flinched as if Aubree's harsh words were a slap on her face. "I'm sorry if you don't like that I'm calling, Aubree, but I must speak to Jack. It's important." A tear fell from Stacy's eye as she spoke. She felt like she might faint.

"I'll see if he wants to talk with you."

Stacy's heart pounded as she went over what exactly she would say when Jack's voice came on the line.

"Stacy, I thought I made it clear I didn't want further contact with you. Aubree is very upset you called."

As Jack's harsh reprimand echoed across the miles, the carefully planned words she'd rehearsed fled. "Jack, I'm pregnant."

The line was silent for a few moments, and Stacy began to wonder if Jack had hung up.

"What? No way!" Jack's words held venom. "Are you sure it's my baby?"

Stunned, Stacy remailed silent.

"I bet you're happy about this, thinking I'll come back to you. Well, just so you know, that isn't going to happen."

Stacy's face grew hot. She didn't think this conversation would be easy, but she was shocked to hear his hateful accusation.

"Jack, there's no question about it. You are this baby's father. I'm calling so we can make a plan for this child when it arrives."

"I don't know what you expect you're going to get from me."

This couldn't be the same man she'd married.

"I've got to go," he said, sounding rushed. "After I've had some time to figure out what needs to be done, I'll call you."

The sharp click caused her to flinch.

Stacy stared out the bedroom window, still holding the phone to her ear. In that moment, she felt Jack's betrayal more than she ever had.

CHAPTER 36

Stefan still felt a little shaken from seeing Frank's bottles earlier that afternoon. Why did Chaplain Miller have them? What were they for? He remembered the only clue the chaplain had given him—that they somehow represented the fact that God keeps his promises.

Stefan left the Sozo building and, feeling the warm evening air, opted to sit in the courtyard. The beach would have been nice but revisiting his memories with Sophie at their beach home was more than he could bear right now.

The breeze rustling the leaves provided some comfort to his spirit. He wished he'd brought a book out with him. Maybe he could get lost in a story and not feel so alone. He briefly thought of going into the lounge of the Sozo building and picking one up, but dreaded possibly running into Frank.

Stefan wasn't sure what he would say to his friend. Was Frank feeling alone too? And how had he felt about seeing the bottle with his wife's name on it?

"Hello, Stefan. Did you enjoy your extra piece of cheesecake or are you still saving it?" Chaplain Miller asked as he sat down in a nearby chair.

Deep in thought, he hadn't heard Chaplain Miller approaching. "That cheesecake was so good. I'm saving it for some time in the near future." Stefan patted his belly.

Chaplain Miller laughed. "I know what you mean, and I still have a good hunk of it left at my house. My sister is a good cook, though."

Stefan noticed the chaplain was carrying the sky-blue bottle with his name on it.

"We spoke the other day about the unpredictable things of life and God's role in orchestrating everything. Did our conversation spur any thoughts, Stefan?"

Stefan tore his gaze away from the bottle and looked out across the courtyard. He cleared his throat. "These things have been on my mind a lot."

"Oh? Tell me more."

"Everything I thought was true about life is in question. I thought we were here to love and support one another, making our part of society a better place. I thought a man was to protect his wife and the helpless ones in his community. I haven't been able to do either."

"Why do you say that, Stefan?"

"I couldn't help Sophie. Watching her endure so much pain broke my heart." Stefan's voice trembled. "I begged God to make her better, and when it became obvious she wasn't improving, I begged God to give me the cancer and not her. God continued to be silent." Stefan's jaw clenched.

"You felt powerless, didn't you? You wanted to help … you begged to help, and you couldn't." Chaplain Miller watched as Stefan barely nodded his head. "Is there anyone else you felt powerless with?"

"I took on a personal injury case where a young woman and her little daughter were seriously hurt because of someone else's negligence." Stefan fidgeted in his seat. "I boldly stepped in and took on her case, thinking winning for these two could somehow make up for what I wasn't able to do for Sophie."

Chaplain Miller remained silent.

"What should have been an open-and-shut case—the award of a large amount of money this young mother needed desperately to care for her daughter's future needs—fell apart." Stefan sagged back into his chair and hung his head. "The jury sided with the defendant over a small mistake I made. It was all my fault that we lost."

Chaplain Miller stood while picking up the sky-blue bottle with Stefan's name on it. "It's clear that you hurt tremendously for your wife and your clients. God sees your pain, Stefan." After a brief pause, he said, "There is something I want you to think about. Sometimes we give ourselves the idea we have more power than we actually do, and when we believe it, we set ourselves up for failure time and time again."

Chaplain Miller laid his hand on Stefan's shoulder. "There are many things in life we can't control. That's why God wants us to depend on him. He *is* in control. God bless you, and I'll see you tomorrow."

As Chaplain Miller turned to leave, Stefan asked, "Why do you have a bottle with my name on it, and what about all those bottles in your house? What are they for?"

Chaplain Miller smiled. "They are containers that hold a liquid more precious than gold."

Stacy had to drag herself to her room after cleaning up from supper. She felt so tired but knew getting to sleep would be difficult. She climbed in bed and gathered the soft quilt around her. Placing a pillow behind her, she reached over to the nightstand for her Bible. Before she could even open it, her cell phone rang. She cringed when she saw it was Jack.

"Jack, I don't know why you're calling. After your earlier accusation, I have nothing to say."

"Ah ... well, I told you I'd get back to you about a plan for our baby."

"So, you now believe you're the father?"

"When you told me you were pregnant, it was just the first thing that popped into my head. I have since had time to process this news, and I think we need to get together and make a plan. How about we meet somewhere in the next day or so?"

"Jack, I've just started my new job. Asking for time off isn't an option."

After a moment of silence, Jack spoke. "I guess Aubree and I could come there and meet you after your shift, but it's not my first choice. I'll check and see about time off from both of our jobs."

After their conversation, Stacy's stomach churned as she thought about what he'd said. *Why does Aubree need to come? It isn't her baby.*

With a trembling chin, she prayed. *Oh, Lord, planning for this unexpected baby is difficult enough, but now I'll have to see Jack and Aubree together. How will I be able to stand it? I have faith you will help but help my unbelief.*

CHAPTER 37

Debbie made her way to Chaplain Miller's office with a light heart. What she once dreaded—meeting with someone in his spiritual position—she now looked forward to.

Arriving at the chaplain's open door, Debbie rapped gently with her knuckle and entered.

Chaplain Miller turned from his computer screen, smiling. "Welcome, Debbie. It's so good to see you this afternoon." He bent toward his screen, taking the mouse in his hand and clicking on what Debbie assumed was the save button. He then turned off his screen, which made Debbie believe he planned to give her and their discussion his full attention.

Thank you, Lord, for placing such a considerate man as Chaplin Miller here at Bethany.

"You look happier ... lighter," he told her.

"Oh, I'm just bursting to tell you. Josh is coming to see me tomorrow!"

The chaplain beamed. "I'm so happy for you! I'm sure you two have a lot to catch up on."

"Yes, I'm so looking forward to seeing him."

Chaplain Miller rotated a bit in his chair. "Tell me how you feel about being here at Bethany R&L now that it's been almost a week. I remember you weren't very thrilled about it when you first arrived."

"You're right, and if I'm honest, there's still a part of my heart that hurts so much about the circumstances that brought me here." Debbie's gaze moved to the floor, feeling ashamed of what she just said.

Chaplain Miller bowed his head a moment, almost in reverence for the heartfelt words she'd just spoken. "That's an interesting choice of words. What you did *not* say was, 'how much my heart hurts about being here.' Instead, you said, 'how much my heart hurts about the *circumstances* that brought me here.' Interesting."

Debbie's eyes moved to the picture that hung on the wall behind Chaplain Miller. She was growing to love the charcoal drawing of Jesus holding the lamb. "I did say that, didn't I?"

Chaplain Miller nodded but allowed Debbie to continue.

"I still feel so rejected and misunderstood by our school's leadership. It really hurts that they didn't even try to get to know me. On top of that, they were taking a verse out of context, interpreting that it stated dedicated Christians must be at every church function or there is a problem spiritually. They just passed judgment on an issue I believe is *not* biblical. I'm also missing Josh so much, and honestly, I blame them for that too."

Chaplain Miller raised his eyebrows. "I think, if I were in your place, I would struggle with those things too." He picked up the notebook Debbie recognized from the day before, opened it to an empty page, picked up a pen, and wrote one word. He turned the notepad around for Debbie to see. *Resentment.*

"The kind of feelings you describe are a natural response to the circumstance in which you have been. If you're not careful, though, they can lead to resentment."

Debbie sighed. He was right. "Yes, I think the seed of resentment has already started to sprout within my heart."

"When you harbor resentment, it's a dead end—emotionally, mentally, and spiritually. The word *resent* originally meant 'to feel again,' almost as if you are saying to yourself whatever you resent over, and over, and over. This is bad because these feelings often lead you on a downward spiral that produces anger, belligerence, bitterness, and more."

Debbie hung her head because, in that moment, she recognized those very things in her own heart.

Neither one of them said anything for a moment, and then Chaplain Miller flipped a few pages forward in his notebook. "Yesterday, we talked about your strength of being compassionate. Did you have any thoughts that came to mind concerning that after you left?"

"Yes," Debbie answered. "The verse in Acts 20:35 about it being more blessed to give than to receive came to mind. It's true, you really do experience a blessing when you give to others. For example, I have one little girl in my class who is living with her grandparents. I happen to know they have had to scrape up any money they can just to have her in our Christian school. So when I saw her shoes were beginning to fall apart, I got her a new pair, and every day, she comes into my classroom and shows them off. But then I thought about how cunning Satan is to interfere with that blessing. When the administration nitpicked some of my flaws, that blessing was tainted, stealing the joy of giving from my heart."

"You're right. Satan doesn't want God's children experiencing anything that's good as a result of following him. Good observation. Now, let's pick another one of your strengths and analyze it. Which one?"

Debbie unfolded her list and read the contents silently. "How about loyalty?"

Chaplain Miller turned and pulled a thick book off the shelf beside him. "I've always been fascinated with word origins and meanings. Therefore, this dictionary. I could find definitions online, but I just haven't wanted to give up this method of discovery."

She smiled. Debbie hadn't used a dictionary in this way since she was in elementary school.

Chaplain Miller flipped through the pages, landing on what Debbie thought must be the L section. He ran his finger down a column and stopped. "It says here that loyalty is 'a feeling of strong support or allegiance to another person or organization.' Is that your understanding of this word?"

Debbie frowned in concentration and thought for a moment. "Yes, it is, but I would add that my allegiance is given because of the actions and reputation of the individual or organization."

"So you're adding conditions or standards a person or organization needs to have in place before they earn your loyalty. I like that addition, Debbie. I think it can be a dangerous thing to give allegiance to someone or something blindly, especially in spiritual matters. This is how heartbreaking things like what happened in the seventies with the followers of Jim Jones come about."

"I remember reading about that horrible event in one of my college courses," Debbie said.

"It had to have broken God's heart." Chaplain Miller paused for a moment, then focused on his book again. "Here's something interesting to add to our definition of loyalty. It says the origin of this word was a legal Latin term meaning a *steadfastness* of allegiance. What do you understand that to mean, Debbie?"

She thought a moment. "Doesn't steadfast mean to stay in place, refusing to budge?"

"Yes! Exactly. So, what do you think the implications are of this steadfastness?"

"Being steadfastly loyal means you're not a 'fair-weather friend.' You stick with the person or organization through thick or thin."

"Nice observation. This can be a very good thing. It makes you reliable. You will be steady in your allegiance. Now, let's switch gears. How can loyalty be a vulnerability?"

Debbie gazed at the notes she had on her paper. "Sometimes, being loyal can cost you a lot. Standing for what you believe can cost you the feeling of acceptance and even your job. Not many people are willing to risk this, so if you continue to stand firm, you may be in the minority."

"When this happens, what does that mean for the one staying loyal?"

"It may shake the loyal person's confidence he or she had originally with that person or organization. You can also feel like you're alone in your support, and it becomes more difficult to be steadfast in your loyalty."

"Do you feel that your confidence has been shaken by some of your school's leadership?"

Chaplain Miller's question hit Debbie right in the heart, and her eyes filled with tears.

"I've always been loyal to God's church and his people," Debbie said with a thick voice. "So when they met with Josh and me that painful night, something I have prided myself in was shaken—so much so, I'm not sure I can be steadfast in my loyalty to the church-run school. At the same time, I am beginning to understand the times I vented with coworkers about Josh's and my frustrations was not helpful for anyone in the long run. It was wrong."

"Yes, I can imagine. Do you think because of these circumstances, Josh has had his loyalty tested too?"

A light bulb turned on right then for Debbie. "I've thought about this situation from Josh's standpoint, but I've been so caught up in my own, I haven't really considered his."

"Maybe that would be a productive and revealing thing to do. Spend some time thinking about all these things we've been discussing, and then talk to Josh about it."

Debbie looked at the clock. She'd been here almost an hour. She smiled and stood.

"I will. Thank you, as always, for your time."

Chaplain Miller closed his notebook. "That's why God has placed me here, Debbie. Enjoy your day with Josh!"

⚕✝⚕

Stacy's day had been full already—she'd told Ruth about Jack and Aubree's visit and had asked Mrs. Turner to leave early tomorrow—and she was feeling worn out.

By the end of the afternoon, Stacy was beat. She guessed that in addition to being pregnant, the added stress of Jack and Aubree's visit tomorrow was taking its toll. On a whim, and feeling like she could use some comfort, she stopped by Chaplain Miller's office before she headed home.

When Chaplain Miller spotted her, he smiled. "Hello, Stacy. Come in and have a seat."

"I didn't come for a long chat. I'm ready to head home and thought if you were too, we could walk together."

"As a matter of fact, I was getting ready to head home, but I'd be more than happy to postpone that if you need more time to talk."

"No, I just thought I'd fill you in on a few things."

"Sounds good." Chaplain Miller shut down his computer then walked to the coffee maker, turning that off as well.

As they made their way from the building, Chaplain Miller asked, "So, how did it go, breaking the news to Jack?"

"Not well, but I honestly didn't expect that it would. He was in as much shock as I have been."

"That's understandable, considering the circumstances you shared with me."

"What I'm really worried about is Jack isn't coming alone tomorrow. He's bringing Aubree with him."

"She was your best friend, if I remember correctly." Chaplain Milled clasped his hands behind him as he walked.

"Yes. And I honestly don't know how I'll discuss this surprise with both of them. Doing so would have been difficult enough with just Jack, but adding Aubree into the picture is almost more than I can bear."

"I can certainly understand that." Chaplain Miller stopped on the sidewalk leading up to the Lewises' home. "Consider this. Tell God what you're thinking and feeling. As your heavenly Father, he cares about you tremendously. He will be working everything involved with this baby for good. You can trust in that."

"I hope so, Chaplain Miller." Stacy sighed. "Because, right now, at a time I should be elated over having a baby, I feel mostly hurt."

"It's truly understandable." As Chaplain Miller turned to walk away and Stacy opened the front door, she heard him say, "Your sorrows matter to God."

CHAPTER 38

Debbie rose earlier than any other day during her stay at Bethany. Josh was coming today! She took her time in the shower, giving her hair an extra shampoo and rinse. As she stood before the mirror, waiting for the exhaust fan to pull out the steam, she put moisturizer on and combed out her light brown hair. She wanted to look her best for her husband.

When she could finally see her reflection, she applied her makeup, put on a pretty blouse and skirt, and dried her hair. Debbie felt like a teenager getting ready for a big date, and her smile in the mirror reflected her happiness.

She slipped on her shoes and headed to breakfast. *Josh said he would be here around eight, so I'll eat and get back here before then, just to double-check my appearance.*

Debbie made her way to the cafeteria where she ran into Stacy. She smiled. "Good morning, Nurse Meadows."

"Nurse Meadows? You're being awfully formal." The two laughed as they got their food and sat down. "Today is a big day for you," Stacy said, stirring the creamer in her coffee. "Will your husband be here soon?"

Debbie's heart pounded with anticipation. "Yes, Josh should be here in about an hour. I can't wait!"

The two women ate and talked about Josh's visit. When she was finished, Stacy wiped her mouth with her napkin and rose. "See you later, Debbie. I hope you and Josh have a wonderful day."

Debbie said goodbye and watched as Stacy made her way out of the cafeteria. At that exact moment, her breath quickened when Josh came walking into the room carrying a bouquet of roses. His smile communicated he had missed her as much as she had missed him.

The couple embraced with no concern about their audience.

"You're here earlier than you said," Debbie said.

"Well, I woke up extra early, and I knew I wouldn't go back to sleep, so I hit the road. I picked up coffee and a breakfast sandwich along the way."

Debbie breathed in the scent of the flowers. "These are so beautiful, Josh. I can use the vase I had for Patricia's flowers. They are starting to wilt now anyway."

"Sounds good, and then we can sit down and figure out how you'd like to spend the day."

Debbie picked up her tray awkwardly with one hand. "Let me get that for you." Josh grabbed the tray, and they made their way out of the cafeteria.

As the couple left the cafeteria, they ran into Stacy, who was in the hall. "This must be Josh."

"Yes, it is. Stacy, I'd like you to meet my husband, Josh. Honey, this is Stacy Meadows, my nurse."

"I've heard a lot of good things about you from my wife," Josh said as he stuck out his hand.

"Oh, that's good to hear!" Stacy bent over to smell the bouquet. "These are beautiful flowers. Josh, you certainly know one way to make a girl feel loved."

Josh beamed, revealing he appreciated the compliment.

"Well, I won't tie up your precious time together, but it's good to meet you, Josh."

"It's good to meet you too."

Debbie and Josh took the roses to her room. She replaced the ones from Patricia with Josh's and smiled.

"I'm so blessed to have you and a new friend to keep me in flowers."

"I knew you'd like them, and they should last for many days." Josh plopped down on the bed. "What would you like to do today?"

"Let's just spend some time together here. Then, there are some people I'd like you to meet."

"Sounds good to me." Josh smiled and drew Debbie to him.

In the early afternoon, Debbie and Josh went by Chaplain Miller's office, hoping he was free.

Debbie saw the open door and stuck her head in. "Hello, Chaplain Miller. I have someone with me who'd like to see you."

Chaplain Miller stood as he saw both Debbie and Josh come into his office, holding hands.

"Hello, Josh! It's good to see you again." Chaplain Miller held out his hand, and Josh grasped it with his free one.

"Why don't you two have a seat. Coffee anyone?"

"No, thank you," Josh said.

"I don't care for any, either, but thank you for offering," Debbie said. "Chaplain Miller can never have enough coffee. There have been very few times I haven't seen him with a mug in his hand." Debbie laughed.

Chaplain Miller poured himself some and sat back down at his desk.

"So, Josh, I know a little more about how Debbie is doing because of working with her here, but I'm wondering how you're holding up being temporarily separated from this lovely woman."

Josh cleared his throat. "It's been difficult not having my best friend around. On top of that, Debbie is such an organized person I've come to depend upon her help in that area, because unfortunately, I'm not."

"Sounds like the two of you complement each other with your strengths."

"Yes, we do," Josh said, while Debbie nodded in agreement.

"Debbie has explained the difficult circumstances that led to her stay here at Bethany. How are you doing in your struggles with your job? I would guess this situation has made the thought of your work at the Christian school a little strained."

"It has." Josh glanced at Debbie, and she squeezed his hand. "I wouldn't be honest if I didn't admit to some hard feelings." He rubbed the back of his neck with his other hand, then leaned back in his chair. "Working at the same school that made this decision is very difficult. I've seen many who have left the church and its ministries permanently because of the challenges they've faced while in this type of work."

"I know it must be hard for Josh, especially because he's so protective of me," Debbie added.

"That's a good thing." Chaplain Miller took a sip of his coffee. "We all have scars that affect how we interact with each other. For some reason, people think those who work in a church or church-run organizations should be perfect, but this incorrect thinking leads to all sorts of problems. Perfection belongs to God."

"I know that, Chaplain Miller, but I just don't know how much I should endure as a servant of Christ and when to shake the dust off my sandals," Josh said.

"You raise a good question—one I can't answer. This is where the Holy Spirit provides discernment. Learning to tap into his guidance will lead you in the way you should go."

Chaplain Miller turned, reached for something on the shelf beside his desk, and set it down.

Debbie's eyes grew wide when she saw the familiar light green bottle and another one sitting next to it—the amber bottle with Josh's name on the label. She had to force her eyes from them to focus on what the chaplain was saying.

"The Lord cares deeply for both of you. Stand on the promise of Hebrews 13:5 that says, 'I will never leave you nor forsake you.'"

Josh and Debbie rose to leave, and just as they walked out of his office they heard, "Josh and Debbie, I sense your pain, and I care."

Once out in the hallway, Josh paused. "Have you found out why Chaplain Miller has those bottles with our names on them?"

Debbie rubbed her chin with her hand. "No, I haven't, and I'd really like to know."

CHAPTER 39

At three o'clock, Stacy headed home. She wanted to get back home in enough time to change her clothes and get her act together before Jack and Aubree arrived.

Stacy was glad Charles and Ruth had both insisted Jack come to their house. They planned to be home and available if Stacy felt she needed them. Stacy had grown to love Charles and Ruth and was grateful for them.

Stacy went straight to her room and changed from her uniform into a simple sundress. She stood in the mirror and turned to view her right side. Was her body beginning to show her baby's growth?

Lord, I dread this meeting. How am I going to keep from falling apart? Just seeing the two of them together is enough to crush me.

As she continued to scrutinize her reflection, a verse from Isaiah 40 came to mind. Stacy grabbed her Bible and looked it up. Isaiah 40:29 read, "He gives strength to the weary and increases the power of the weak."

Lord, it seems this verse was written just for me. I need strength and power. Help me to trust you will do as you promise.

Stacy made her way to the patio where she heard her hosts chatting.

"You look refreshed," Charles said.

"I hope so." Stacy took a deep breath to calm her nerves as she felt her stomach tighten. "I don't want to come across as a nervous wreck, even though that's exactly how I feel."

"We'll be praying for you the entire time Jack and Aubree are here," Ruth said. "I've freshened up the living room so you all can have some privacy, but please know, we'll be here the whole time."

"Go and get settled in the living room," Charles said with a calming tone. "I'll answer the door when they get here and bring them in." Stacy could sense and drew strength from the feeling of protection Charles had for her.

"Thank you, both. I don't know what I would have done without you."

She'd passed by the living room before but hadn't spent any time there as Ruth and Charles preferred to relax on the patio. She liked how the elaborate cream drapes hanging in the windows softened the room's décor and how the light drawn into the room from these windows gave it an airy feel. Stacy sat down on a wingback chair, biting her lip.

Before she was ready, the doorbell rang. Charles's steps could be heard as he went to answer the door. She could hear men's voices, and then Charles walked into the room with Jack. Her heart lurched. Stacy stood and put on what she hoped was a pleasant face.

"Hello, Stacy," Jack said as Charles left.

There was the man she'd fallen in love with almost a decade ago—the one she pledged to be with until death. She knew seeing Jack would be difficult, but Stacy hadn't anticipated such a rush of emotion.

Stacy looked over Jack's shoulder, dreading her encounter with Aubree. When she didn't see her old friend, she asked, "Where's Aubree?"

"She didn't come. We both decided it would be better for just the two of us to talk."

Stacy felt a wave of relief flooding over the emotions she'd just experienced. Perhaps God had truly heard her prayers. "Have a seat."

He sat on the sofa, moving stiffly as he got situated.

"How are you doing?" Jack asked, sounding unsure of how to begin their conversation.

"I'm doing well, Jack." Stacy felt surprised at the realization that she was, indeed, doing well. "I like my new job at Bethany and the people I work with."

"That's good." Jack glanced around the room, and Stacy noticed how rigid his body seemed, betraying how uncomfortable he felt.

Stacy realized how hard this must be for him too. She prayed God would help them both.

"I assume you've given some thought to the coming baby."

"I have," Jack said, clearing his throat. "Aubree and I both feel that we should have primary custody of the baby when the court-determined age is reached."

Stacy caught her breath as her assurance quickly fled and panic filled her. "Primary custody? What? You can't be serious."

"I am, and I've already consulted a lawyer. He's prepared to go to court if you fight me on this. You don't have your own home, and, I believe, you no longer have transportation. Just those two facts alone make it obvious I should have legal and physical custody after the baby is weaned. Clearly, this will be in the best interest of the child."

"That's absurd. I thought we should have joint custody." Stacy's words grew louder as her face grew hot. "Are you kidding me? You know being with me would be better for our baby, regardless of my current living and transportation status."

"Aubree and I both see your living situation as up-in-the-air, and even then, we just don't like the idea of bouncing the baby between two households, several hours apart."

His words stung. "First of all, Jack, I don't really see how what Aubree thinks should be factored in here. You and I are the parents, not her. Secondly, I plan to get my own place as soon as I can, as well as a car, so those things are irrelevant."

Jack stood, dismissing further conversation. "You need to understand, I'm prepared to fight for the custody of this child. And when I am awarded custody, I'll expect child support from you, as well."

Stacy jumped up, swaying on her feet. Her skin had turned clammy. *The mother is the primary caregiver. There's no way a judge would grant Jack custody of their baby. Would he?*

Not waiting for a reply, Jack stormed out of the room and back out the way he came in.

Stacy fell into the chair, her ears buzzing. *Oh God! I need you more than ever!*

CHAPTER 40

Stefan pulled a brush through his hair and gave his reflection an appraisal. He'd enjoyed his time with friends yesterday but hadn't slept well. Stefan's own thoughts were his judge and executioner. A part of him felt it wasn't right for him to enjoy something.

You forgot about Sophie and her suffering for several hours, and what about poor Allie Barker, who probably spent her afternoon and evening struggling to help Lauren with all her needs?

With a heavy heart he made his way to his appointment with Dr. Walker. He was surprised to see Chaplain Miller sitting with a softly crying Frank. Stefan hurried through the room, not wanting to infringe on their privacy, but he couldn't help but hear Chaplain Miller say, "God understands your pain and is deeply concerned for you."

That man always says God is a loving and caring God. Could God still be at work in his children's lives when people choose to do horrific things like Frank's wife did?

Stefan didn't know Chaplain Miller's complete view of God, but he knew the contempt he had felt for his creator since Sophie's death and his lost court case was now in question. Did God care about him after all? Deep inside, he truly hoped so.

⚱†⚱

Stefan sat in the courtyard after lunch, reflecting on his therapy session that morning. Dr. Walker had encouraged him to get into the habit of assessing the validity of each thought he had. The doctor said this exercise would be difficult at first, but if he committed to working on it, Stefan could rewrite his internal dialogue to reflect truth rather than his statements of judgment. He also explained to Stefan he should look for ways to have fun and feel happy—that this is what their loved ones would want them to do, and stating that many people who have experienced loss erroneously think this is betraying the memory of one they deeply loved. Stefan had not considered this.

As he continued to think, Stefan was interrupted by musical notes coming from his cell phone. He pulled it out of his pocket, not surprised to see his son, Mark, was still trying to reach him. Mark had been calling him on and off for several days, and Stefan had not answered. But hearing his ringtone this afternoon, the love he had for his son shoved out fear and conflict. He answered his phone.

"Hello."

"Hey, Dad. Where are you? I've tried to call you on numerous occasions, and you haven't answered. I happened to be in California on business, and thought I'd stop by to see you. Now my time to return is getting closer, and I'll have to fly home."

"Oh?" Stefan felt sweat break out on his forehead. He knew he would have to tell his sons where he was and why, but he was not prepared to answer Mark's question.

"When you didn't answer my calls, I went by your office and was shocked to see it was locked up, with no one there. I drove home and knocked, and then I finally let myself in. It doesn't even look like anyone lives there. What's going on, Dad? Are you all right?"

Stefan didn't reply at first, but sooner or later he would have to tell his kids what he'd attempted to do and where he was.

"I'm in Klauthmos Bay for a while," Stefan said.

"Wow! You haven't taken a vacation in years. What about your practice?"

"I needed to take some time off from work. Mrs. Warren needed some time off too."

"You know, Dad, you could have come to Virginia for a visit. What's in Klauthmos Bay? I don't remember either you or Mom ever saying you'd been there."

"It's complicated, Mark."

"I don't understand."

"I'm staying at a place called Bethany R&L."

"Oh, okay. I've got to finish up with some meetings this afternoon, but I'd love to join you for a bit. Are you going to be at the resort for a while? I can change my plane ticket and visit with you for a day or two. Colleen won't mind."

Stefan cleared his throat. "Bethany R&L isn't a resort, Mark."

For a few moments, only silence came through the other end of the phone. "What sort of place is it?"

"Bethany R&L is a behavioral healthcare facility." Stefan took a deep breath. There was no turning back now. "I'm here because I tried to take my own life." Stefan was ashamed to tell Mark this news, but he deserved the truth.

A moment of silence passed. "Oh, Dad … why didn't you call Robert and me? We would have gladly flown out to be with you and support you. I had no idea."

Stefan took a few moments to compose himself before answering.

"I wasn't ready to tell you. I didn't think you'd understand. I also was afraid you would not want to see me after I chose to isolate myself from you and your brother."

"Oh, Dad. Robert and I would never feel this way. I'll come up first thing in the morning and we'll spend some time together."

Stefan did not have the energy to say anything more.

"I'm sorry I haven't been there for you, Dad. I hope to change that, starting right now. I'll see you soon."

His son ended the call, and Stefan continued to sit in the courtyard for a while. He couldn't believe Mark felt he had not done enough for *him*. Could he and his brother forgive him for distancing himself and, ultimately, for attempting to take his own life?

A more important question was, did God forgive him from the same two things? For the first time in many months, Stefan hoped he did.

CHAPTER 41

Debbie hadn't anticipated how lonely she'd feel once Josh left. She pushed her lunch around the plate with a fork and stifled a sob. After they'd said their goodbyes last night, Debbie had gone to her room and fallen apart. She must have cried for a couple of hours.

She hadn't slept either, and her exhaustion and loneliness contributed to a rough start this morning. Unfortunately, she wasn't feeling any better as the day progressed.

Debbie took her dishes of partially eaten food over to the counter and wandered outside. Stacy stood in the courtyard, shuffling through some papers on her clipboard. When she looked up, Debbie noticed her red eyes and tear-stained cheeks.

"Stacy, are you okay?" Debbie asked.

The nurse swiped a cheek with the back of her hand. "I will be. How are you doing? I'm hoping you had a wonderful day with Josh."

"It was incredible, but ..." How much should Debbie tell her?

Stacy raised her eyebrows. "But what?"

"Today, I'm so out of sorts. I miss him so much, and the pain is unbearable."

Stacy reached out and lightly touched Debbie's shoulder. "I understand why you feel that way. I'm sure he misses you just as much." Stacy consulted her clipboard and then asked, "How was your session with Dr. Murphy this morning?"

"I'm not sure I would say it helped me take any steps forward. I mostly talked about my pain of being separated from Josh."

"I wouldn't consider that discussion as not being a positive step forward. Identifying our emotions helps us process them. You've been learning ways to process emotions so they have a healthy place in your life. This is good."

Debbie swallowed, giving herself time to think. "You're right."

Stacy lifted her clipboard again and scanned her notes. "I see you have an appointment with Chaplain Miller at two o'clock. Have you found his counseling helpful?"

"I have," Debbie answered. "He's helped me move in a positive direction spiritually, and his approach to our relationship with God brings healing with it."

"Yes, Chaplain Miller has a spiritual gift of discernment. I'll be checking in on you later. Have a good afternoon."

"You, too." Debbie hoped Stacy had someone checking in on her too.

⚰✝⚰

Debbie arrived at Chaplain Miller's office right at two o'clock but was surprised to see Chaplain Miller wasn't there. As she was about to turn and double-check the schedule on his door, she spotted a wooden crate on the floor by his desk. She could make out the tops of glass bottles. Looking over her shoulder to ensure no one was around, she moved closer.

The box held twenty bottles or more. Debbie spotted a light green bottle about two thirds full of liquid with her name on the label. Right next to it was Josh's amber-colored bottle.

Debbie backed away from the crate and went out into the hallway.

I really need to find out why Chaplain Miller has these bottles.

Her thoughts were interrupted by Chaplain Miller's approach. "I'm sorry I'm running a little late, Debbie. Another patient had an emergency, and I was needed there. Come on in," he said, stepping to the side of the door to allow her to enter first. "How was your day with your husband?" Chaplain Miller smiled as he sat behind his desk.

Debbie focused her eyes on Chaplain Miller. She didn't want them to stray to the wooden crate, suggesting she'd already been in the room.

"Wonderful! We had such a good day."

"I'm thrilled to hear it. Experience has taught me, however, that today probably hasn't gone as well for you. Am I correct?"

Debbie nodded, tearing up. "Yes, it hurt so bad to say goodbye last night, and I didn't sleep very well either."

"I can understand that. There's a reason why you feel this separation sharply. God has put the two of you together, and now, you are one. Separation pulls against that bond, and naturally, it hurts."

"It certainly does." She tried her best to keep her chin from trembling.

"Besides the feelings of longing you have for Josh, do you have any other feelings you can identify?"

Debbie thought for a moment, and then pursed her lips together. Chaplain Miller waited silently, allowing her to find the words she needed to answer his question.

"Honestly, I'd have to say I'm angry today—even more so than I was when I was 'required' to come here."

"Why do you think that is, Debbie? Do you feel you haven't gained anything worthwhile from your stay at Bethany?"

"No, it's not that." Debbie reflected. "I think it's the way they made it come about. I feel Pastor Hughes and Mr. Jennings are wrong in attributing total church attendance as being a command of God's word. I think so many Christians take it into their heads they know exactly what other people need to do, rather than focusing on themselves."

Chaplain Miller nodded. "It's often easier to see the weaknesses in others before we see our own. I think what's really causing you some anger is that you *expect* followers of God to be different than they are."

"Is it wrong to expect those in leadership of Christian ministries to be committed to following God's word?"

"Can a person be committed to following God's Word and do and say things that are in opposition to the Word?" Chaplain Miller asked.

"Yes, but shouldn't they know better than to treat other followers of God the way they've treated Josh and me?"

"Debbie," Chaplain Miller said softly, "haven't you treated other followers of God poorly? Have you always acted in a godly manner toward them?"

Debbie hung her head. Chaplain Miller was right. She had acted in a similar manner to those she'd accused of the very same thing a few minutes ago.

"Something else to consider, Debbie. Have you had some expectations in your mind of how God should have acted in your situation? Remember when we were discussing your strengths and potential vulnerabilities?"

"Yes."

"One of yours is loyalty. You feel a deep sense of allegiance to those you're close to. Could it be you're actually accusing God of not being loyal to you?"

Chaplain Miller turned, reached into the wooden crate by his desk and pulled out the light green bottle that had

Debbie's name on the label. "God cares deeply about you and all his children. Sometimes, when life gets very difficult, it's easy for us to conclude God isn't concerned with our lives and our struggles. I use bottles like this one with your name on it to remind us of the verse in Psalm 57:8 that tells us God is so concerned for us, he even collects our tears in a bottle."

Debbie let his words sink in.

"Rejoice, Debbie. God not only is aware of your pain, he collects your tears, showing how much he values us and the events that happen in this life."

CHAPTER 42

The next morning, Stefan continued to mull over the conversation he'd had with Mark. He missed his son terribly, but found he was nervous about seeing him. On his way through the lobby, Jerry waved with an envelope in his hand.

"Hey, Stefan. I noticed when I was picking up a letter over here in the mail cubicle that you have one too."

Stefan stopped short and blinked several times.

Seeing his confusion, Jerry urged him to come and see what he had. "I'm sure you must have been told mail is delivered here and sorted according to room numbers."

Stefan nodded, remembering how he'd been shown where mail could be picked up. He assumed he would not receive any mail. He looked in slot 2023 and sure enough, there was a letter—forwarded from his law office. There was no return address.

"Thanks for pointing this out, Jerry." Without further conversation, Stefan headed to his room.

Once inside, Stefan sat on the bed and read the letter.

Dear Mr. Krause,

I wanted to write and thank you for all you did for Lauren and me. I know we were both shocked at how the trial turned out, but I know you did your best for us. I don't hold you responsible for the outcome in any way.

You went over and above the line of duty for me and Lauren, and I will never forget that. Please don't worry about us, we'll get by. Lauren is actually improving and may, indeed, walk again one day.

I'm forever grateful for all you did for us.

Sincerely,

Allie Barker (and Lauren)

Stefan folded the letter and put it back in the envelope, his hands shaking.

She isn't blaming me for what happened at the trial. How can that be?

Stefan wept again out of guilt, forgiveness, and the possibility of hope. Then he looked at the letter again.

Lauren is doing better?

He turned toward the cafeteria but decided food didn't appeal to him right now. He felt such relief over Allie and Lauren but was also nervous about Mark's arrival. He also needed to go by the nurses' station and change his therapy session with Dr. Murphy.

After taking care of his appointment, Stefan headed back to his room to prepare for seeing his son, thinking it might be nice if the two of them went to Lakewood Park. Would Mark recognize the sound of the swings in motion as he had? For some reason, this seemed important to Stefan.

With one last glance in the mirror, Stefan made his way over to the main lobby to wait for Mark. He took a seat at a distance from a group of people who had already gathered there.

He surveyed the room as he waited, his mind going back to when he first arrived in Klauthmos Bay. The feelings of anxiety and desperation washed over him again.

What am I going to say to Mark? Seeing the disappointment in his eyes is going to kill me. Lord, if you really do care about me, I need your help now.

Twenty minutes went by before Mark entered the room through the front doors. Stefan's heart jumped as he recognized so many of Sophie's features in his son's face. Father and son embraced, reestablishing their bond. They sat side by side on the sofa, ignoring the tears that came to both of them.

"Dad, I don't know what to say. If I'd known, I would have been there. I'm sorry I've let you down." Mark hung his head and cried.

Stefan put his arm around his son's heaving shoulders, sharing his son's hurt and grief. "Mark, this isn't your fault. I've had a really difficult time dealing with your mother's death. I'm sorry I overlooked both Robert's and your grief and that I shut you both out of my life."

They sat for a moment, before he realized how public a place the lobby was.

Stefan stood. "Why don't we take a walk? There's a park a few blocks away that has several benches, and we can have some privacy there."

Mark stood and wiped his face with a handkerchief Stefan handed him.

As they started down the road, Stefan turned the conversation away from himself for the time being. "How is Colleen doing?"

"She's fine. She's busy working with several clients, writing up copy for whatever their needs are."

"That's good. And you? How is your accounting business doing?"

"Very well. That's why I'm out here on the west coast. I was attending the American Accounting Association's annual conference meeting."

Stefan nodded, remembering other occasions that both of his sons had attended conferences such as this one.

As the two passed Chaplain Miller's house, Mark gasped.

"What in the world is up with the person who owns that house? Look at all the bottles in the windows. I've never seen anything like that!"

Stefan nodded. "That home belongs to Chaplain Miller. He works at Bethany. He's a kind and knowledgeable man. When I've asked about the purpose of his collection, he has only shared they represent that God keeps his promises and that their liquid is as valuable as gold to him."

"Surely there is more to this collection than that."

"I agree. I hope to find out more about them because the chaplain never does anything in his work with God's people that doesn't have a spiritual and often practical purpose."

They crossed the street and approached the bench where Stefan liked to sit, near the playground swings.

Stefan grinned, hearing the sound of boys' voices, clearly competing with one another. He dropped down on his favorite spot. "Do you remember your mother and I taking you and Robert to the park when you were young? You two competed on the swings just like those boys are now."

Mark grinned. "I do. It was hard to swing higher than Robert—his legs were longer than mine."

They both sat for a moment, listening to the boys playing.

"Dad, can you tell me what's going on with you?" Mark asked gently.

Stefan was dreading this conversation, but it was best to get it over with.

"As you know, watching your mother suffer through her battle with cancer was heart-wrenching. I saw a strong woman get weaker and weaker. Her body just disintegrated, and I couldn't do anything to help her. On top of that, the very God your mother and I had dedicated our lives to didn't help."

Mark put his arm around his dad's shoulders. "You know Mom would be horrified to hear you say those words about God. You can't mean them."

After a few minutes, Stefan took a deep breath. He needed to be honest with his son, even if the truth hurt.

"Yes, Mark, I did. I think this is why I isolated myself from you two boys. I prayed your mother would be healed, or at least, not suffer as much as she was, but God remained silent. I begged him to give me the disease and pain, but that request was ignored too. If God chose not to help, I had to do everything I could for your mother, and I completely failed at that. On top of everything, both you and Robert still held onto your faith like your mother did. I couldn't, and I was ashamed and, honestly, angry, so I withdrew from both of you."

"Dad, you didn't fail Mom." Mark swallowed. "You were the best husband and support to her. She would never think you had let her down. As far as Robert and I are concerned, we would be able to understand this crisis of faith you were having. We would never have turned our backs on you."

"I just couldn't take away her pain, and I felt so helpless." Swallowing the lump in his throat, Stefan searched within for courage to continue. "The months that followed her passing were a type of death for me until a personal injury case involving a young mother and daughter came my way.

"This woman's daughter was seriously injured in a car accident that could have been avoided. There had been negligence on the car dealership's part. I determined that even though I couldn't help your mother, I could help this woman and her child. I believed their case would be the key that would help me cope with your mother's death."

"What happened?"

"I fought the car manufacturer and its dealership with everything I had. To make a long story short, I lost the case on a technicality. I should have known better. The guilt and grief of losing this case just became too heavy. To my dying day, I'll never forget the hopelessness I saw on my client's face when the verdict was given."

Stefan hung his head.

"I sank into a dark hole. I prayed for help ... I prayed for a miracle. I prayed out of desperation, but I heard no reply. I became so distraught that one day, I walked out on the beach and into the water, trying to end my guilt and pain. All I remember is the water washing over my head."

"Oh, Dad, I didn't know." Mark pulled him closer.

"None of that was your fault. I was in such a dark place that ending my life seemed like a better option. Obviously, I wasn't successful. I woke up in the hospital and was told a young man had saved me from the waters. There I met Chaplain Thomas. He recommended I come to Bethany for a while, so I did."

"Dad, I'm so sorry I let you down. I should have made more of an effort to call regularly and to come out to see you. I guess I was hurting so bad that the thought of talking to you made all those feelings surface."

"I understand, son."

"But God's not at fault for not healing Mom or for you losing your court case. You know as long as we live in this world, bad things will come our way. These things hurt deeply but the astonishing thing is God can use these circumstances to produce good. I think this is happening now with you and in our relationship. This is very good!"

"I think I'm just beginning to understand this. Now that I think of it, God did bring me here to get help, and I'm learning things about him I may never have known otherwise, and you're here too." Stefan hung his head in humility.

The two sat for a while longer, eventually sharing memories of a wife and mother who left this world too soon. Stefan enjoyed talking about Sophie, because it made her feel closer to him.

"Let's go and get something to eat, Dad. Are you allowed to leave the area?"

"Of course, I can," Stefan said a little too forcefully. Realizing his mistake, he added softly, "I can come and go as I please, so yes, let's go get something to eat."

The two men got up and made their way back to Mark's rental car. Just as they entered the Bethany R&L parking lot, they met Chaplain Miller.

"Hello, Stefan. How are you, my friend?" Chaplain Miller said, extending his hand and smiling.

Stefan shook hands. "Chaplain Miller, this is my youngest son, Mark."

"Nice to meet you, Mark. Your father has told me about you. He's so proud of you."

Smiling, Mark shook Chaplain Miller's hand. "Good to meet you too."

"We're spending the day together," Stefan boasted.

"That's wonderful!" Chaplain Miller said. "I won't keep you from your visit. I'll catch up with you later, Stefan." Chaplain Miller continued walking toward the cafeteria.

"That chaplain seems like a genuine person."

"Yes, he is," Stefan agreed warmly.

CHAPTER 43

Stacy didn't know how she'd made it through these last few days without breaking down. She'd come close but staying busy had helped.

As Stacy sat in her room, she thought back to the conversation she had with the Lewises after Jack left the other day. They both stated Jack's rationale for having full custody was ridiculous. Stacy smiled a bit as she remembered Charles' words.

"Stacy, don't worry. We have several attorneys in our church, and we'll put you in contact with one of them, so you'll have help with drawing up a plan for when the baby arrives."

Even though she was tired, she needed some fresh air and decided to go out for a stroll.

She stepped out on the road, thinking she'd go to the beach, but then changed her mind. Picturing the benches at Lakewood Park convinced her to head in that direction.

As she walked, she played through the scene with Jack again and again. She'd experienced a series of so many emotions. She felt shock, anger, worry, and determination, and then she'd cycle through them again. Her reflections now turned to prayers.

Lord, I need your help. I'm scared to death Jack and Aubree will wind up with my baby. Please hear me and send help. I'm desperate.

At that moment, Stacy reached Chaplain Miller's Bottle House. She gazed at all the beautiful bottles and remembered what the chaplain had said. These bottles were, in part, a symbol of the fact that God does care about his children. The thought comforted Stacy.

"Stacy, hello!" Chaplain Miller called as he stepped out his front door. "It's such a pleasant evening. I thought I'd sit out on the patio. Would you care to join me?"

"Sure," Stacy said as she stepped over to the seat where she'd rested that first day she arrived in Klauthmos Bay.

The two sat down, and Stacy sighed.

Chaplain Miller leaned in. "From the look of stress on your face, can I assume your meeting with Jack and Aubree didn't turn out well?"

Stacy's gaze moved to the window of the house adjacent to the patio. The bottles displayed there reflected the setting sun. "No, it didn't, but one good thing happened. Aubree didn't come with him."

Chaplain Miller nodded. "Did you two make a tentative plan for when the baby comes?"

"*We* didn't make a plan. Jack was only interested in telling me what *his* plans were for the baby. He said he's going to fight for full custody when the baby is born." Stacy's voice quivered as tears gathered once again. "What a mess!"

Chaplain Miller didn't say anything for a moment, but then stood and picked up a stray feather from the ground. He sat back down, examining and twirling it briefly.

"Stacy, I'm holding one of God's promises right here. Do you know what kind of feather this is?"

"No, I don't know much about birds at all."

"This is a feather from a sparrow—the most common bird in the world. They're everywhere, nesting in top windows of our cities' tallest skyscrapers, and they have even been found in some underground caves, probably flying in by mistake."

Stacy stared at the feather while listening.

"Because these birds are so common, people have a tendency to not value them—you know, the economics of supply and demand. In light of that, I think it's interesting Jesus himself speaks about them. In Matthew 10:29, he says God is aware of each sparrow that may fall to the ground." Chaplain Miller paused and studied the feather again, then placed it on the patio table. "Jesus says next that God even knows the number of hairs on our heads and even though he cares about sparrows, he values people all the more."

She reached over and picked up the feather, running her finger gently along the soft edge.

"Stacy, God values you and your child more than you will ever know. Cry out to him, and tell him your hurts, fears, and worries. He longs to help you in your difficulties."

She nodded. "I know in my head those things are true, but when it comes to my everyday life, it's much more difficult."

Stacy twirled the sparrow's feather. She'd keep this feather as a reminder that God did, indeed, care about her.

She longed to have a relationship with God like the Lewises and Chaplain Miller had. Their faith made it seem so easy, but Stacy knew everyone faced challenges. She just felt she wrestled more than she needed to.

Lord, I want to trust that you care about me—that you feel my struggles and fears. Please, could you help my faith? I want to lay this burden of heartache down, and I'm not sure how. Help me!

CHAPTER 44

For the first time, Stefan didn't mind the idea of meeting with Chaplain Miller. His conversation with his son not only encouraged him but also shed some light on the fact that he may have jumped toward too many wrong conclusions concerning God and his relationship with him.

He walked into the chaplain's office just as the older man was putting something into a wooden crate.

"Hello, Stefan. Have a seat."

Chaplain Miller finished what he was doing, placed the crate on the floor beside his desk, then settled into his chair. "Coffee?"

"No, thanks." Stefan was surprised when Chaplain Miller didn't go over and pour himself some.

"Your son, Mark, seemed like a fine young man. Does he favor you or Sophie more?"

"Fortunately, he looks more like Sophie." The two men chuckled.

"How was your visit?"

"It was a difficult one." Stefan noticed the edge to his voice. "I hadn't told my boys anything about the circumstances that brought me here."

"Oh? Why is that?"

"I didn't want them to see me in the state I've been in. I've been ashamed of my behavior, and I'm sure it would have shamed Sophie too."

"Why do you think your grief and difficulties are things to be ashamed of?"

"I had the idea that because I'm their father, I'm supposed to be strong and not the man I now find myself to be."

"You speak in past tense. Did something happen to change your opinion?"

"Yes, a little."

"Tell me more."

"As a father, I thought I should be someone who makes good decisions, works hard for a living, and when the difficult things in life come, make a plan and carry it out."

"These are good things."

"Yes, but since Sophie's death, I didn't realize how angry I was at God, and it was this very thing that encouraged me to isolate myself from my boys." Stefan's voice quivered.

The chaplain nodded and waited for Stefan to continue.

"This anger and isolation has been eating me alive. I didn't realize how much of a danger this thinking and feeling was. I never wanted to cause more hurt for my boys, and I think this was God's way of also alerting me that I was hurting myself too."

Chaplain Miller cleared his throat, then leaned forward. "It sounds like you have realized that people cannot always be strong, always make the right choices, and always be successful. This is part of living in a fallen world—one turned upside down by Adam and Eve in the Garden of Eden, and we have followed in their footsteps. Paul said correctly in Romans that we've all sinned and fallen short of the glory of God."

"I think I'm beginning to understand this a little." Stefan fidgeted as a moment of silence passed. "What I don't understand is did God allow us to be flawed by giving the opportunity to do wrong to Adam and Eve?"

"Yes, and no," Chaplain Miller said. "He created man for his glory, and part of that glory is man can choose to follow him. Adam and Eve had a choice, and so do we. Unfortunately, we often make the wrong choices, and then we have to live with those consequences."

"I know a man who yearns for faith in God shouldn't ask this but why would God want to create a world he knew was going to turn out like this?"

"Stefan, that's a good question ... one people have asked throughout history. What I wonder, though, is if this is really the question people are asking God, or is there, perhaps, something else?"

Stefan said nothing as he contemplated the question.

"I think what they really want to know is whether or not God is truly good. And if he is, does he care about the things we care about?"

"Yes! I'll admit it." Stefan sat up straight. "Even though I have a slightly different view now on the importance of admitting when we struggle, I still don't understand how God can just sit there in heaven and watch horrible things happen to those he says he loves."

"I appreciate your honesty." Chaplain Miller smiled. "You're asking some good questions. This means you're not settling for the easy Sunday school answers that some do. I want to challenge you to give this some consideration now that you have begun to understand some important things."

Stefan looked at the clock. Time for him to go.

He stood and walked toward the office door. He turned back to thank the chaplain but he was busy, bending over and picking up the crate he had been working with when Stefan entered. The chaplain placed it on his desk. He picked out two bottles and set them down, side by side.

The sky-blue bottle had Stefan's name on the label, and the one on the teal bottle read "Mark."

"You have a bottle with Mark's name on it too. I don't clearly understand their purpose."

"You will understand more in time, but it's important you know the promise of God and his concern for his children also includes Mark."

Stefan left Chaplain Miller's office thinking about the beautiful bottles.

CHAPTER 45

Debbie awoke with the same feelings she'd battled the previous days. As she moved about her room, a cloud of resentment and pain followed her. She arrived at the cafeteria for breakfast, hoping she wouldn't need to interact with anyone.

Returning to her room, Debbie forcefully kicked off her shoes and sat down hard on the edge of the bed. She stared out the window while anger and fear spilled from her eyes.

It's not right that I should be here when I belong at Josh's side. The pain of rejection and misjudgment is deep.

Debbie pictured the meeting with the members of the school board the night that her world turned upside down and her heart began to race. She got up and paced the room, playing out the scene in her mind over and over again.

Finally, Debbie's thoughts and body began to slow down. She decided to take a chance that Patricia would be home, hoping to gain some guidance concerning her thoughts and feelings.

As soon as Debbie was outside, she began to relax a little. She moved down the pathway leading to Cayce Road. As she approached Patricia's house, relief filled Debbie at seeing the older woman working on a flower bed.

"Good morning, Patricia."

The older woman sat back on her heels, wiped her forehead with her gloved hand, turned her head, and smiled. "Such a nice day the Lord has given us. It's so good to see you, Debbie."

Patricia's eyes held such care, Debbie's pain came back to the surface and bubbled over. Tears pooled in her eyes, and she stumbled.

Patricia removed her gloves and set them down next to the bed she was working on. She stood and met Debbie on the front walk. Putting her arm around the younger woman, Patricia guided her to the porch swing.

Patricia spoke soft, comforting words and allowed Debbie to cry. She grabbed some tissues from a box on the nearby table and handed them over.

Dabbing her eyes, Debbie began to pull herself together. "I'm sorry, Patricia. I didn't mean to fall apart. It's just, I'm not having a very good day."

"Is it because you so enjoyed your time with Josh and now you're lonesome for him?"

Debbie nodded. "I knew saying goodbye would be hard, but I didn't expect it to be *this* hard."

Patricia patted Debbie's hand.

She squeezed the wad of tissues. "It hurts so bad to be separated from my husband, but I'm also struggling to forgive those who instigated my stay at Bethany." Debbie's voice trembled. "God must be so unhappy with me right now."

"Why would you say that?"

"As Christians, we're supposed to forgive, and I thought I'd forgiven those men, but now I'm not so sure."

Patricia shifted herself on the swing and faced Debbie. "What do you think forgiveness is?"

Debbie looked off in the distance. "I think it means I give up the right to revenge and no longer hold their actions toward me over their heads."

The older woman nodded. "That's not a bad definition, but now I'm going to ask you a very important question. Is this *giving up* a one-time act?"

Debbie's mouth fell open, but she quickly closed it and studied the floor.

"Let me see if I can help you with it. Do you remember that I told you my husband, Henry, and I have a son?" Patricia gazed out over her garden. "We were thrilled when we found out Wesley was on the way. We fixed up a nursery and did all the things new parents typically did. Wesley grew up in this house, and though we tried to encourage him to choose his friends wisely, our son got in with the wrong crowd."

A wave of dread washed through Debbie's body as Patricia used her foot to push off the porch floor, setting the swing into a gentle motion.

"About six months after Wesley had committed several small legal infractions, we got a call in the middle of the night." Patricia swallowed. "There is nothing more alarming than a call at that time. It was the police. Wesley had been arrested for armed robbery."

The two women sat silently on the slowly moving swing, allowing Debbie a minute to think.

"Henry and I had to go through the painful process of getting a lawyer for Wesley, going to court, and worrying about how this would affect his future. These facts alone were difficult to handle, but something else happened that hurt just as much—that was the attitude of some members of our church when they heard this news."

Debbie grimaced. "Oh no."

Patricia shook her head. "I want to say clearly many in our church were supportive and helpful, but the few who weren't said and did things that hurt us badly."

The older woman stretched out her arms as though she might be working out the kinks from gardening that morning. She then let her hands fall on her lap. "Henry and I had a very difficult time dealing with the things individuals said and did until we realized we needed to forgive both the people who said such hurtful things *and* our son."

Debbie shifted a bit on the swing. "How in the world were you able to forgive in those circumstances?"

"This is where I learned an important lesson about forgiveness, Debbie. I found forgiveness is not a one-time act. Forgiveness is something you have to do over and over and over again."

Debbie frowned.

"What I'm hoping you can pick up from this conversation is you're not a disobedient Christian because you have to choose to forgive someone repeatedly. Though we are the temple of the Holy Spirit, we still have Adam's sinful nature, and we must renew the grace of forgiveness, perhaps many times, to those who have harmed us. That's the essence of forgiveness."

Debbie leaned back, closed her eyes, and took a deep breath as the swing continued its slow rhythm.

"Where is Wesley now, if you don't mind my asking?"

Patricia sighed. "When he got out of prison, he came home looking for a fight. He thought Henry and I should have bailed him out of jail that last time, and he made his feelings clear in no uncertain terms. Because we'd refused to help and enable him in that instance, he made the decision to never let us back into his life. Henry never got to see his son again."

CHAPTER 46

Stefan frowned as he left Dr. Walker's office. The doctor had given Stefan some exercises that, if practiced, would allow him to gain a small gap of time between cause and effect so he could act in, rather than react to, situations that came his way. He shook his head, not totally understanding.

In the courtyard, Stefan paused and took his phone out of his pocket to see the time. Doing so, he noticed he had a voice mail message from his oldest son, Robert. Though Stefan had some time before his two o'clock appointment with Chaplain Miller, he decided to listen to it later. He knew his son was at work right now, and he needed to give his last meeting with the chaplain a little more thought. He would definitely get in touch with Robert later in the day.

A short time later, Stefan stood outside Chaplain Miller's office. Though he had a lot of respect for the man, Stefan wasn't completely sure where his own relationship with God was and, at this point, wasn't sure where he and God stood. There was a part of him who would be glad to get back home and back to normal life. Yet ... what was normal life? He took a deep breath and stepped in.

Chaplain Miller immediately looked up from what he was doing and stood. "Hello, Stefan. I'm glad to see you."

Stefan knew that people said this, but often they weren't really glad to see anyone. He had even said these words to others, too, but Stefan was convinced this man, Chaplain Miller, truly was glad to see the people he ministered to.

After offering the chair opposite him, Chaplain Miller picked up some papers from his desk and scanned the first page. "I notice on your schedule you had an appointment with Dr. Walker earlier this morning. How are those sessions going for you?"

Stefan crossed his arms. "I guess they're going all right, but they seem to open a door within to some things that make me feel uncomfortable."

"Is being uncomfortable a bad thing?"

He thought for a moment. "I'm not sure if I can answer that."

"Comfort is a word that's used a lot these days." Chaplain Miller laid the papers back down on his desk. "We have comfort foods, beds designed to be more comfortable, spas to help us unwind, soothing music, and even meditations designed to soothe us."

Stefan shifted in his chair. "For the past two years, comfort has eluded me. I don't think there's been a day when I haven't cried out to God for it, but it's seemed that nothing changed. I wouldn't say comfort has become my norm."

Chaplain Miller did not appear to be disturbed by Stefan's statement. "Let me ask you another question. What does comfort mean to you?"

A minute went by while Stefan considered this. "I don't know. I guess what I mean is the pain I'm experiencing disappears."

"You're not alone in thinking that's a good definition." Chaplain Miller turned and reached for what looked like a reference book of some kind. He placed it on his desk, opened it, and thumbed through the pages.

Stefan strained to see but the print was too small.

"Ah, here it is." Chaplain Miller's finger paused on the text. "Among several Greek words the New Testament uses for comfort, two are *parakaleo* and *paraklesis*. They are legal terms."

The part of Stefan that belonged to his vocation sat up and took notice.

"These words communicate a summons a person gives to another requiring him or her to stand by in a supporting role. Knowing that Paul tells us in 2 Corinthians 1:3–4 that God is the 'God of all comfort,' the implication is God has a legal obligation to comfort. But what is this comfort to which God is obligated?"

Frowning, Stefan thought he knew the answer to the chaplain's question and didn't like it. Instead, he said, "What kind of God would repeatedly ignore the cries of his children? How is that the God of comfort?"

"Stefan, the difficult news is when God promises comfort, it doesn't mean he uses an emotional eraser within us, and our difficulties are gone. That is not a reality in this life. The good news is he *does* promise he will stand beside us and go through the process of pain with us." Chaplain Miller shook his head. "What I have a hard time understanding is why God thinks I am so valuable that he's willing to stand with me through my pain."

Taking a reflective breath, the chaplain continued. "In all the universe, among the billions of people on this earth, considering all the pain that exists in this life, God has chosen to be with me, beside me ... always. In the joys and pain, *Emmanuel*, 'God with us,' is right by my side. That alone brings me comfort."

Stefan thought then of Sophie. Hadn't she said the same thing?

"Let me say one more thing, Stefan, and I'd like you to give this some thought." Chaplain Miller wrote something on a scrap of paper and folded it. "Initially comfort doesn't start with a feeling, it's a knowing. I feel comfort because I *know* God is beside me, fully understanding my pain."

Stefan slowly stood, thinking of what the chaplain had just said. As he turned to leave, Chaplain Miller handed him the folded piece of paper. He did not look at it until he was in the courtyard. Once there, he opened the note and saw six words. *God sees your deep hurt and cares.*

Stefan sat down hard on a chair, feeling drained.

⚰✝⚰

The voice message Robert had left mostly stated his concern for his father, and Stefan felt grateful his son seemed to hold no judgment. He would give Robert a call this evening.

Stefan decided to rest a little before dinner, so he walked into the lounge of the Sozo building. He wasn't prepared for what he saw.

Frank sat on the sofa as if pinned there by some unseen force—head tilted back, arms splayed, eyes firmly shut. A moan of pain came from deep within his friend.

Stefan's hands became clammy and his blood pressure soared. *What should I do?* Without even thinking he prayed, *God, please show me what to do. Frank desperately needs help, and I don't know what to do.*

He remembered there was a list of emergency contact numbers in the kitchen by the phone. His shaking finger ran down the list, then he picked up the phone and called the number listed next to Frank's name. His voice sounded a lot higher than normal. "Frank Snider is in a crisis. He needs help right now. He's in the lounge of the Sozo building."

While Stefan waited for help to arrive, he decided to sit with Frank—the only support he could think of. *Why aren't you showing me what to do, Lord? You say you are a "A very present help in the time of trouble." Don't you care?*

He sat silently, surprised he seemed to absorb some of his friend's pain. Frank didn't seem to notice his arrival. Though Stefan knew despair, his friend's pain seemed to reach to the depths of hell. Tears flowed down Stefan's face as he considered this.

It wasn't long before Frank's doctor arrived and helped him get up and leave.

Stefan stood and left the building too, knowing he wouldn't be able to rest as he had planned. He found himself headed for Klauthmos Beach.

Once there, Stefan didn't bother to remove his shoes and socks. He marched to the edge of the tide. He felt as if his soul had been cut wide open, and he might bleed to death. Frank's moans of agony played repeatedly in his thoughts.

Exhausted, Stefan fell to his knees. Without realizing, he threw his head back, closed his eyes, and spread his arms apart. A moan similar to Frank's burst out of his being.

If God cares about my misery, where is my comfort?

In a voice not more than a whisper, Stefan heard, "Just as you sat by Frank's side, I'm sitting by yours."

"How do I know that, God? Give me something tangible that will help me believe you."

No answer came.

CHAPTER 47

Stacy hung up the damp kitchen towel she'd been using to clean up the supper dishes and went out to the patio. Ruth sat bent over her needlepoint, and Charles was reading the evening paper. Stacy rubbed her shoulder, trying to work out some of the kinks. *I would give anything to have a marriage like they have.*

"Stacy, come join us." Ruth patted the seat beside her.

Stacy sat down, sighing softly. She had not noticed how sore her feet were until this moment.

Ruth set her handiwork in her lap. "When you got home today, you looked like you had a lot on your mind. Care to share it?"

"I was so tired after today's shift I was looking forward to an easy stroll home, but then I noticed I had a phone message from Jack."

Charles lowered the top corner of the paper and raised an eyebrow. "I hope he's come around to being more sensible concerning the child."

"He wanted to let me know he's hired the attorney he had originally consulted to help him in the custody battle over the baby." Stacy let out a long breath and laid her hand protectively on her belly. "He said I would save a lot of money and time if I would just go ahead and agree to his terms of taking full custody. What am I going to do?"

Charles folded his paper and placed it on the coffee table. "We didn't want to bring this up at supper because we wanted you to relax a little after work, but I've been in touch with Philip Jackson, a member of our church. He's an attorney who specializes in child custody cases. I don't know who Jack has placed on retainer, but I doubt he has the credentials Philip has."

Stacy sat up straight, her heart pounding. "Do you think I can afford an attorney of his caliber?"

Ruth smiled. "Charles and I already discussed this, and we want to finance the fees you'll incur."

Stacy's throat tightened. "You both have already done so much for me, but this will likely be a huge expense."

"You let us worry about that, Stacy." Charles smiled.

As Stacy sat taking this all in, Psalm 23:5 came to mind.

Lord, it appears that you truly are "preparing my table" before Jack and Aubree. I am truly grateful that you keep your promises even though my faith is sometimes weak.

What will Jack think when he realizes I have an attorney already and one with the experience Mr. Jackson apparently has?

⛎✝⛎

The next morning's rounds with the patients on Stacy's caseload were a mix of encouragement and concern. Because of her own suffering, she longed to support each one, knowing how vital that was in life. Stacy knew she was blessed God had led her to Bethany. Working with Chaplain Miller and living with the Lewises were beyond what she'd hoped her new life would bring her. In spite of this gratitude, however, Stacy still battled feelings of loneliness and abandonment.

Verse six of Psalm 23 came to Stacy's mind. *Surely goodness and mercy shall follow me all the days of my life and I will dwell in the house of the Lord forever.*

Stacy shook her head, so grateful God wanted her with him forever. It filled her heart with hope.

THE BOTTLE HOUSE

By late afternoon, the day had grown warm, and Stacy began to slow. *I do need to take a break from time to time.* She stepped out of the building and found a seat on a stone bench near the main entrance of Bethany R&L.

Her shoulders slumped and she longed to put her feet up. She focused on her ankles, thinking they surely must be swelling.

Stacy felt the cool stone beneath her and closed her eyes, concentrating on her breathing. Dr. Davis had suggested some specific exercises to try whenever she could. She needed to keep practicing them because Stacy had found they helped calm her.

Hearing the breeze through the surrounding trees, part of Psalm 23:5 came to mind. *Thou preparest a table before me in the presence of mine enemies.*

Stacy had already reflected on the fact that Jack and Aubree were enemies, in this sense. It was a good reminder, though, that God had control over the situation and would honor her in spite of them.

This new realization gave Stacy some hope. Yes, her ex was making this unexpected pregnancy more difficult and, she thought, might do so for many years to come as their child grew up. In spite of this, Stacy smiled. She realized she was not alone and that God freely offered his help.

Stacy's breathing calmed.

Looking back up, she smiled when she saw Chaplain Miller coming her way with two bottles of water.

"I saw you from the cafeteria window and thought you could use some cold water." The chaplain handed Stacy one of the bottles.

Stacy opened it and took a long drink. She could feel the cold liquid moving through her body into her stomach. "Thank you."

"You're welcome. Do you mind if I join you for a minute?"

She smiled. "Please do."

The chaplain pulled out a heavy chair and sat down. He opened his bottle and took a drink, then focused on Stacy. Though she couldn't be sure, she thought she read concern in his face.

"How are you doing, especially physically?"

A sigh escaped from her. "I have to admit I get tired this time of day and hope this isn't a pattern for my entire pregnancy."

"Let me see if I can help obliviate some of your worries. Mrs. Turner deeply cares about each nurse on her staff. If you find this exhaustion becomes a regular part of the next several months, go and talk with her. She'll work with you in creating a schedule that functions well for both you and your patients."

Stacy swallowed and attempted to rein in her emotions. "It's so humbling that you, the Lewises, and Mrs. Turner are so gracious and willing to help in so many ways." Stacy looked down. "Though I feel that I don't deserve all this support, I am grateful."

"It's not about anyone deserving any good gift from God. That's what grace is all about, Stacy. I wonder, though ... do your worries stem from Jack's aggressive actions concerning the custody of your unborn child?"

"That's part of the problem, Chaplain Miller. The Lewises have placed a lawyer—Philip Jackson—on retainer on my behalf, but my doubt makes me feel I'm ungrateful for God's provisions."

Leaning toward Stacy, Chaplain Miller nodded his head. "Well, just so you know, Philip Jackson is one of the best and most experienced family law attorneys around. Be assured, your situation is in good hands."

Stacy felt ashamed, and her voice became softer. "God must be so disappointed in me. I have doubted on and off that he has my best interests at heart, and sometimes I've even wondered if he truly cares about the pain and hurt in my life."

"God understands our pain and weaknesses, Stacy. He loves you and your unborn child deeply, in spite of what your circumstances look like." The chaplain took another drink. "Your thoughts are shared by many other people, and I'll be discussing this topic at a very special chapel service Sunday morning. I think it would help you in your struggles. I hope you'll consider coming."

"I'll see you then."

After Chaplain Miller walked away, Stacy went back into the building and finished her afternoon shift feeling lighter and stronger.

A ping on her phone caused her to break out in a cold sweat. A voice message from Jack. Stacy knew now was the time her new faith would be tested.

CHAPTER 48

Debbie had finished her session with Dr. Murphy and, seeing there was a little time before her ten o'clock appointment with Chaplain Miller, took a seat in the courtyard. She sat back in a wrought-iron chair, closed her eyes, and listened to the soothing splash of water coming out of the fountain. Debbie was glad to take an emotional break, even if only for a few minutes.

The sound of a door closing startled her. She rubbed her eyes, realizing she had dozed off. Checking her watch, she saw she still had time to make it to Chaplain Miller's office for her appointment. She stood and made her way through the hallways.

Debbie knocked on the open door before stepping inside. After greeting the chaplain, her eyes immediately went to the framed sketch of Jesus holding the lamb. She loved the feeling of comfort and safety it gave her. Chaplain Miller followed her eyes to the picture.

"It sure is a wonderful image, isn't it? Jesus holding the lamb close and with such tenderness and love. A former patient here at Bethany drew it for me and I had it framed."

"It's beautiful. I love that the nail print in Jesus's visible hand is included."

"What, specifically, does it say to you, Debbie?"

"It reminds me Jesus had to suffer death on a cross, making it possible for sinful sheep to be held in his arms."

Chaplain Miller nodded. "It's amazing to me that God's Son chose to die for us—the sheep who have gone astray. He longs to give us forgiveness if we ask. That's called grace."

Debbie nodded. "Patricia Harmon and I were talking about forgiveness yesterday. She pointed out that Christians often have to forgive many times the same people who have wronged them."

"Yes, it's in direct contrast to how God forgives." Chaplain Miller took a sip from his coffee mug. "David had it right. He points out that if we ask for forgiveness, God throws our sins as far as the east is from the west. David ought to know—God forgave him of adultery and murder."

Debbie hung her head and looked at the floor.

"What's troubling you?"

"It's hard for me to understand why God thinks I'm important enough to die for. I certainly wouldn't if I were God."

"It's funny that you used the phrase, 'If I were God.' We often play god, even if subconsciously, when it comes to our day-to-day experiences." He rose, offered Debbie some coffee—which she declined—refilled his mug, and sat back down at his desk.

"It's easy to assume God thinks the same way we do. Because we feel unforgiving, then God must be unforgiving. We feel angry about certain things, then God must be angry about them too."

"Yes, now that I think about it, I *have* done that very thing."

The chaplain set his mug on his desk and looked directly into Debbie's eyes. "What is it that you're assuming about God? What thing are you believing that, if you weighed it using Scripture, you'd find was incorrect?"

Debbie felt ashamed of the idea that immediately dominated her mind. "I've been struggling over whether God notices my suffering or not. And if he's aware, how does he react to it?"

Debbie's throat tightened with emotion.

Chaplain Miller looked down at a crate beside his desk, and Debbie's eyes followed his gaze. The container held numerous colorful bottles.

"Debbie, I have a special Sunday service planned tomorrow at nine o'clock in the chapel. I encourage you to attend because we're going to wrestle with the very things you're finding so difficult."

Debbie stood, wiping her eyes with a tissue she took from Chaplain Miller's desk.

"I'll be there."

CHAPTER 49

Stefan moved through supper in a fog. What he'd seen and experienced with Frank today had been the depths of anguish. The moment seemed to add to his justification of anger toward God and cut deep into his heartstrings. Why didn't the same thing happen with God? When he saw all the pain and suffering in this world, how could he overlook it? Stefan felt that God was indifferent to the pain of his children. Sophie's pain and suffering had seemed to mean nothing to God because he'd chosen not to do anything to help her.

Realizing he no longer had an appetite, Stefan took his dishes with his half-eaten food and deposited them in the correct place.

He decided to go the park, hoping he would find a little comfort. As he walked, his thoughts felt like a jumbled mess.

You're legally supposed to be by my side, supporting me, God. Where are you?

"Hello, Stefan. It's good to see you."

Startled, Stefan was surprised to see he stood just a few feet from the Bottle House. Chaplain Miller was standing on his patio with a book in his hands.

"Do you have time to join me here on this beautiful evening?"

Nodding, Stefan sat in the chair the chaplain had pulled away from the table for him.

"What are you reading?" Stefan asked, looking at the book but not seeing the title.

"I'm reading the memoir of a woman whose son planned and carried out a multiple-victim killing spree."

"Isn't that a little bit morbid? There is so much evil in the world. Why do you want to immerse yourself in it more by choosing to read something like that?"

The chaplain sighed. "It is a difficult book to read emotionally, but I wanted to better understand the suffering one feels as a direct result of the actions of family members."

Stefan cringed as his thoughts went immediately to his sons and what they must be feeling about his attempted suicide. His next thought went to Frank.

Clearing his throat, he said, "I witnessed suffering on a level I've never seen or heard this afternoon with Frank. I will never forget the sounds and sight of his anguish. Where is God's comfort in Frank's living hell?" Stefan's hands clenched into fists.

"What did you do when you witnessed Frank's distress and asked God for help?"

"I remembered that emergency numbers for everyone were posted by the phone in the kitchen, so I looked up Frank's and called."

"Is that all you did?" Chaplain Miller tilted his head, encouraging Stefan to remember more.

"Well, I didn't know what else to do, so I just sat with him while ..."

"While what, Stefan?"

Suddenly, Stefan realized the implication of his statement. "I sat with him while he grieved, providing what I hoped was support." His fists unclenched, and he leaned back against the chair.

Chaplain Miller leaned forward. "Do you think Frank was aware you were there?"

Stefan rubbed his jaw. "I'm not sure, as he was in such agony—anything else would be hard to notice."

The chaplain nodded. "I have two challenges for you. Spend some time reflecting on your last statement as to whether Frank knew you were there or not. Did that make your actions less effective? Second, I'm having a special service tomorrow morning in the chapel. We'll be examining the exact issues you've raised today. I hope you'll come and be a part of it."

Stefan looked at the bottles in the nearby window, then he tore his gaze away and focused on Chaplain Miller. "I'll think about it."

CHAPTER 50

The next morning, Chaplain Joseph Miller set his crate filled with small bottles on the floor next to his pulpit. The echo of them gently bumping into each other reverberated through the empty sanctuary. As was his custom before each Sunday service, Joseph walked between each row of seats and prayed that those who would soon occupy them would have ears to hear God's words and hearts receptive to his healing.

With his *Amen*, Joseph checked the clock and saw his congregation would soon arrive. He moved to the lectern, set up a card table beside it, and then arranged his Bible and notes. The chaplain bent and picked up the crate of bottles and set it gently on the table.

Chaplain Miller looked up from his task as people began to arrive. As he greeted them, Joseph took another opportunity to pray for each person, lifting their specific needs and hurts before God.

"Hello, Chaplain Miller," Stacy Meadows greeted him.

"Good morning, Stacy!"

Lord, please fill Stacy with courage. Remind her that even though she has been betrayed by some important people in her life, you will never leave her nor forsake her.

Debbie Young walked in right behind Stacy. "Hello, Debbie. It's good to see you."

"Hello."

Rejection and criticism are heavy loads to carry, Lord. I ask that you use your words and my comments to bring healing to Debbie. Help her to see herself as you do.

Several others arrived and Joseph continued his greetings and prayers.

As the clock indicated it was time to begin, Joseph was relieved to see that Stefan came in the back door and sat down.

Thank you, Lord! Please use your word this morning to resurrect Stefan's faith. May he realize in ways he never has that you care about him and the suffering he has endured. As he continues to hurl judgments upon himself, please save him from self-destruction.

After singing "Amazing Grace," Joseph stood a few moments, looking out at this congregation.

"This is the day the Lord has made," he recited.

"We will rejoice and be glad in it," the congregation replied.

He paused once more and made eye contact with each person there.

"Today, we'll visit an event in the Bible that both amazes and disturbs me," Chaplain Miller said.

Several people shifted in their seats, seemingly surprised that anything in the Bible would disturb this man of God. But he prayed his vulnerability would open their eyes.

"If you have your Bible, turn to the Gospel of John, chapter eleven." Joseph opened his and waited for others to find it.

"The disciple, John, records an event that many of you who have attended church throughout your life will find very familiar. The chapter documents the raising of Lazarus from the dead."

Joseph immediately noticed that Stacy's eyes widened. *Lord, I see you at work already! Thank you.*

"There are so many important lessons in this chapter, it's easy to get lost in all of them. I'll do my best to focus on only a few rather than the whole.

"John 11 tells us a good friend of Jesus, Lazarus, is sick. Just to put this event in context, Lazarus lived in Bethany with his sisters, Mary and Martha." The chaplain absentmindedly pushed up his glasses on the bridge of his nose and then looked down at the text. "Other references in Scripture acknowledge Jesus is a close friend with this family, and he probably visited with them on more occasions than the Bible reveals. As Lazarus's illness became serious, Mary and Martha did what many of us do when we face critical circumstances, they cried out for Jesus."

Looking back at his congregation, he continued. "Jesus finally shows up after Lazarus had been dead three days. If I were one of the sisters, I would be angry at him for not coming when they sent for him."

Debbie Young nodded and Joseph whispered a quick prayer for the right words to encourage this young teacher.

"Mary and Martha must have been frustrated, as I assume, and in great distress. Both sisters make statements that oozed from their souls. They both say, 'If you had only been here, our brother would not have died ... if you had only been here.'"

In the back of the chapel, Joseph saw Stefan hang his head. *Lord, speak to him.*

Chaplain Miller paused reverently at the lectern giving some who were weeping a moment.

Clearing his throat, he continued. "Most of us know that in a few short verses, Jesus will command Lazarus to come back from the dead, and he does. Jesus is the resurrection and the life. This wonderful treatment center that has helped many heal was named after this event. Bethany R&L—the resurrection and the life."

Chaplain Miller smiled. "This is the part of the story that amazes me. It lifts my soul to praise God, but what do I find disturbing within these verses?"

He noticed Stefan had raised his head and was now frowning.

"Jesus asks Mary to show him where Lazarus was buried. Once there, John tells us what later became the shortest verse in the English Bible. 'Jesus wept.' Through the years, this short verse has disturbed me. What did Jesus do? He went to the tomb and wept. *Wept.* Why?" Chaplain Miller paused to let the question sink in.

He noticed Stacy dabbing at her eyes with a tissue. He turned to the crate and lifted out the red bottle that held her name. He heard the young nurse gasp.

"This is why Jesus wept." Chaplain Miller's hand pointed first at Stacy's bottle and then tilted the crate for the congregation to see it was full of beautiful bottles.

Debbie's softening face made it clear to Joseph that she'd spotted her light green bottle among the others.

Drawing the people's eyes back to Stacy's bottle, Joseph continued. "Psalm 56:8 tells us that God collects all our tears in a bottle. These bottles represent the lives of each one here and those associated with them. The liquid within symbolizes your tears that God collects and remembers." The chaplain pointed at the liquid in the red bottle. "These exist so in times of sadness and heartache, your bottle can remind you that your Creator does more than just notice your tears—he saves them and cherishes them, not because he likes his children suffering, but rather, because he has placed such a value on you he acknowledges the pain we go through in this life."

Chaplain Miller paused, allowing his eyes to sweep across the listeners. His attention was drawn to Stefan who now sat with his arms crossed. *Lord, soften this wounded man's heart. May he understand better how much you love him.*

Pushing his glasses back up his nose, Joseph looked back down at his Bible a moment, then focused back on the congregation. "Jesus wept at Lazarus's tomb because he was sharing the grief and hurt his friends were experiencing. God sees our sorrows and weeps over each one."

Whispers of astonishment moved through the room. Many seemed struck with awe, but Joseph was taken by surprise when Stefan stood, his cheeks red.

"Chaplain Miller, that's nice God sees our suffering. It's touching."

Joseph couldn't help but notice the sarcasm that spewed out of this man's mouth.

"It's one thing to notice our suffering, but what about him? Why would an omniscient and omnipotent God care about the billions of individuals on this earth? How could he, or better yet, *why* would he care about us?"

Out of the corner of his eye, Joseph noticed Debbie's head slightly nodding.

Stefan's fists clenched at his sides. "Yes, Jesus probably got caught up in the moment and wept for the suffering his friends went through before he raised Lazarus from the dead, but what about those of us who receive no miracle? I don't see a bottle up there that represents God's tears." He stood shaking as everyone moved their focus from Stefan back to the chaplain.

Taking a moment to bow his head, Chaplain Miller allowed a short time to dissipate the smoke from Stefan's burning words. He raised his head, picked up another bottle, and moved over to the door of the chapel.

"If you ever wonder how God feels about all the suffering he sees down on this earth, follow me."

The group got to their feet, unsure of where Chaplain Miller would lead them but curious enough to follow. The chaplain led the worshippers down the hall and out of the building. He made his way down Cayce Road.

Before they knew it, he had led them all onto the beach. When everyone was gathered, they formed an impromptu semicircle facing him and the ocean.

The chaplain gazed up to the heavens and took a deep breath. "Stefan has asked a question that is not only thoughtful but honest."

The chaplain looked at Stefan and nodded his head.

"We don't have trouble believing God knows all that transpires in our lives, but we can be very troubled when we assume he has no feelings about it. Years ago, I harbored the same feelings that Stefan has bravely stated. Does God care about the things that happen to us?"

Stefan held his focus on Chaplain Miller's face.

"Jesus seemed to care as he walked this earth. But the question remains, is God our Father ever moved with tears? When he sees the despair, the destruction, the neglect, and the abuse on this earth, how does he react?"

His voice was strained as he spoke through his emotions.

"It's because of questions like these that I started the practice of procuring a unique bottle for each person who comes through the doors of Bethany R&L and those in their families who suffer with them. I wanted for each person to know the words of Psalm 56:8 are true. God collects our tears. He can account for every one."

The chaplain focused on Stefan. "No, I don't have a bottle to represent God's tears, Stefan. No bottle could contain and store the number of tears God sheds over all the hurt he sees we endure and cause here on earth. But he does weep for those who don't know him. For failed marriages. For the hurtful mistakes and choices people make."

Chaplain Miller paused, then he turned around and made a sweeping motion with his arm toward the ocean. "Here is where God's tears are stored."

As a wave crashed onto the shore, the chaplain's words washed over the people.

He turned to watch Stefan look at the waters. The same waters that had almost became his grave. Stefan fell to his knees. Joseph felt tears of gratitude fall from his eyes as he saw Frank and Jerry move toward their friend and each place a hand of support on their friend's shoulder.

The chaplain then looked at Debbie and smiled, seeing her face shine with what had to be joy, relief, and gratitude.

And then he saw Stacy, her eyes closed and her hands covering her unborn child. Joseph detected a slight swaying back and forth as if she were being rocked by God himself.

And in the holy moment, Joseph raised his head and said, "And God will wipe away every tear from their eyes."

EPILOGUE

"Chaplain Miller! I'm so glad you could make it." Stacy shifted her one-year-old baby girl, Kaylee Ruth to her hip.

"Hello, beautiful girl!" The little girl giggled as the chaplain tickled her under the chin. "I wouldn't miss Kaylee's birthday. I'm just so glad you invited me."

Gazing at her baby's face, Stacy smiled. "God surely turned a bad situation around, didn't he? I never thought I'd have a baby without Jack or have my own apartment, but now here I am. Ruth and Charles have become Kaylee's surrogate grandparents and since I joined their church, she's also got many uncles, aunts, brothers, and sisters. What a blessing."

Ruth clapped her hands to catch everyone's attention. "Don't forget the cake, everyone. Kaylee can't eat it all."

Stacy laughed as she moved with Chaplain Miller to the table holding the food. She had already kept the chaplain up to date on her life, telling him that Jack and Aubree had married and were now expecting their own baby. Though the events of the past year still hurt, Stacy tried to focus only on what she could control—being a good mother and competent nurse.

"Is your custody situation with Jack working out?"

Stacy nodded as she picked up a piece of chocolate cake.

"Yes, I'm glad the Lewises found me a very competent lawyer. God truly does see our sorrows and cares deeply.

Every time I look at my small red bottle, I am reminded of this. Thank you so much for the work you do ministering to me and the people of Bethany R&L."

Debbie straightened up, rubbing the sore spot on her lower back.

"Now that we've gotten some iris bulbs for you, let's take a break," Patricia suggested.

"Sounds good to me." The two women walked to the porch swing and sat down.

"These bulbs are going to be beautiful along the front of our new house. Believe it or not, Josh loves flowers too so all these bulbs and cuttings from other parts of your garden will be thoroughly enjoyed." Debbie smiled, picturing their own house with a wrap-around porch and swing.

Patricia pushed off the floor and started the swing in motion. "Tell me how things are going since you both left teaching at the Christian school."

"As you know, Josh and I felt that moving on to other schools would be best. He's now teaching physics at the high school, and I'm teaching third grade at one of the local elementary schools."

"I bet your mother must be happy since you finally moved to teaching in public schools."

"Yeah, well. You would think she would be happy but, as always, she's on to something else she feels needs fixing within me." Debbie laughed.

Patricia smiled. "In that one sentence, I detect a change in your spirit. What's different?"

Debbie nodded. "Several things I learned, while here those four weeks with Chaplain Miller and Dr. Murphy, taught me that I cannot control other people nor their reactions. I guess I'm learning to recognize I don't need my mother's approval to be content within. I've got more work to do in this area but it's a good start."

"I am so happy to hear this. These types of lessons make navigating this life a little easier." Patricia patted Debbie's hand. "Now, let's get back to the garden and find some more plants you can use at your new place.

⚱︎✝⚱︎

"Stefan!"

Stefan looked up to see Frank racing toward him.

"I was afraid you had gone already."

"No, but I'm heading out soon. It's been a good summer, but it's time for me to start living again." Stefan thought about spending one more time near the swings but decided he better get back to his room and pack if he wanted to catch his plane.

He'd decided to sell his house and move to the east coast to live near his sons. He'd open up an office there to practice law and would enjoy spending time with his sons and grandchildren. He hoped to join a church there and become an active member in God's house once more.

"I heard from Jerry yesterday," Frank said, falling into step beside him.

"How's he doing?"

"Good. He said to wish you the best and to keep in touch."

Stefan stopped at the entrance to his building. "You stay in touch too, okay? I'll email you my new address soon."

Frank nodded and rubbed his neck with his hand. "Aren't you going to miss your life here on the west coast? I'm not sure I could make that big of a move."

Stefan considered his friend's words for a moment. Yes, he'd miss being able to visit Sophie's grave, but he knew she was no longer there. Sophie was enjoying life in her *eternal* home, and she'd want him to live his life here—to the fullest.

Frank nodded, clapped his hand on Stefan's shoulder, and then walked away.

Chaplain Miller walked up then and handed Stefan his sky-blue bottle.

"I purchase two bottles for each person who is associated with Bethany. I do this so I can give one to my patients when they leave, and the other takes a place of honor at my home, the Bottle House. I hope it'll remind you of your time here and all that you've learned and healed from."

Stefan took the bottle and held it up to the light, knowing each time he'd see it he'd think of the ocean. Not that fateful day when his life almost ended, but the day he realized God's care for him.

ABOUT THE AUTHOR

Susan Grant is a graduate of Columbia International University and a former Bible teacher in the public schools of North Carolina. Susan has written for devotional magazines such as, *Unlocked—Daily Readings for Teens*, and *The Upper Room*. She has also had her writing published in the *Bangor Daily News*, and several online magazines. Her first book, *100 Minutes with God*, was a #1 new release on Amazon. To receive her daily "minutes," sign up at susan-grant.com. She can also be found on Facebook.

Susan teaches middle school language arts and lives on the coast of Maine with her husband, Randy, and her little red dachshund, Boone.

Made in the USA
Middletown, DE
27 December 2022

20480347R00177